MARK MY WORDS

Also by Muhammad Khan

I Am Thunder

Kick the Moon

MARK MY WORDS

MUHAMMAD KHAN

MACMILLAN

Published 2022 by Macmillan Children's Books
an imprint of Pan Macmillan
The Smithson, 6 Briset Street, London EC1M 5NR
EU representative: Macmillan Publishers Ireland Ltd, 1st Floor,
The Liffey Trust Centre, 117–126 Sheriff Street Upper
Dublin 1, D01 YC43
Associated companies throughout the world
www.panmacmillan.com

ISBN 978-1-5290-2994-9

Copyright © Muhammad Khan 2022

The right of Muhammad Khan to be identified as the
author of this work has been asserted by him in
accordance with the Copyright, Designs and Patents Act 1988.

1 3 5 7 9 8 6 4 2

A CIP catalogue record for this book is available from the British Library.

Printed and bound by CPI Group (UK) Ltd, Croydon CR0 4YY

'Whatever a patron desires to get published is advertising;
whatever he wants to keep out of the paper is news.'

– anonymous quote found on a placard on
the desk of L. E. Edwardson, day editor of
the *Chicago Herald* and *Examiner*, 1918.

CHAPTER 1

Hopping off the bus early, I head down the street with an artificial spring in my step, armed with a determined smile. I run through a mental checklist hoping to nix the odds of a back-to-school-fail; brand new backpack, peng hijab, multicoloured flashcards, and a contractual obligation for zero PDFs (Public Displays of Foolishness).

Man, did September roll around fast. One minute, I'm enjoying the summer holidays — working morning shifts at the local cafe, spending evenings watching K-dramas curled up on the sofa with Mum — the next I'm faking enthusiasm for the first day of term at a brand-new school. Like who goes to a new school for the *final year of their GCSEs*? Even if it is the 'better' school on the 'better' side of town . . .

My phone buzzes and another message pops up from my best mate, Liam.

Where are you?

I begin to text back, not noticing the massive traffic cone right in front of me. 'Argh!' I cry, lunging to prevent myself from hitting the pavement. A couple of primary school kids laugh.

PDF Count: 1.

'Dua?'

Glancing round, I find lovely Liam beaming at me, mouse-brown curls fluttering in the September breeze, dressed in the royal blue and gold colours of Bodley High and proudly sporting the faint green paint stain on his sleeve from last year's art project. I sigh. It's finally happened: the growth spurt Liam's been talking about for years has turned him into a six-foot bean pole. I grin as we bump fists.

'You are *so* ready for the new year at *Minerva College*,' I say, hyping him up.

'*And* I've got these!' He jabs his thumbs at his hearing aids like cartoon arrows. 'State-of-the-art Bluetooth.'

'Nice! You're practically a cyborg,' I say with a wink.

'All thanks to Auntie Aisha. If she hadn't kept on with all them emails, they probably would've fobbed me off with an ear trumpet.'

'Mum's always doing the most,' I say with a slight eye-roll. I spot some friends across the street and give them a wave. The Year Eleven Bodley High exodus is real and, good or bad, there's no turning back. 'Once she's found a cause, she has to see it through.'

'Reminds me of someone else I know . . .' Liam says, nudging me.

I laugh. 'Dunno what you're chatting about, mate. Year Eleven Dua has zero plans to be up in other people's business.'

I don't mention the ban on PDFs, since that's already a lost cause.

'And be less bossy?'

'Did I say you could speak?' We both crack up.

Liam's eyes travel across the street. 'Look at them, watching us like we're savages.' Four Minerva students in pristine maroon blazers train their eyes on us briefly. 'What you looking at?' Liam barks.

I smack Liam in the chest. 'Leave off. They have every right to check us out. We are *invading* their school.'

'Not by choice,' he says, bitterly. 'Swear down, if they say anything—'

'They will. You just better not say anything back.' I signal a thank you to a bus driver who's letting us cross. 'So beyond all the snapchats you sent me, how was Blackpool?'

Liam's face lights up. 'It was the best! Nan showed us around her home town and we played Bridge, which is actually kind of cool when you get the hang of it.'

'OK, Boomer.' I laugh.

'Honestly, it's kind of fun! I took her for a walk down Blackpool pier to remember the good old days when Grandad was still around and everything. But every now and then, she'd get confused.' He lapses into a glum silence. 'There was this one moment when she looked at me funny . . . like she didn't even recognize me.'

'Man, I'm sorry.' This has been worrying him all summer. His mum already struggles with caring for his nan's dementia, so she might have to move her into a care home to cope. I'm praying it doesn't happen any time soon or my guy is going to feel lost.

'So, what did you get up to while I was away?' he asks, changing the subject. 'Let me guess: loads of basketball in your new Jordans?'

'Super rare Kobes, actually. And no. Drills can get boring when you've got no one to play with.'

'Hope you're not trying to guilt-trip me into playing, cos I'm tired of having my skinny white arse handed to me.'

A smirk lifts my lips. 'OK – so you know that online magazine: *This Uni Life*? Well, they ran a competition for an amateur writer to get an article published. And I entered . . .' I purse my lips, feeling my cheeks tingle. 'I submitted "A Newbie's Guide to Surviving Your First Week at Uni".'

He nearly chokes on his chewing gum. 'But you're fifteen! You literally know nothing about uni.'

'As a proud member of Gen Z, I know how to harness the

power of Google.' I poke my temple. 'I call it "intellectual appropriation". Anyway – it worked! I won.'

'Oh, my days, Dua! Congrats for beating legit uni students to the prize.' He gives me a high five and then wiggles his brows. 'What did you win?'

'Annual cinema pass, fifty per cent off pizza voucher and . . . um . . . some useless crap,' I mumble, waving a hand dismissively.

He looks at me expectantly. 'Don't hold out on me, fam.'

I blush, looking around to make sure no one is walking directly behind us. 'You tell anyone about this, I'mma hunt you down. Understand?'

He nods solemnly and we slow down.

'Three condoms' – he gasps sarcastically – 'which I *obviously* binned. Can you imagine if Mum found them? She'd think my PG-13 life is a lie.' He barks out a laugh.

I take a deep breath. Minerva College is on the east side of town, built on top of a beautiful hill, which gives it a super dramatic look, but it's a pretty intense trek. Next time we're bussing it. With perfect timing, the large electronic gates swing open to let us in. Like the Minerva school blazer, they're a regal shade of maroon.

The campus beyond is spacious and perfectly colour-coordinated, making Bodley's clashing vibrancy seem like a messed-up Rubik's cube. There are lush green spots everywhere and even a crystal-clear lake edged by a grassy verge. Large modern-art sculptures are dotted around, making the place feel more like a fancy park than a school.

'Forget this!' Liam panics, pulling a sharp one-eighty.

'You're a cyborg, remember?' I insist, wheeling him over to our lot. 'If anyone can survive this, you can.'

'Swear down, if them posh teachers start talking shit, I'mma turn my hearing aids off!'

'Morning, Miss Rowntree,' I say brightly to my Bodley High chemistry teacher, as she loops her shoulder-length hair behind her protruding ears and ushers us into the hall. A crap teacher by anyone's standards, she's the type to take it personally if you ask questions. Without Mum, I'd be failing chem.

'Hello, Huda,' she answers robotically, pale eyes darting wildly. I hadn't even considered it before, but I realize Bodley staff must also be nervous about coming onto Minerva turf.

'Miss, her name's *Dua*,' Liam says, vexed. 'That's Huda.' He points to a pretty Pakistani girl in a glamorous hijab with a glittering rose pin just ahead of us, who, at the sound of her name, turns towards us and blinks her false eyelashes with disdain.

'That's what I said, isn't it?' Miss Rowntree says sharply, flashing her eyes.

Bless Liam for taking offence on my behalf. Some people see the hijab before they see the person: it is what it is. I wonder if the Minerva teachers will be any more aware. Doubt it.

Minerva's interior is just as impressive as the outside. Every wall is painted pale grey without a smudge or swear word in sight, and the trophy cabinet is fit to burst.

'That shoulda been ours,' Josiah says, pointing to the football cup. Our school team captain is back from the summer sporting a great twist fade and, like Liam, has grown about a foot.

'Don't touch!' Miss Rowntree snipes. 'They won't appreciate your greasy fingerprints.'

Josiah narrows his eyes.

'Allow it,' I whisper. 'She's a cow, but don't give her a reason.'

He considers this then smiles. 'Thanks, man.'

The large medieval-looking doors of the hall creak open and we file in. The walls are decorated with stunning paintings in gilt frames, each with a little panel displaying the name of the artist. I gawp, realizing this is *student* work. They wouldn't look out of place at the Tate Modern.

We are directed to fill up the pews on the left. The almost hallowed silence combined with the stained-glass windows depicting religious scenes makes even the rowdiest kids behave. The Minerva students, who we Bodley kids have taken to calling the 'Blue Bloods', are already occupying the pews on the right. Some watch us, smiling with polite curiosity, while others avert their gaze. Just like the affluent east side of town, the majority of them are white. Are their home lives as perfect as their school appears?

'Crocodile smiles,' Liam whispers.

Soaring above the wooden stage at the front of the hall is a large plaque of the school's coat of arms with a shine that suggests a summer paint job. A tall, silver-haired man rises from his seat, maroon, black and gold academic robes fluttering as he strides over to the illuminated lectern with all the confidence of a monarch.

'Look at that fool!' Liam seethes. 'Thinks he's Dumbledore!'

I roll my eyes. 'Let's just hope he doesn't make us sing the Hogwarts school song cos my voice *will* shatter all that stained-glass.' A couple of Bodley kids chuckle and I smile, glad to have lightened the mood.

Our principal, Mr Aden, joins him at the lectern and I can't help feeling a little proud. He's a tall Somali guy with a neat little beard, dressed in an expensive-looking air force blue suit. Our dear Mr Aden: master of entertaining assemblies and psychedelic ties, and keeper of a mystical bottle of lollipops for when you're down in the dumps. In short: a legend.

'Good morning and welcome!' booms the beardless Dumbledore. 'I am Sir Reginald Unwin – proud headmaster of Minerva College. And this is Mr Aden, principal of Bodley High.' Mr Aden waves briefly as Sir Reg continues. 'As you are aware, Minerva has formed a Learning Trust with Bodley, which we are very proud of, and we are delighted to welcome Bodley's Year Elevens to our site while building work is undertaken at their school. This arrangement will benefit both schools by enriching our shared experiences and hopefully raising attainment.'

I snort. Everyone knows it has nothing to do with results – it was rushed through to avoid austerity cuts.

Aden moves a little closer to the stand and speaks. 'In some cases, Bodley students will retain their existing teachers and class sets. In others, they will be mixed in with Minerva classes and share their teachers. And, wonderfully, our sports teams will now have the benefit of training on the same state-of-the-art grounds.'

A murmur of horror sweeps across the Bodley and Minerva students. 'They kept us out of the footie county championships with their dives. And now we'll be sharing a pitch? Disgusting,' Josiah mumbles to me.

'Bodley, you are going to show our partners how well-behaved and focused you can be,' Mr Aden instructs with firmness. 'Our hopes for glowing GCSE results rest on your capable shoulders.'

Sir Reg gives a short spiel about Minerva making us feel welcome and how good this will be for both schools. Just the look on Liam's face tells me he's not buying it. He sees Minerva as the enemy. It's easy to hate on entitled people who were born to win at life but as long as they don't treat us horribly, I'm going to keep an open mind. It's our last year, and I want to make the most of it. Mr Aden sits down at the back of the stage and Sir Reg moves onto Minerva news.

'At the end of last term, the Minerva rugby team participated in the Under Eighteens London Championship.' The Minerva kids lean just a fraction closer as the atmosphere shifts. 'And to tell you all about it, here is our captain: Hugo!'

Minerva goes *wild*.

The blond boy who walks onto the stage is so tall that at first I think he's a teacher. Massive shoulders fill out his blazer but the fine cut of his tailoring hints at a slim waist. Glancing round, I see adoration on the Minerva kids' faces.

OK, we get it – he's peng.

Hugo describes his team's uphill battle to win the finals and it suddenly becomes clear why Minerva is so obsessed. Though his voice is deep and resonant, it crackles with energy, summoning the match before our eyes, taking us through every heart-racing tackle and try. I don't even know the guy but he has me reluctantly rooting for the win.

'So did we win?' he asks the entranced crowd. 'Does *this* answer your question?'

Suddenly the entire rugby team pour onto the stage, bringing the championship cup with them. Raucous applause, stamping feet and euphoric screams drag me along for the ride. Liam has to nudge me to bring me and my hands back to earth.

'Now,' Sir Reg says, his cheeks tinged with colour as he gestures for order while the rugby team leave the stage. 'You may be aware that our very own school newspaper, the *Minerva Chronicle*, won a prestigious award over the summer. Here to tell us more about it, and a very exciting opportunity, are Keira Walsingham and Renée Harris-Lords, editor and deputy.'

As if struck by a taser, I'm sitting ramrod straight. Liam looks over at me, aware that kismet is at play here. This is *it*.

'Good morning!' says an enthusiastic and entirely flawless blonde girl into the microphone, making everyone feel included with a friendly sweep of her eyes. Behind her, a slideshow begins, flashing up pictures of her news team receiving the Omega Young Journalists of the Year award at the Savoy in London. Her tone of voice and body language is on point, keeping us engaged. I start making mental notes.

Up on stage, Keira is cracking back-to-school jokes. *Hilarious!* Her expression shifts as she talks about this year being scary but seriously important. *Relatable.* Then she hands over to Renée, a stunning mixed-race girl, who gives us a brief visual history of the *Chronicle* via quirky pictures of student reporters from way back when the world was sepia-toned. *Enduring.*

'This is why the *Minerva Chronicle* is so dear to our hearts,' Renée says, folding delicate hands over her chest. 'Winning awards and being part of that legacy is a humbling honour.'

Keira starts clapping and, taking our cue, we all join in.

'Thank you, Renée,' Keira says. 'The *Minerva Chronicle* has flourished where sadly other school papers have disappeared, because we never shied away from maintaining the highest standards.' She looks out into the hall. 'That's where you come in! We are hoping to welcome two new recruits to our dedicated news team. This position is open to both Minerva *and* Bodley students. Needless to say, it will look impressive on sixth-form applications.'

'So how do you apply?' Renée asks rhetorically. With a delicate flick of her wrist, the slide behind her reveals application details. 'All you have to do is go to the *Chronicle* website and upload an original article. Something that shows off your awareness of current affairs and your voice.'

'The deadline is this Friday,' Keira adds.

'That's not enough time!' I protest in a voice like a foghorn. A flurry of laughs surround me, and there are shocked faces from the right side of the hall. Aden shoots up in his seat, eyes scouring for the Bodley culprit. I sink lower, using the lower part of my scarf like a niqab to hide my identity. PDF Count: 2.

'True,' Keira says, unperturbed. 'But the mark of a good journalist is producing excellent copy on short notice. Nobody wants to read old news.'

The rest of the assembly is a blur. All I can think about is getting on the *Chronicle*. That kind of pedigree would not only make me a shoo-in to do my A levels at Minerva, but it couldn't hurt when seeking a big break in the actual world of adult journalism.

I. Am. *Stoked*.

People start filing out of the hall. 'Bodley students, please stay behind for some housekeeping,' Aden announces at the lectern.

I watch Keira and Renée exit through the door on the far right. Rowntree has just clocked Huda's make-up and is threatening to send her home and Aden is organizing six students to hand stuff out.

'Cover for me!' I tell Liam, ignoring his protests as I dart across the hall after my future employers (fingers crossed).

'Excuse me, ladies!' I call out, catching up to Minerva's answer to the D'Amelio sisters.

Renée's beautiful olive-green eyes appraise me, lingering on my hijab, while Keira smiles with what I think is warmth. 'Yes?'

Suddenly at a loss for words. I blush, desperate not to blow up the PDF Count any further. 'Hey, so I'm Dua.' I give a little wave. 'I was super-impressed with your presentation and I'd really like to submit an article. But you didn't say what the cut-off point on Friday was. Friday evening would best, obvi—'

'It was on the slide, wasn't it?' Keira asks Renée, her brow arching.

'Pretty sure it wasn't,' I chime.

'Nope, it definitely was,' Renée states matter-of-factly before wagging a finger at me. 'Gotta improve your observational skills if you want to join the team.'

I feel my eyes water and audibly swallow. 'So if you could remind me, I'll have it ready for your perusal stat.'

'Friday midday,' Keira says. 'Good luck!' She turns, her ponytail swishing glamorously.

Renée continues to stare at me with a mixture of amusement and curiosity. Then, spinning on her heels, she executes a perfect flick of her silky burgundy tresses before joining Keira in a synchronized strut.

You don't like me, I think. *But that's only because you don't know what I can do.*

CHAPTER 2

I wave tiredly to Liam as I hop off the bus. Liam's my bestie and all, but listening to him banging on about Bodley being the 'proletariat' and Minerva the 'bourgeoisie' would give even Comrade Marx a migraine. I mean, he's not wrong, but we have to stay positive if we're going to survive the year – and honestly, our first day wasn't even that bad. Liam's just annoyed he didn't totally hate it.

I pull out my slightly creased copy of the back-to-school edition of the *Minerva Chronicle*. Not cheap at two pounds, but hardly surprising considering it's printed on glossy paper with tons of meaty articles. But it feels dated and stuffy, like a teacher was calling the shots instead of a teenager. There's stuff about dressage shows and skiing competitions – like, who can afford that? There's self-help that comes off as preachy and triggering, and a think-piece *praising* Churchill – the Murderer of Bengal. If Keira takes me on, we're going to have to make some changes.

As I walk up our drive, my brain ticks over with article ideas. Homework's gonna be an unfortunate casualty tonight, but it's a detention I will gladly sit if it means landing a spot on the *Chronicle* team.

'Mum!' I call, closing the front door behind me.

Silence.

Weird. She's definitely in because her red Qashqai is parked in the drive. I inhale the familiar scents of jasmine ittar and fragrant spices, then call again as I drop my bag. Still no reply. Maybe she's enjoying a soak in the tub. Mum's school started back on Monday, so a herbal bath bomb and a few tea lights might be her prescription for the evening.

So why is my skin prickling?

I hear a sob.

'Oh no . . .' I exhale, tracing the worrying sound to the front room.

Mum gets low sometimes. It's painful to watch but even harder to pick up the pieces. I didn't think it would happen so soon into the school year.

She's on the sofa, a letter embossed with the Gwaine Academy school crest open on her lap. Snail trails of drying tears glisten on her cheeks, her brow a Tube map of frown lines. My heart sinks. This is a face I've seen before. The last time it made an appearance was just before the summer holidays began, but I put it down to end-of-term exhaustion.

'Mum, don't be sad.' I pull off my two-piece hijab as I sit down beside her, my fingers interweaving with hers. Cool air prickles my scalp, filtering through my loose curls.

Mum jolts as if surprised to find me sitting beside her. She wipes her eyes with the corner of her hijab. 'Dua! How did your first day go?'

'It was all right, yeah.'

'Great! I know you had your heart set on going there.' She pulls the pins out of her hijab and slips it off, trying to pull herself together.

'I mean, it's a year early, and technically I'm still at Bodley, but I'm hopeful.' I ignore her attempt to distract me, worry grazing my throat. 'Mum, why've you been crying?'

'Oh nothing, beyta. I'm just tired.'

'At the start of a new term?'

She falters, a twitching cheek muscle betraying her nonchalance. 'Well, teaching is a stressful job. There's a reason it has one of the highest resignation rates of any profession. Would you like a snack? Spring rolls or pakoras? We've got both.' As she rises, the official-looking letter tumbles off her lap, landing at my feet, and I pounce.

'Don't touch that!' she demands.

Disobeying my mother doesn't come naturally, so I flinch before a phrase leaps off the page and then I can't stop myself.

GROSS MISCONDUCT
Dear Aisha Iqbal,
Last term you were placed on capability procedures. Your performance caused concern after you took a total of 123 days of absence and failed to mark mock examination papers in a timely manner. The school also received a number of parental complaints. You were invited to a meeting in which you were informed that this amounts to gross misconduct, as clearly set out in the school's disciplinary policy (attached). Your line managers have lost confidence in your ability to perform to our high expectations.

This is to inform you that you will have two months to convince us otherwise. A senior colleague has been assigned to coach you to meet the standards you are failing. If after this probationary period you continue to underperform as verified through observations of your lessons, your contract will immediately be terminated and you will be dismissed from your post.

Yours sincerely,
Mrs Berol Bertram
Principal
Gwaine Academy

My heart hammers. I look up at Mum, hoping there's been some kind of mix-up, but she turns away, her face contorted with shame. 'I guess I don't know how to teach any more.'

'What you on about? You're the best chemistry teacher in Enley!'

'Maybe that was true once . . .' she says, sitting back down beside me.

'You're the KS4 coordinator!' I counter. 'It doesn't get much better than that.'

Her lips quiver. 'I'm not. They relieved me of those duties last term.'

I blink in surprise. 'But you never said anything!' She sinks into herself and my anger rises. 'Look, I know you don't want to, but you *have* to tell them about David. You need to make it clear that your head of department is a bully.'

She exhales, smiling sadly. 'Teachers are supposed to be able to cope with complex emotions.'

'Complex emotions and bullying are two very different things! David is a racist, Islamophobic thug! If he's like that with you, Mum, imagine what he's like with kids of colour.'

The downturned corners of Mum's mouth sink deeper. 'I shouldn't've told you.'

'Mum!' I cry in frustration, angry that David has somehow mind-swapped my confident, capable mother with the self-doubter I see before me. 'You're the one who's always telling me to never take anything lying down – you have to fight!'

'You think I didn't try?' Mum shakes her head, her eyes welling up with tears again. 'I should've left with my reputation intact when I had the chance. Your Nana and Nani always said arguing was my problem. It's why they disowned me.'

I calm myself down and take her hand. 'I thought that was because they thought Dad was beneath you?'

Mum sighs, putting her other hand over mine. 'Rashid is from a different caste. That made him "unsuitable" according to my parents. Anyway, my stubbornness eventually frustrated your dad too.' She taps the letter. 'And now it's cost me my job.'

I shake my head, lost for words.

She smiles sadly up at me. 'I'm sorry, beyta.' She gently strokes my cheek with a trembling hand. 'I'm just so *tired* of fighting.'

Liam has always told me I'm rubbish at being sensitive and he's not wrong. But even I can see now is not the time to convince Mum to fight back. So I just hug her instead.

In my mind's eye, I see Mum's case on the front page of the *Minerva Chronicle*: TOP SCIENCE TEACHER BULLIED BY RACIST COLLEAGUE. I need to get on the team and draw attention to stuff like this. Schools are meant to be safe spaces. We should be using our platforms to help create and maintain that safety.

But I'll have to think about the *Chronicle* tomorrow. Right now, Mum needs me.

CHAPTER 3

I wander through the maze of corridors. Being in the top set for English feels like a slam dunk – a real opportunity to show the Chroniclers I've got game. I'm still waiting on some inspo to drop an article into my head, which is a little worrying, but I'm confident I'll get there.

Wish I was as confident about finding my English classroom, though . . .

Thankfully, the younger Minerva kids are super helpful. Like cherubim, they practically fly me over to my lesson, their giant backpacks acting like beacons. Quickly adjusting my hijab, I knock on the door and poke my head inside.

Everyone turns to look at me, including the teacher who's taking the register. Mid-flow, he raises a finger, indicating he'd like me to remain standing till he gets to the end. *Whatever you say, Teach . . .*

I scope out the class. A small proportion of Bodley kids are mixed in with this very serious-looking Minerva lot. I smile at Liam before spotting Indira Jones and wondering who she paid off to end up in Set One. She smiles satanically, her asymmetric black bob a shattered helmet on her head, crimson highlights like streaks of blood. Indira's a spoiled princess who only ended up at Bodley because, like me, she flunked the entrance exam at Minerva. The difference is Indira's never counted herself among us – she's supposedly 'better'.

Two seats are available: one next to a strikingly good-looking Black boy with a square jaw, glasses and waves – I vaguely recognize him from the rugby team that jumped onto the stage in assembly. The other next to Ms Minerva Chronicle herself: Keira.

'You must be Dua Iqbal,' Dr York surmises, rising to his feet. Dressed in Harris tweed, he's as thin as a crack in a mirror. I get a vision of him in gum boots, tramping up the muddy moorlands at dawn, a bloodhound at his side, shotgun at the ready.

'I said would you prefer to sit next to Oba or Keira?' he repeats, making me realize I zoned out.

Hot Boy or Boss Gal: Distraction or Intimidation?

'I really don't mind, sir,' I tell Dr York with what I hope is a convincing shrug.

He raises his shaggy eyebrows and tips his head at the space next to Keira. As I install myself beside her, Keira briefly returns my smile before focusing back on Dr York. I throw an apologetic glance at Oba to show it's nothing personal and he smiles kindly.

Doing a double take, I realize Liam has forgotten to give Dr York his transmitter to wear round his neck. Without it, Liam could miss out on important stuff. I remind him with a gesture but he knits his eyebrows together obstinately.

'We're going to start with an activity that is as fun as it is meaningful,' says Dr York with unbridled excitement. 'In each envelope, you will find jumbled Shakespearean quotes. Your task is to match them up with the correct play. First pair to finish wins a teabag!'

'A teabag? Is that it?' calls out Harrison, a Bodley kid with a fiery explosion of freckles on his nose.

'Yes, a teabag of the finest Ceylon Earl Grey from Sri Lanka,' Dr York says proudly. 'Once tasted, never forgotten. And next time, dear boy, raise your hand if you have something you'd like to ask.'

'I got a question,' Mo says, asking about homework. Mo is Huda's boyfriend and an all-round nice guy. He used to come to

Mum for science tuition in Year Eight when he was struggling.

Once the envelopes have been handed out, Dr York produces a pocket watch from his jacket, a thumb hovering provocatively over the plunger. 'Your time starts *now*.'

I split the envelope and scatter the pieces between me and Keira. 'Get the kettle boiling, hun, cos we're winning that teabag.'

Keira smiles thinly before moving pieces of paper around with a perfectly manicured nail. *Don't screw this up, Dua!* I think. *This is practically a job interview.* We get it sorted in three minutes straight. I can't help the grin across my lips: clearly we work well together.

Throwing both hands in the air I cry, 'Done!' Dr York glides over, eyebrows wriggling like eels in fur coats as he checks.

'Good show, ladies!' he concludes. 'Here is your prize.' The teabag lands between us. 'The rest of you have five minutes to catch up.' #TeamDueira – the unstoppable journalistic duo no one knew they needed. Scratch that – sounds a little too close to *diarrhoea*.

Keira's face is as expressionless as a mannequin. Could that be Botox or is she genuinely not impressed with me? I prod the teabag. 'You want?'

She shakes her head. 'I've a collection at home just festering away in a jar.'

A small silence settles between us.

'So . . . how did you get to be editor of the *Chronicle*? Did you volunteer?' I ask, squirrelling away the teabag with pride.

'No, the process was *far* more rigorous,' she scoffs. 'There was a long application form and you had to submit an article on one of three topics. Then shortlisted candidates were interviewed by the previous editor and a teacher.'

'Sounds intense,' I say, impressed. 'We always wanted a paper at Bodley but there was never a teacher willing to supervise.'

'That's so sad,' she says, pouting. 'Well, good luck with your submission. I mean, *if* you're OK with the deadline?'

I grin confidently. 'Wouldn't miss it for the world.'

Of course, Mum's letter nuked any plans to knuckle down last night, but Keira doesn't need to know this. With Mum agreeing to take the day off to get advice from her teaching union, I can focus my energies on coming up with something special tonight.

'Come on, ladies and gentlemen!' says Dr York, snapping his fingers. 'Are Keira and Dua the only two competent students in the room?'

My skin tingles with pride, repping Bodley.

'So . . . how was your summer break?' I ask, keeping my voice beneath a whisper.

'Oh my God, it was completely wonderful: New York is stunning,' Keira says, touching her throat. 'We did the Statue of Liberty, catacombs by candlelight, lots and *lots* of shopping. Then one of Dad's friends gave us a private tour of the *New York Times* offices.'

I cover my mouth. 'The Gray Lady? That's mad!' She's talking about one of the most influential papers in the whole fricking world – the one Times Square was named after.

'How about you?'

'Nothing that compares to that,' I admit with a bashful smile. 'We did Alton Towers, I played basketball, made a little extra working at the local cafe and–' Wait for it, wait for it . . . – 'I had an article published in *This Uni Life*.'

Boom.

I'm expecting Keira to congratulate me, or at least ask what the article was about, but her interests lie elsewhere. 'Why did you need to make a little extra?' I blink at her.

For the editor of a paper, she's not doing a very good job of picking up on the important parts of this chat. How many more hints do I have to drop before she realizes I'm the ideal recruit?

'I'm saving up for uni. I don't want to be paying off my student loan till I become a "Gray Lady" myself!'

'Won't your parents take care of that?' Keira asks with concern, completely missing my witticism.

'Why would you automatically assume that?' I say, finding it hard to hide my annoyance. 'If that was the case, student loans wouldn't be a thing. Right?'

Keira nods. 'Touché. I guess having you Bodley kids here is a great eye-opener.'

Wow. *That* opened her eyes? Maybe that's why the *Chronicle* is so one-dimensional. Just another reason why someone like me could be an asset.

'OK, everyone!' Dr York calls out as Oba and Harrison hand out shiny new textbooks. 'In the light of that abysmal failure, I'm going to scrap my lesson plan. Open your textbook to page thirty and begin reading *in silence* while I print off some worksheets.'

The moment he leaves, the room erupts.

'Are you going to the Rumbal?' Keira asks Oba.

What the heck is a Rumbal?

'Who's hosting this time?' he asks with a mischievous grin.

'Rah, not me!' snaps the surly girl next to Liam. It's almost physically painful hearing 'rah' in such a posh, RP voice. 'Mother's still cross about the Breezer stains on the Tibetan sheepskin.'

'It's at Renée's,' Keira says, fully in her element. 'Everyone *chill* is welcome.'

'I'm chill,' Liam says, trying to be smooth. 'Can I come?' If he had said it to someone other than Keira, I might've cringed for him. But there's no way a journalist with Keira's integrity would do Liam dirty.

'Yeah, the invite's in the mail, Bodley bastard,' says a guy at the front, setting off a round of laughs, the loudest of which is

Indira's. Mo's mouth drops open.

I look at Keira, expecting her to jump in and defend Liam. She stays silent.

'She said *chill* not *chav*,' says the girl beside Liam. 'So no Bodley scum.' Indira's laugh goes from being the loudest in the room, to silent.

'That's discrimination!' barks Harrison.

The girl shakes her head. 'Actually, there are plenty of Minerva kids who join you on the blacklist. Katie and Elspeth over there, for example. Simon is a pervert, so obviously *he's* cancelled. Tanya "leaked" her own nudes so we don't need to see any more of her, either—'

'Hey, I'm cool with the Brides of Dracula,' says a boy, leering at Katie and Elspeth, who haven't uttered a word. They're both serving E-girl vibes through make-up and accessories. 'We can play three in a coffin!' He bucks his hips, making disgusting sex noises while people laugh. Oba puts his head in his hand.

'Did he really just say that?' Mo asks, blinking indignantly.

I can't believe my eyes. Katie and Elspeth look hurt and literally nobody is challenging these Minerva arseholes. Outrage fills my throat as I prepare to cuss the boy out.

'You'll only make it worse,' Keira says conspiratorially, putting what I think is meant to be a calming hand on my arm. 'There's no shaming the shameless.'

So me and the Bodley crew watch in horrified silence as the polished veneer of Minerva cracks and splinters right before our eyes.

I try to catch Liam's eyes to send some silent comfort his way. Then Dr York returns, and it's like none of it happened.

Packing up my stuff at the end of the lesson, as Dr York talks about our first assignment, I hover beside Keira.

'Hey, congratulations on winning the coveted teabag,' Oba

says as he passes our table, his eyes sparkling.

'Thanks,' I say easily. 'It's going on the mantle between my Orwell and Pulitzer.'

He laughs then joins his rugby mates in the corridor.

'So where do you usually hang out at break?' I ask Keira as she packs away the last of her things.

She raises her eyebrows, deliberately avoiding eye contact. 'Mm? Oh, I've no time for that. I'm interviewing the new PE teacher. The buzz is he was on the Olympic archery team. Enjoy the brew.' She bustles out before I can even suggest tagging along.

Indira whispers as she walks past: 'No one wants to be friends with an oppressed girl in a hijab.'

She's gone before I can even process what she's just said.

Liam is hanging by the door. 'I see you're making new pals while I still have breath in my body. The *betrayal*.' He dramatically mimes being stabbed in the heart.

I roll my eyes. 'It's called networking, bestie. Don't worry.'

'Really? Cos it looked a lot like arse-licking to me.' I give him a chuckle, trying to ignore the weird feeling in the pit of my stomach. All the arse-licking in the world wasn't going to get me any closer to Keira. 'Oh yeah? Well what about you and Chantel Adiche last year? Remember all the mouth-to-arse resuscitation? There were memes, fam.'

'That was different. I was *in love*, not trying to mooch my way onto some posh school paper.' Furrows rut his brow. 'There were memes?'

I'm about to crack a joke when I realize we're alone with Dr York and Liam looks uncomfortable. He's not usually one to linger . . .

Of course.

I drag him over to the front of the room, ignoring his confusion. 'Um, Dr York?'

'What can I do for you?' he asks, smiling at us both.

'Liam needs you to wear his transmitter next time so he can hear you better but he doesn't like making a fuss,' I say. Liam cringes but seems relieved.

'Ah!' Dr York says, looking at Liam with new eyes. 'I completely forgot. My apologies. Won't happen again.'

'No worries,' Liam says, going red.

I bite my lip. Snitches *do* get stitches, but I can't let it go. 'Plus, the boy who was sitting over there said some really disgusting, misogynistic things to Katie and Elspeth when you were out of the room . . . it was messed-up.'

Dr York blinks in astonishment. He takes a minute to absorb what I've just said. 'I shall have to pick him up from his period five class. Thanks for letting me know!'

His surprise makes me wonder what else goes under the radar here. Keira definitely didn't seem bothered. I'll have to write something about that.

SUBMISSION FOR THE MINERVA CHRONICLE

'Western Beauty Standards Have Left the Chat' by Dua Iqbal

Before we begin, full disclosure: I'm not that cute Asian girl you see on ads looking like she just sashayed off a Bollywood set. You know the type: golden skin tone, perfect teeth, hair to rival Rapunzel's, and snatched cat eyeliner. My complexion is a couple shades darker, my teeth aren't some glued-on polar veneers, I stopped being interested in having my face painted like a cat back in primary school, and I choose to keep my hair covered with a hijab. Still reading? Good, because my words are no less important.

When people like me enter a room, questions of religion, ethnicity and even stereotypes often get thrown in our faces on a sliding scale from mildly offensive to aggressively dangerous. Some days it seems everyone is entitled to a verbal poke and prod so <u>THEY</u> can feel comfortable with our 'otherness'. Well, this article isn't for those people. This one's for <u>us.</u> We have plenty to work on in our own community, without having to deal with Islamophobic behaviour too.

None of my grandparents want a thing to do with me. Did I do them some egregious wrong? I hear you ask. Not unless you consider a leaky nappy a hate crime. The only thing I'm guilty of is being born.

Let me explain: Desis will proudly tell you the caste system has been confined to the annals of (a shameful) history. But we know that's not true. It's alive and kicking in much of South Asia where you're expected to marry someone from your own 'tribe' to ensure your culture and family traditions don't get wiped out or 'lost'.

My parents met at uni and wanted to tie the knot. Instead

*of being delighted that my mum had found someone she
wanted to spend her life with, my grandparents forbade her
from getting hitched because Dad is from a 'lower' caste.*

*But those aren't my mum's values. The things that made
her 'swipe right' were Dad's religious commitment, kindness,
and sense of humour. You'd think that fifteen years down the
line your grumpy gramps would get over it. Not in this
community! We hold onto vendettas to a point where we rival
the corniest South Asian drama series.*

*What bothers Nani-Ji the most is that I've inherited my
dad's beautiful darker skin tone and wider nose.*

*Enter my wealthy aunt, who came to rescue me from the
bigotry of our community, likening herself to Cinderella's
fairy godmother. Fresh from a trip to Pakistan (and a
pit-stop in Seoul), she fluttered in with her 'magical' gifts to
fix the problems 'causing distance' between us and the
family:*

1) Luxury skin-whitening cream

*This product is from a major international brand that
was quick to post a black square on their Insta, claiming
'Black lives matter' during the global protests. The cream
promises to kill my wicked melanin, leaving me looking 'fair
glowing and lovely'.*

2) Non-surgical nose-corrector clip

*Picked up in South Korea, this popular item is supposed to
be worn every day until my disrespectful nose learns to
behave thinner.*

*3) A taffeta silk shalwar kameez with intricate
embroidery.*

*Bibbidi-Bobbidi-BOO-HISS! With the exception of
#3 – which is the one zardozi lining in this soufflé of storm
clouds – these gifts are brutal. In her head, she's 'just trying*

to help me marry a nice Pakistani boy' so that the family can finally ignore the part of me that belongs to my dad.

Oh, Auntie. I'd much rather a shattered glass ceiling than some glass slippers.

Let's be real: trying to reconcile the characteristics you're born with, the expectations placed on your shoulders, and the person you want to become is no mean feat. And being a woman of colour in Britain takes it to a whole new level. But even free from the eyes of the British, I'm still subject to scrutiny. There's no way to ever make everyone happy: I'm too dark, too Muslim/not Muslim enough, too tall, too 'covered up'/not covered enough and always way too mouthy.

Well, I'm ripping up the rule book and blasting stereotypes with a blazar cannon. I hereby solemnly swear to rock every facet of my identity and live my best life. I am an empowered British-Pakistani, I am an unapologetic Muslim, and I am a woman of many talents. I don't owe you 'cute' or an explanation. If that offends you, I suggest you follow Western beauty standards and leave the chat. Don't let the virtual door hit you on the way out.

CHAPTER 4

'You OK?'

I pull myself out of my reverie as I stumble out of biology. Mum couldn't get out of bed again this morning. Last night, I *had* to finish my homework and left her on her own downstairs. The guilt's been weighing on me all morning. 'Huh?'

'You've always been a Monday Person,' Liam says. 'What gives? Are you worried about the *Chronicle* announcement?'

We give a wide berth to a group of Thespians, who seem to be arguing with a bunch of Musicians about whether their grime-musical adaptation of Cinderella is a 'game-changer' or 'woke trash'. Man, Minerva's Clique Wars are like something out of an American high-school movie, not real life.

Wearily rubbing an eye, I shake my head. 'Nah.'

'Good, cos your article was fire. It's gonna help a lot of people feel seen and make others check themselves.' He scratches at the green paint on his blazer sleeve. 'Did your auntie really give you that nose peg and shit?'

I nod. 'Hey, don't tell my mum, OK? She's got enough to worry about and Auntie Irum is, like, the only relative who still visits.'

'Yeah, what is up with your mum? Waved to her in Lidl on Saturday and she blanked me like she was zonked or something!'

That terrible sinking feeling starts again.

Mum is a ferociously private person but I've been carrying this alone for nearly a week and it's already feeling too heavy. Besides, if I can't trust Liam, who's left?

So I spill the tea. I tell him all about Mum's ongoing troubles with her school and how it's worn her down to the point where she's not acting like herself any more.

Liam can barely contain his fury. 'You've gotta take them to court!'

'You don't understand. It's like she doesn't have the energy to fight her case,' I explain.

'Nah, your mum is like Boudicca in a hijab.'

'That was before.' We walk into the playground, daylight dazzling my sore eyes. 'She's lost faith in herself. And I didn't notice.'

He puts his arm around my shoulders and calms me down a little. 'Listen, don't kill me, yeah? But I think you should tell your dad.'

I fry him with a hefty dose of side-eye. 'You know the separation was ugly and Mum's vexed at Dad for all the times he missed childcare.'

'They separated, what – four years ago now? Look, I'm not saying he'll fix everything, but you won't feel like you're having to deal with it alone. Trust me – when things are really bad with Nan, my cousins are always around to help. It makes the world of difference.'

Liam doesn't get it. Back in Year Seven, Dad promised me everything would stay the same between us even though he and Mum weren't together any more. Every weekend he'd have me over to tell him how I was doing at school over a delicious meal he'd prepared. Then we'd shoot a few hoops at the park or watch a cheesy movie. Once the initial horror of having separated parents was over, Dad showed me that life could still be sweet.

Then the apologies began.

I couldn't go over at weekends cos he was busy with work. He'd send me expensive gifts I knew he could barely afford, but that was no substitute. I began to see less and less of him as he vanished behind a mountain of excuses. He even stopped paying child support. Then one day I decided to close the door on him. No Dad was less painful than one who kept letting you down.

That afternoon, as we're sitting in class getting confused while Rowntree tries to show us how to create an efficient revision timetable, the school tannoy system crackles to life. Rowntree nearly jumps out of her skin, clutching her heart, which makes a few people laugh.

'Miss, don't worry! They're going to announce the winners of that newspaper competition, not announce World War Three!' Huda tells her, trying to muffle her laughter.

The nervous excitement coursing through me feels lethal.

'It's in the bag,' Liam whispers, giving me a nudge. Is it? For sure my article is the best thing I've ever written and is ten times braver than the one that got published in *This Uni Life*. But was it too different for the *Chronicle*?

'Yeah, good luck, Doo-doo!' a mocking voice calls from behind us – Indira. Her demonic Cheshire Cat grin is back.

'What'd you say?' Liam asks, bristling.

'Are you *deaf*? Oh, right . . .' Indira chuckles at her own discriminatory joke. I start to clap back but Liam puts a hand on my shoulder, turning me back to face the front. I bristle.

Indira has never needed a reason to start beefing but here she's a Bodley kid whether she wants to be or not. She's one of us. Why choose now to go into full bitch mode?

On the tannoy, Keira and Renée are starting their announcement. My breath catches in my chest.

'I just want to take a moment to thank everybody who submitted an article, both from Bodley High and Minerva College. We read every piece with interest and they were all special in their own way.'

Polite filler from Keira. *Just get to the good bit already!*

'So without further ado, here are the names of the two students we are proud to welcome to our award-winning team today,' Renée says, like it's the fricking Oscars.

I knock my fists together, trying but failing to ease the tension.

'*Chloe Padgett-Price of Minerva College and Indira Jones of Bodley High!*'

There is a sound ringing in my ears like the aftermath of a bomb. A pressure swells behind my forehead, nerves misfiring as the world swims in and out of focus. Indira bounces to the front of the classroom and curtsies, waving her hands, demanding applause.

'The winners will each receive *Minerva Chronicle* lanyards with press ID badges inducting them into the British Press Association of Journalists, Photographers and Documentary Makers,' the voice on the tannoy squeals.

Liam rubs my back, pushing a tissue into my hand. 'It's a fix, man. Don't cry.'

Crying? Who's crying? It takes me a hot minute to realize that *I* am. Indira and her mates laugh, mocking me with finger-tears dragged down their cheeks.

It's all too much.

I have to bail.

Rowntree blocks my way, hissing for me to sit down. Dodging her, I run like a girl possessed, claiming sanctuary in the toilets.

Sitting on the loo with the seat down, I pull my two-piece hijab off and wait for the tears to end. How many people saw my breakdown? Not many, I guess. Rowntree's frog-like expression as I dodged round her springs into my mind and an uncontrollable torrent of hysterical laughter blasts out of my guts.

'Right, I'm coming in!' I hear the toilet door rebound off the door frame, feet slapping across the tiles, and a determined rap on the cubicle. 'Dua? Dua! Open up or I'm climbing over.'

I open the door. Our gazes meet and Liam slaps a hand over his eyes. 'Your hijab!'

Oops! Slamming the door shut, I smooth down my curls and loop my hijab over them. A moment later, I re-emerge.

'You're in the girl's toilets,' I say. 'They'll send you to the gallows for this.'

'Wouldn't put it past those medieval weirdos,' he says. 'You OK?'

I shrug, a shuddering sigh escaping me. 'I gave it my best shot and it just wasn't enough. Not to mention I shared a side of myself I don't normally feel comfortable talking about.' I hold my head in my hands. 'I'll never be good enough for them.'

'Screw them and their stuck-up paper! You're the best writer at Bodley – end of!'

'You're just saying that cos—'

'I'm speaking *truth*. Your writing is amazing, and you know more about real life than Keira ever will – plus you'd make a better boss. You're going places, Dua, even if those bigots can't see it.'

Bigots? They went out of their way to tick all the boxes. One Minerva recruit, one Bodley. One white, the other mixed. And like most people who tick boxes for the sake of ticking boxes, they've made sure no one will challenge them, their views or perceptions. They can keep publishing stupid horse-riding, out-of-touch stories and keep Bodley experiences at arm's length.

Wait. Back up.

What did Liam just say?

'. . . *plus you'd make a better boss.*'

'What?' Liam asks, sensing a shift in my internal universe.

But the idea is only starting to form, so I shake my head.

CHAPTER 5

We're standing under the bus shelter outside Minerva College, defending our positions at the front of a throng of kids as we're jostled by late arrivals seeking cover from the splattering rain.

'Can everybody moooove, please!' booms a girl, joining the queue. 'Rah! You lot are rude!' she trills when nobody shifts. 'Y'all gonna get bumped.'

Luckily the bus pulls up and Liam and I jump onboard, our cards beeping as we quickly tap in. I notice some of the passengers pulling their kids closer and clutching handbags as if we're feral. To be fair, some of us probably are. But still.

Liam and I head upstairs and crash across the prime seats at the front. I grab Liam's wrist and use his hand to wipe the steamed-up windscreen.

'Oi!' he cries in fake protest, until he laughs, using both arms like windscreen wipers before frowning. I follow his gaze to the silver minibus parking in front of our bus, plumes of blue smoke wafting from under its hood. Painted on the side in maroon and gold is the Minerva College emblem. A bald man with a giant sports umbrella gets out, jogs up to our driver's window and knocks. His voice is so loud we can hear it from all the way up here.

'Sorry, engine trouble. Got enough seats for fifteen boys?'

The Minerva rugby team pours out of the minibus, laughing and ducking, their bright yellow shirts and maroon shorts instantly drenched in the deluge. The other Minerva kids passing by say 'Hey' or exchange high fives. Fascinating. I've seen tons of

Minerva cliques hating on each other these last couple of days, but it seems the rugby lot get a universal free pass.

'Six seats upstairs,' the driver replies. 'Should be another bus along in a bit.'

The coach counts six boys onto our bus and instructs the rest to wait under the shelter.

'That's all we need: a bunch of entitled pricks spoiling the ride home!' Liam complains. I shrug.

The stairwell vibrates as the jocks arrive, hunting for seats. They're so huge and intimidating that absolutely nobody tries to block them with a bag or legs up on a seat. My nostrils are suddenly filled with a fresh but musky scent. I glance round and watch Hugo sit down a few rows behind us and signal for Oba to join him.

I mean he seems like a chill guy . . . but he's Minerva's golden boy. Probably a know-your-place kind of person like the rest of them.

Liam clutches his nose. 'God, one of 'em's gone a bit hard on the aftershave!'

'Stupid bus driver can't count! There're only five seats,' one of the players complains. 'Oba, go downstairs!'

'Why me?' Oba asks, quite fairly.

'Oh, don't make it a race thing!' he scoffs. Oba raises a brow. Liam and I roll our eyes. 'You missed that catch last week. We needed that mark,' the irate player says, tugging at Oba's shirt to make him get up.

'Oba's ten times the player you are,' Hugo says, batting the jock's hand away. 'Plus you stink like piss, mate. Get downstairs before I knock you down there myself.'

The guy hesitates for a moment, then storms off down the stairs.

'That whole school is white as hell,' Liam mutters as we turn back around. 'And coming from *me*, that's saying something. Aden shouldn't have sent us here! They don't even have a fingerprint system for the school lunches, how B-Tech is that?'

'I thought you'd be happy. At Bodley I believe you called it an "infringement of your civil liberties".' Liam's a bit of a conspiracy theory nut, but he's no flat-earther. It's much more fun than that. He just thinks differently.

'The only people happy about this whole thing are the Minerva kids: now they can call us "Poundland Kids" up close and personal. One of those rugby idiots told me my mum's so poor that when he stepped into a puddle she said, "What you doing in my bathtub?"'

'Arseholes.' I glance over my shoulder and glower at the team. Hugo has his arm round Oba's neck.

Suddenly, I'm distracted by the rugby top pulled taught against bulging pecs and the way he throws his head back as he laughs at something on Oba's phone.

My cheeks prickle as for one moment Hugo's incredible blue eyes meet mine. Maybe it's all the wet bodies on the bus, but steam shimmers in the air, framing Hugo like the star of some cheesy Eighties music video. I turn my back on this thirst trap *fast*, adjusting my hijab like a cloak of invisibility. Luckily, Liam's still seething so doesn't notice.

'She's in my English class,' I hear Oba telling him. 'She's really smart.'

I've managed to get through high school without crushing on anybody (except for Adam Saleh, but that was only cos half the girls at mosque were into him) and now suddenly this posh rugby guy thinks he can mess with that with his rent boy aftershave and his ridiculous biceps? *Miss me with that nonsense!* I have things to do. I *won't* get distracted.

The bus stops at East Enley Rugby Ground and I get another whiff of what I've realized is Hugo's intoxicating aftershave as the team departs. Feeling a tug on my scarf, I whip round to glare.

'Your hair was showing.' Hugo explains with a gentle smile before staring at my creps. 'Kobes? Those are like collector's items! Bryant was the GOAT.'

'Omigosh I'm forever telling my dad that!' I babble. 'He thinks nobody can touch Jordan.'

'No way. Bryant had the edge. Rest in power.' He makes a fist of solidarity and in spite of my reservations I feel something warm inside.

'Stop flirting with the Bodley girls!' shouts a meathead, bumping Hugo from behind. 'We've got a match to win.'

'As if you'd fall for a total prick!' Liam jeers once they've gone before catching the slightly dazed look in my eye. 'Oh my God. Were you two having a moment?'

'Of course not!' I snark. 'I was just being polite.'

Shaking the whole thing off with a shudder, I glance behind. *Depressed Bodley Kids, I see you.* Everyone looks homesick, the usual banter we enjoyed on the ride home absent.

On the opposite side of the road, the bus to Bodley High is arriving. 'Come on!' I say, dragging Liam by the arm.

'What? Why?' he stammers, coming along for the ride anyway.

'We're going back to Bodley.'

Ten minutes later, the rain patters to a stop as me and Liam hop off the bus, and nostalgia strikes like a wrecking ball. I am so not prepared. Bodley kids tear towards the bus, booming with laughter, gabbling with gossip, and chasing each other like headless chickens. It feels like coming home – a home you were forced to leave. I breathe in deeply and feel myself relax for the first time all week.

'Man, less than a week at Minerva and I already forgot what Bodley was like!' Liam says, gesturing at a couple of kids sneaking onto the bus through the exit doors.

'Y'all wild!' I tell the kids, laughing as they bustle past us.

We thread our way through the escaping carnival and towards the school gates.

'So you gonna tell me what we're doing here?' Liam asks. I could hug him. This one would follow me to the heart of Mount Doom without explanation.

'I have an idea,' I tell Liam seriously. 'And if you refuse to pledge your undying support, my heart will break. No pressure.'

He looks at me with bewilderment, trying to figure out whether I'm joking, but gestures for me to continue.

'I want to set up a paper for Bodley kids. Something *real* that talks about our lives. One Bodley addition to the *Chronicle* is hardly going to make us feel seen.'

'Especially when that token is Indira,' Liam agrees. 'But how are you going to get Aden to agree? You asked in Year Eight and he said no.'

'Yeah, that was Year Eight me. Do you remember how annoying I was?'

'*Was?*' I fake hit him on the arm and he laughs.

'I'll approach him as a mature Year Eleven young woman with my equally capable *deputy editor*,' I announce with more confidence than I'm actually feeling. 'We'll hold Aden to his "open door" pledge.'

Liam suddenly goes pale. 'We? As in you and me? Nah, bruv. I don't know the first thing about journalism.' He adjusts his right hearing aid. 'I don't think I can write good enough—'

'What you on about? You're in Set One for English at Minerva of all places! You're always questioning the version of the news we get and curious to know how things happen,' I tell him, waving a fist like a mace. 'We may not have money, or sexy cologne —'

'What?'

'– but Bodley has no lack of talent,' I finish, purging Stupid Sexy Hugo from my thoughts.

Liam doesn't seem convinced but follows me to Mr Aden's secretary's desk anyway.

Legend.

'Ah, Dua! Liam!' Aden says, smiling with delight as he welcomes us into his office.

Settling into a seat, I take a deep breath, delivering my elevator pitch. When I start floundering, Liam freestyles it, strengthening the case for why we need our own school paper and proving to himself that he has all the skills necessary to be deputy.

'And presumably you would be editor of this hypothetical newspaper?' Aden asks me, raising his eyebrows.

'Unless you think there's somebody who could do a better job?' I smile as nervous sweat gathers in my underarms.

'You're a brilliant student, Dua, and any school would be proud to have you.' He smiles kindly, building up my hopes. 'It's certainly a nice idea and I respect your tenacity, but as I told you before, we simply don't have the resources or a member of staff with time to supervise such a venture.'

'With all due respect, Mr Aden, we're in Year Eleven. You've already instilled important values in us, so we won't need such close supervision. And we'll be one hundred per cent digital.'

Aden strokes his neat little beard. 'I can't have you devoting time to a school paper when you should be revising for your finals.'

'Revision time is sacred – no arguments there,' Liam says. 'But we could do this for extracurricular. To broaden our experiences and prepare us for uni applications.'

'Plus we'd recruit other students to lighten the load so no one misses out on revision,' I add. 'It'd really boost the Bodley school spirit at Minerva.'

'Hmmm,' says Aden, hunching his shoulders. Now to clinch the deal . . .

'Look, sir,' I begin, 'we understand our community; the best and worst of it. Bottom line: we need to make more noise about both. Like when one of us wins a prize or contest or something, other kids need to see it and believe it could be them.'

'There are refugee kids on our side of town living under lies and rumours that they get five-star accommodation and govern-ment handouts,' Liam says. 'Anonymous interviews would help people understand what it's like to be them and that they was literally running for their lives.'

'And that's just one example,' I say, picking up the thread. 'You learn about some of this stuff in PSHE, but if you really want to make a difference, you have to keep the conversations going beyond the classroom. And they're *definitely* not happening in Minerva classrooms.'

Aden glances at Liam, who nods. 'Come on, sir. Give us a chance, eh?'

Aden sighs, leaning back in his chair, but I can tell we're getting through to him. 'If I agree to this,' he says doubtfully. 'I don't want it to be seen as direct competition to the *Minerva Chronicle* – especially since they've taken on Indira. I do, however, think the lower years would be curious to read about your *positive* experiences at Minerva. All articles must be submitted to me for final approval before you upload them, as I am answerable to the governors. Any suggestions I make will need to be acted upon without exception.'

My mouth drops open. What kind of a control freak is he?

'In addition to that,' he continues, as if he hasn't spoiled the idea enough already, 'you will need to make sure all content is fit for general consumption. That means it must be appropriate for Year Seven eyes and more importantly their parents.'

WTF? Their parents can read their own boring adult newspapers without sticking their beaks in ours!

His eyebrows twitch, the ghost of a smirk wavering over his delicate features as he studies me. 'I can see you want full control of the reins, and one day, when you're working as a professional editor, I'm sure that will be the case. However, for now, I must hold final say. That is the deal: take it or leave it.'

The red pill must be swallowed.

'We'll take it.'

'You was so gonna tear him a new one!' Liam teases as we walk home now that's it's stopped raining.

I scowl. 'Seven, actually – one for every day of the week.' Liam cackles and I scowl harder. 'The nerve of that man! It's our idea, our time, and our effort.'

Liam stops laughing. 'Look, if you're that vexed, we can forget the paper. Not like we signed any contracts or anything.'

'We'll do the paper, all right, just the way Aden likes so he doesn't have to get his principal knickers in a twist. He'll get bored soon enough, and when he does, that's when we start publishing the *juicy* stuff.'

A respectful grin spreads over Liam's face. 'I pity the teacher that gets in your way. But you told Aden we're gonna recruit other kids. Not gonna lie: most people will think this is lame.'

'Not if we sell it to them in the right way.'

'How? We can't put posters up at Minerva, my follower list could fit on the back of a postage stamp, and you aren't any more popular.'

Lightbulbs appear above our heads as we chorus, 'Roshni!'

CHAPTER 6

At lunchtime, I spot my quarry exiting the refectory. Roshni Arora, aka She Who Must be Stanned, is like the Arishfa Khan of Bodley. This social media influencer boasts a *mega* following for her beauty and party vlogs, lip-sync TikToks, and her hilarious clapbacks.

She stalks past, long hair fluttering like a silk curtain in the magnificence of her own slipstream. Somehow she's maintaining a three-way convo with mates at either elbow while also tapping away on her rose-gold phone with flawless acrylic thumbnails. Multitaskers are exactly what our paper needs.

'Hey, Rosh!' I begin, peeling off from the wall.

She blinks her magnificent feline eyes scornfully. 'Yeah, don't ever call me that again.'

I clear my throat, attempting to get back on track. 'I hear you're the go-to girl for all things social media.'

'If you're looking for a like or a follow, forget it. My brand is authentic.'

'Pfft! Everyone knows that – which is why I have a business proposition for you.'

She gives me an icy stare which I somehow manage to hold without breaking a sweat. 'You've got five seconds.'

'All I need, but it's for your ears only.' I give her friends a dismissive jerk of the jaw.

Roshni maintains the frosty glare for a beat before shimmying her delicate shoulders, dismissing her lackeys. 'See ya later, babes,' they say, wasting their best dirty looks on me. I try to stay relaxed.

'So the proposition is this: I'm going to be the editor of a chill online newspaper for Bodley and I'd like you to signal boost so people know I'm recruiting.'

She stares at me for a full three seconds. 'This about you not getting the Minerva paper gig? I heard you had a meltdown.'

Ouch. Guess more people noticed than I realized. Or Indira's getting a kick out of telling the story.

'And why do you think that is, Roshni?' I say, rallying. 'Why do you think girls like me and you, people with way more talent than Indira, always end up overlooked?'

An unspoken acknowledgement of the way things are passes between us.

She draws her beautiful hair back. 'OK. What do you need and what do I get out of it?'

My heart does a backflip. Roshni is a tougher sell than Aden and her unique skill set could make or break the paper. 'I need you to get my words out there. You help us grow and we return the favour. We'll do an exclusive article about you – the most followed teenage influencer in Enley.'

'See, I'm gonna need more than that. Assuming your online paper doesn't bomb, I'm gonna want a permanent role. Something I can put on sixth-form applications.'

I breathe a sigh of relief. For a moment there, I thought she wanted a salary.

'Done!' I put my hand out. She stares at it cautiously, like it might be unsanitary, before asking for my number.

'Send me your advert by six sharp,' she says, pinging me a text. 'If I think it's any good, it'll be up on all my socials.'

'You sure you'll reach the right sort of people?'

She rolls her eyes. 'There won't be a kid at our school who doesn't know about it. Getting them interested, well – that's down to you.'

*

Last period of the day is PE and it's honestly such a relief to be back in Bodley company so we can be ourselves. When the Blue Bloods are around, everyone – including teachers – acts differently. Not that they have it perfect. I was shook when I found out Minerva girls don't get to play basketball.

After a thrilling match, I get dressed and make a beeline for the doors. Roshni's 6 p.m. deadline is killer and I'm going to miss it unless I catch the early bus home. Liam's going to be pissed, but I'll just have to text him. Careening round a corner, I skid to avoid a couple of girls – oh no.

It's Keira and Renée.

'Oh, Dua! Sorry you didn't quite make the cut for the *Chronicle*,' Keira says, smiling sympathetically.

Renée's eyes glint. 'Yeah, but a paper lives and dies by its reputation. Your article was just a tad lacking in the grammar department.'

Keira hushes her, placing a hand on my upper arm. 'Are you OK?'

Her concern throws me. 'I'm fine. Wait. What? Lacking in the grammar department?'

'There's a rumour going around that you took it really badly. Ran out of tutor period bawling like a baby,' Renée says with Machiavellian relish.

'I needed the loo,' I say flatly. 'Now what did you say about my grammar?' Subconsciously my fists find my hips, my feet planting themselves in a boxer's stance.

'Your gram-mar,' Renée says, leaning forwards like I don't speak English. 'Colloquialisms and slang make for bad copy.'

Keira shakes her head. 'Your piece was great but the quality of the winners just pipped you to the post. It happens, I'm so sorry.'

Fake Sympathy or Brazen Mockery. Hard to say which is

worse. I square my shoulders. The voice in my head is telling me to drop it, go home, and work on the advert, but there's a righteous anger brewing in my belly which will not be denied. 'Come on, Keira, there's nothing wrong with my grammar, and besides, you said you wanted something written in my voice. What did Indira's piece about her shopping trip to Dubai tell you about her voice, other than that she really likes buying handbags? But I guess maybe mine isn't a voice you really wanted to hear . . .'

'If I remember correctly,' Keira says, furrowing her brow, 'the tone of your article was a tad aggressive. You started out well, and your style is definitely engaging, but you quickly descended into radical politics. Extreme points of view, particularly over religion and race, will alienate our readership.'

Now I'm mad. 'So basically what you're saying is that my article was great but you write for a white middle-class readership and don't want anything to do with the real world?'

Renée glares. 'We're not going to change our minds, so you might as well take that attitude back to the ghetto.'

I round on her. 'What, just because you speak with a posh accent and you have a lighter skin tone, that makes you better than me?'

Renée's hand flies to her mouth, a sound of outrage escaping her lips.

'Look, apologies for Renée's lack of decorum,' Keira says levelly. 'Your writing is good but reactionary. A journalist can't afford to let her emotions colour her reports. You'd be a liability for the paper, and as editor I have the unenviable role of making tough decisions. If that makes me a bitch, then so be it.'

'Plus your identity politics suck,' Renée adds. 'Blaming white people for your own failings is counterproductive.'

'Again, I'm sorry,' Keira echoes as they walk past me.

'You will be,' I call after Keira. 'The real reason you passed up on my article is because you feel *threatened* by me. You know, I could've been an asset: a friend who challenged you to produce your best work instead of massaging your ego like that slimy sycophant. You did me dirty, Keira. Mark my words: karma's coming for you.'

Neither girl shows any sign of having heard me as they mingle into the mass of swarming bodies.

Bodley's got talent and your school paper needs YOU!
   Calling all aspiring journalists, content creators, bloggers, vloggers, cartoonists, enthusiasts and people with a voice who want to be heard.
   We are creating an exciting online newspaper made by Year Eleven Bodley students at Minerva! Not only will it look amazing on your CV but you'll be working around passionate creatives who get you. If you've ever felt under-represented, ignored, or silenced, answer the call NOW.
   Register your contact details HERE.
   Share your skills, shape the world.
   (Karens need not apply)

I grin, imagining Renée going into cardiac arrest over the deliberate grammatical errors. I pick up my phone to run it past Liam— *Shit.* Liam! In my haste to get home and prove Keira and Renée wrong, I missed one crucial thing.

Cursing myself, I dismiss all thirty-seven missed messages from Liam in my inbox and FaceTime him. The phone rings endlessly and then, just when I think he must be on Do Not Disturb, an angry face appears and says with a harsh bark, 'What?'

'I'M SO SORRY,' I cry with shame.

He snorts. 'I waited at the bus stop till four. *Four!* Where was you?'

I cringe. 'I'm SO sorry! I got the earlier bus. Roshni gave me till six to come up with an ad for her socials. Again – I'm really sorry.'

'I looked like a right loser sitting at the bus stop, waiting for you!' he growls. 'This random old lady asked me if I'd just been dumped.'

'Well, at least she didn't offer herself up as a replacement!'

Liam stifles a chuckle.

'Please help!' I beg. 'I've got twenty minutes to complete our begging-not-begging ad before Roshni blocks me forever and I can't come up with a name to save my life. Any ideas?'

'Not till you apologize properly.'

'Bruh! Help now, apology plus cupcake tomorrow.'

'Red velvet from M&S?' Liam drives a hard bargain.

'I'll get you *two*.'

He considers it for a second. 'OK, what you got?'

'*Bodley News* and *Aden's Dictatorship Press*. Do you see my problem?'

He blows air through his nostrils. 'Ah, this is why you *need* me. I've already figured it out.' The suspense is killing me. 'How about *Bodley Voices*?'

Bodley Voices.

'Raaah! You're a genius!' I quickly add it to the ad, blow up the font size then fire it off to Roshni. 'I'm getting you three cakes. FOUR!'

By the time I've finished praying that evening and can finally settle down to start planning out *Bodley Voices*, I find Mum in the front room staring at the TV, laptop on her knees, teacher planner by her side. I sit quietly on the arm of the settee, my heart sinking when I see 'Lesson 1' at the top of a blank screen. She snaps the laptop shut with a smile.

'Hey, how was school?'

Her cheerful tone makes me hopeful. Maybe Mum isn't as out of it as I feared? 'OK, I guess. No new friends.' *But two new enemies*, I think sadly.

'Really? You've only been wanting to go there since Year Seven! Come on, tell your old mum what's wrong.' Hesitantly, I shift from the armrest onto the seat beside her and Mum slips an arm round my shoulders. My game face slips and suddenly I'm as vulnerable as a five-year-old.

'Minerva's beautiful in a private school sort of way and if I'm honest the teachers so far are brilliant.'

'But?' she cocks an eyebrow.

'The politics bother me.'

'Politics? Like friendship groups and general snobbery? Or do you mean the teachers are politicizing their subjects?' She frowns.

'Not the teachers.' I trace the swirls on my mother's shirt with a finger, searching for the right words. 'I mean, I get it. If a bunch of newbies suddenly came on my turf, I'd feel a bit threatened, maybe even resentful?'

'Well, it's silly,' Mum says, firmly. 'The Minerva-Bodley Trust is a two-way street. Both sides benefit. Just be your usual charming self and try to treat each Minerva student as an individual.' She rubs my shoulder with a thumb then stops. 'Something else happened, didn't it?'

I pause for a moment. Mum doesn't need anything else weighing on her mind. 'Nothing I can't handle, Mum. I'm OK, really.'

She insists on making dinner. For a while I'm lulled into a false sense of security. I don't want to have to worry about Mum on top of everything else. But the dinner tastes awful and she keeps drifting off mid-conversation.

What should I do?

The phone rings and I run to get it.

'Don't answer that!' Mum cries after I've already lifted the receiver.

'Aisha?' says the man on the other end. 'Look, you can't keep calling in sick. I've had to field calls all afternoon from angry parents! Just do everyone a favour and resign.'

'David?' I ask.

'Yes. Who is this?'

'Listen up,' I say, not giving away my shock that Mum was off again. 'Don't you dare harass my mum with your aggressive phone calls! She's sick, OK? *You* made her that way. So. Back. Off.'

A frustrated exhale. I picture a thug in a dress shirt, pretending to be something he's not. 'Put your mum on,' he orders.

'So you can abuse her again? Forget it.'

'Then we'll have to start legal proceedings.'

A hundred of the dirtiest cusses bubble up my throat. I slam the phone down before any can escape.

Mum appears in the hallway looking worried. 'Who were you talking to?'

I stare at the phone, then at Mum.

'Just some woman who wanted to know if I'd been in an accident that wasn't my fault.'

'Oh,' Mum sighs in relief before looking guilty. 'I thought it might be David again.'

'You mean you didn't go to work again?' I ask, unable to keep the judgement out of my voice.

Mum gives me a sheepish look. I fight tears. This is so not her. 'I couldn't find the energy. I feel so bad!' Her hands form tight fists. 'It's a vicious cycle. I worry about my students and feel physically sick until I'm incapable of preparing their lessons or going in to teach them.'

How do you react when your rock, your inspiration, turns to jelly? I'm fifteen. I might be able to recite the Periodic Table and give you all the key dates of the Second World War, but I have no clue how to support my mum's deteriorating mental health.

Mum presses her temples. 'Never took a day off for the first eight years of my career. Your dad used to say I had the immune system of Captain America or some other comic-book character. I was going places,' she intones. She dabs at her eyes with the tissue I hand her. 'Dua, so much in life isn't about merit, but who you know and whether your face fits.'

If ever I needed evidence that Mum is at an all-time low, this is it. She's always told me I can achieve anything I put my mind to.

Embers of irritation glow in her sore eyes. 'David and Mrs Bertram may have joined forces to push me out, but if I leave, it will be of my own volition.'

There's her fighting spirit. Maybe Mum hasn't been conquered after all. 'Promise me one thing. Go see the doctor tomorrow, yeah? She'll understand where you're coming from and give you a medical certificate. Then those evil shitfaces won't be able to harass you for a while.'

'Swearing is haram, Dua.' Just when I think I'm going to have to tell her about David's phone call after all, even though I'm petrified it may bring on a massive panic attack, she speaks up. 'It's been a while since I've seen Dr Jeyasingham. A little catch-up would be nice.'

I spend the evening googling how to manage intense anxiety, my homework lying unopened in my bag, *Bodley Voices* a pipe dream.

CHAPTER 7

'Are the chicken paninis halal?' I ask the dinner lady at lunchtime, scanning the quaint chalkboard menu overhead.

She clucks her tongue. 'Course they are with you lot coming here!'

I'm guessing she means Muslims. Hadn't really given it much thought, but while there's a large number of hijabis at Bodley, so far I've spotted only a couple sisters at Minerva. From her attitude, I'm guessing our presence has rubbed this woman up the wrong way. 'You know what? I'll have a Quorn noodle broth instead, thanks.' Can't go haram with Quorn.

The dinner lady rolls her eyes and slaps a corrugated pot on my tray, causing a strip of Quorn and a couple of beansprouts to jump out. 'Next!'

Glancing to my right, I notice Keira and blush, having threatened her with the almighty power of karma. *Awkward.* Luckily she's too busy goading Oba into going to another Rumbal than to take any notice of me.

'Don't be such a stick in the mud,' she berates. 'Your pole dancing was on point.'

'You know I wasn't in my right mind,' he says, chuckling.

They pass out of earshot, leaving me wondering why he wasn't in his right mind.

Somebody places a bag of fruit on my tray.

'Gotta get your five a day,' Liam says with a large smile.

I glance at his tray. 'Hate to break it to you, but hot dogs aren't a food group.'

He chuckles and we head over to a vacant table. 'You're in a surprisingly good mood,' I say.

'They finally sorted out a cashless payment system. Now I can grab grub without being trolled for my meal vouchers.'

'Can't believe Minerva kids would take the piss over something like that. You were right, they *are* a bunch of snobs.'

He smiles and bites a hunk off a hotdog, a generous amount of ketchup dripping down his chin. 'Anyway, today's the big day, Ms Editor-in-Chief! You nervous about the big *Bodley Voices* meeting?'

'Nah,' I feign, realizing 'nervous' doesn't even begin to cover the troupe of frogs performing an amphibious cancan in my belly. I try to take a nonchalant sip of soup but it goes a *bit* wrong.

Choking on a spoonful of broth is never a good look, especially when it results in an entire sprig of parsley flying out of your left nostril. I hide my nose behind a napkin. Indira, sitting with the *Chronicle* crew, points me out, tittering behind a hand. Renée rolls her eyes, mouthing '*savages*' to me.

'OK, so I'm bricking it,' I admit. 'Suppose no one turns up or they have these big expectations, realize I can't deliver, and bounce.'

'Mate, even Aden believes you can pull this off. Remember that time in Year Nine when you won the big debate? The judges called you "formidable".'

'Code for "mouthy little cow". Probably only gave me the award because they felt guilty for eliminating the other Asian kids in the earlier rounds.'

'Nah man – that's that imposter-syndrome shit. Half the time when I get good grades or win something, I'm like: did I do a good job or are they just feeling sorry for the deaf kid? But you know what? I worked hard, and I deserve it. And so do you.'

As always, Liam makes me smile. We eat our lunches, swapping ideas about how we're going to handle the after-school meeting.

Science is in the Faraday Building. The Christie Building, a whole five minutes away, is where we all have English. It's also the location of the impressive school library where Aden has booked our first *Bodley Voices* meeting. All through chemistry, my eyes are fixed on the clock, tracking the minute hand like the progress of an enemy ship on radar, knowing that at precisely 15.05 it must be intercepted. As the hand strikes the fifth minute past the hour, I bolt.

'Oi, Huda! Come back!' Rowntree shouts. When she tells me off tomorrow, I'll simply remind her she called for Huda. It's not my fault she can't be bothered to get my name right.

Like a bat out of hell, I flap my way out of the science block and barrel towards Christie. By the time I've made it up all four flights of stairs, my legs are spaghetti and my lungs seared steaks. But one look at the incredible library is enough to recharge my batteries. It's like something out of *Star Trek*: smooth grey panels broken up with blue strip lighting and a completely mad amount of books. I've never seen a school library so well-stocked. As I stride over to the horseshoe-shaped reception desk, I take in the glowing self-checkout units and poster-sized LCD screens advertising Minerva's Book of the Week, clubs and events in rotation.

'Can I help you?' asks the tiny librarian.

'I hope so,' I reply, living for the climate control which vaporizes the sweat on my upper lip. 'Our head, Mr Aden, booked one of the meeting rooms for us?'

She consults her computer screen and nods. 'You're in room three. Was there anything else?'

'Actually, yeah. Do you have like an archive of old issues of the *Minerva Chronicle*, please?'

She points the way.

Randomly picking three copies from different years, I head to room three. Each meeting room has glass panels so you can see what's going on inside. Pushing open the door, I'm impressed with the large table, row of computer stations, flip chart and frosty lighting. Seriously professional.

Nervously, I glance at my watch then get up and scrawl 'Bodley Press Meeting' on the flip chart. Just my luck it's a yellow pen.

'Hey!' Liam says, swinging in. 'You writing up disses in invisible ink?'

'Might as well be,' I say gloomily. 'Nobody's gonna show.'

But I'm wrong.

A cluster of students in blue blazers are soon making their way towards us.

I'm feeling a whole bunch of PDFs coming on.

'Be yourself,' Liam whispers. 'Well, the yourself that's people-trained.'

There's a knock at the door and Morowa Sarpong, a Ghanaian girl with large eyes and strikingly symmetrical box braids decorated with silver hair cuffs, pokes her head round. 'Hi, Dua. Is this where the meeting for the new school paper's being held?'

'Hi, Morowa! Yes,' I say cheerfully. 'I really hoped you'd join.' Last year Morowa was a UNICEF ambassador and owned assemblies with her provocative poems. Bringing that energy to our newspaper would be a gift.

I almost don't recognize Jenny Lim, who sat next to me in Year Seven manga club. I'll never forget the Hello Kitty stationery she got me for my birthday while visiting her grandparents in Beijing. Back then she wore shiny blue ribbons in her plaits and never spoke above a whisper. Now ruffling her incredible rose-pink pixie cut, she's showing Liam a keyring her girlfriend got her from a video games festival in London. Being a gamer, Liam is hanging on her every word.

Next to her is a bald mixed-race boy with thick, laminated eyebrows and lips glistening with gloss. I think he's called Max and, from what I've heard, he's a bit of a loner. I wonder what hidden talents he might have.

Our final recruit is a Somali kid called Abdi Awale, who's wolfing down a slice of pineapple pizza, a cat's cradle of cheese looping together his fingertips. Even thinner than Liam, he has closely cropped hair, and easily gets mistaken for a Year Eight kid, which helps him jump the lunch queue. Liam and I both grin because Abdi's a *genius* with computers. Pride unfurls in my chest as I clock the quality of our recruits. I clear my throat.

'Thanks for coming, guys. In case you don't know: I'm Dua Iqbal, your editor-in-chief, and this is Liam Ball, your deputy editor. I've been on at Mr Aden for literally ages to let us have our own Bodley paper and last week he finally agreed.'

'Probably from the guilt of sending us here!' Morowa says, getting a chorus of 'Facts!'

Roshni swans into the room, chatting on her phone. 'Bye, babes. I got this meeting now. I know, right? It's with that bossy Dua-girl.' She puts her phone away and looks at my unimpressed glare. 'What?'

'You're late,' I reply.

'Be glad I'm here at all,' she mutters, grabbing a seat.

Liam gives me a soft nudge, reminding me not to react. 'So why do we want our own paper?' he asks.

'Representation?' Morowa says.

'A place to vent?' asks Max, fiddling with a twinkling nose stud.

'Please!' Roshni chirps. 'It's so obviously because Indira beat Dua to the *Minerva Chronicle*. Just sayin'.'

'Bull!' Jenny says, running a hand through her pixie. 'That whole thing was a fix. Indira's been friends with Keira and Renée forever.'

'That's a pretty big accusation to be throwing around,' Liam says diplomatically.

'And I have the facts to back it up,' she retorts. 'Over summer, she posted a pic on her story of all three of them in the business-class queue at Heathrow. They were flying to New York *together*. Mighty fishy, if you ask me.'

Casual acquaintances don't go on family holidays together even if they are loaded. No wonder Indira was baiting me before the announcement. *She knew*.

'The past is the past,' I say, grappling with a sudden suffocating rush of anger. 'The future is where it's at. This will be our safe space. At Bodley, we had the student voice, where tutor reps went to meetings with teachers but basically reported back whatever the teachers had already decided.'

'Exactly!' Morowa says, rolling her eyes. 'How stupid did they think we were?'

Liam quickly pushes on: 'This will be our opportunity to talk about things that really matter to us. We can be critical of stuff but never rude. If we want change, we have to offer alternatives. We'll make creative decisions but Aden has the final word on what gets published.'

The entire room groans. 'So basically we're making a Bodley version of the *Minerva Chronicle*?' Max asks.

'So we're Aden's PR group then?' Abdi asks sceptically at the same time, licking his slender fingers.

'Nope. So long as we give him the articles *he* wants us to write, there's no reason we can't write stuff we find important too. We'll figure it out as we go along,' Liam says, helping calm the room a little.

'The *Chronicle* comes out monthly. You could pick up this month's issue and compare it to an issue printed ten years ago and you wouldn't find much difference. Check out exhibits A, B and C,' I say, tossing the issues I borrowed into the centre of the table. 'Journalism isn't about time capsules; it's about reporting on the here and now. We'll make our mark by being one hundred per cent in the moment, and the best way of doing that is to put new content out weekly.'

Jenny shakes her head. 'That's a pretty big ask given we're in our final year and homework is ten times harder at Minerva.'

There's muttering round the table, a general consensus that weekly would be impossible.

'Not if we keep the articles short and snappy,' I explain. 'Leave it any longer and interest will fizzle out. I need you guys to be committed. Aden is half expecting us to fail.'

'Do we get paid?' Abdi asks, grinning.

'Yeah, heard they get gift vouchers and cinema tickets over at the *Chronicle*,' Roshni says, looking up from a sneaky status update.

'You'll get paid good vibes from all the people you'll be speaking for,' I reply. 'Liam and I will edit your articles; fact-check your sources, and support you in any way we can. Like you, we'll be doing it for the love.'

'So what's the point?' Morowa asks.

'You get to be part of history,' Liam says. 'One of the seven *founding members* of a paper – it'll look insane on sixth form and uni applications.' Everyone pauses for thought.

'There are two rules,' Liam continues, raising his fingers in a V.

I clear my throat. 'Rule number one: no profanity or Aden will shut us down. Rule number two: no slander or Aden will shut us down. You sensing a theme here? Bottom line: do not get us shut down. Criticize whatever you want, within reason, but no naming names unless you can back it up with hard evidence.' I pause, letting that sink in. 'OK, I think most people know each other but let's go round the table, introduce yourselves and say what you want to write about.'

Abdi's narrow face stretches horizontally with a broad grin. 'I'm Abdi Awale, and I'm here for the graphics.'

'Yes!' Liam says. 'Nobody can touch you when it comes to coding and software.'

'True, true,' Abdi says, puffing his chest.

'Hi, guys! I'm Morowa Sarpong and I'm like hot sauce – you either love me or hate me,' she says with a cheeky wink. 'I want to write articles exploring Womanism and why feminism has failed women of colour.'

'LOVE,' I say, clapping. 'Your poems in assembly last year gave me chills.'

'I'm Jenny Lim,' Jenny says, making a V sign and posing like a celeb.

'Girl, your hair is *werking*!' Max says before apologizing for the interruption. His voice is soft with a gentle American twang.

Jenny smiles. 'I'm researching the differences in the way the local council treats the two sides of our town. We all know the rich people live on the east side. The roads on the west have so many craters you'd swear you were on the moon. Every winter there are a whole bunch of accidents because they're so slow to grit them. Coming over here, the difference jumps out.'

Liam raises a power fist. 'It shall be published.'

'By the way,' Jenny says to Morowa, 'You might want to add that feminism has failed the LGBTQIA+ community too.'

'I'm Max Benítez and I want to be your fashion and beauty guru.' He does the Grace Face pose.

Abdi bursts out with mocking laughter, making Max shrink into himself, his cheeks reddening.

'Something funny?' I ask Abdi archly.

'Nuh-uh, it's cool,' he says, folding his arms tightly across his chest. 'But what girl's gonna want fashion tips off a bald boy?'

'Look at your own five-finger forehead before you throw shade at Max,' Morowa scathes. 'FYI, plenty of make-up artists on YouTube are boys.'

I notice Max has gone very quiet, his chin tucked into his neck, his eyes watery.

I put my pen down. 'OK, as your editor, I need to remind you that this has to be a safe space. Everyone is invited to the party. I want you guys to own your uniqueness. Out there, difference is viewed as a weakness; in here it'll become your strength. Bring me your weirdest, craziest, realest selves. We will not live in shame or fear, no matter how much better the Blue Bloods think they are. This paper is for *us*.'

The room nods and Abdi mutters an apology over to Max.

'Max, the exquisite perfection of your eyebrows alone is enough to tell me your fashion and beauty column is going to kill,' I say. 'Prove me right.'

He perks up and I see something approaching respect in everyone's eyes. Even Roshni has put her phone away. Enthusiasm builds as everyone starts talking about what else we could include – movie reviews, top fives, sports, local events, bargains, a quiz. Friendly banter replaces suspicion, and mutual compliments start to flow as our ideas reach critical mass. For the first time since the meeting began, I start to relax, watching these guys thinking and acting as a team.

'Hey, know what we should do?' Morowa asks. 'Something like a celebrity roast of Minerva.'

'Satire?' I ask.

'Yeah. Like you said, it's not the easiest thing in the world being here. The snotty attitudes are suffocating. But we can't openly criticize them for obvious reasons. So we cover it with comedy.'

In my mind's eye, I see Mr Aden wagging a finger at me. I close the door on him. 'Putting smiles on Bodley faces is why we're here. I'm in.'

CHAPTER 8

'The Host Roast' by Dua Iqbal and Morowa Sarpong

Warning — failure to place your tongue firmly in your cheek before reading this article may result in scrambled brains and eighth-degree burns. Proceed with caution.

After a summer free of inhibitions, Bodley moved in with Minerva and gave birth to a beautiful Year Eleven baby. Discussions about names are ongoing — Borva or Midley? Everybody's a winner, right? In a cultural exchange of minds reminiscent of any of the Step Up *movies, Bodley's kids learn the fine art of snobbery while Minerva kids learn to act more 'road'. And that's not all! Bodley's students gain access to better facilities (expect anything not bolted to the ground to be resold on eBay) while Minerva learns for the first time in their silver-spoon-fed lives the value of 'sharing is caring' (and yoga in the face of rising stress levels).*

Sadly, this fail-proof transitional period has run into what some might call 'teething problems'. Grab yourself a biscuit, cos here comes the tea!

Minerva College proudly boasts a high-school hierarchy straight out of a Nineties teen movie. You have the Jocks, who can crack open walnuts in the crook of an over-muscled arm almost as quickly as they lose IQ points while headbutting each other in a bizarre pre-match ritual. Then you have the Tina Fey-approved Plastics who prance around like they're on the red carpet, telling absolutely anyone who'll look their way that 'Yes, my blazer was designed by Versace and my tartan kilt is Burberry.' There are the Journos, who are so desperate to be included with the other two crowds that they'll print anything to curry favour – including last year's news. There's a smattering of Emos and E-girls who get slated for expressing an opinion through an eye-catching aesthetic, and finally the Accomplished Ones whose academic focus is laser-sharp and likely to burn anyone who dares ask them for help. 'Someone call 999, we have another nerd-related injury!'

So in answer to your question: yes! Bodley's finest are having the time of their lives stepping on eggshells that are set to blow up in their faces like landmines. Did we mention there's also enough homework to carry you through to retirement?

Will the warring sides leave behind a school field of shattered egos and a double album's worth of diss tracks, or will the two schools end up in a group rendition of kumbaya? Only time will tell.

Tune in next time for more nonsense from Enley East!

Swearing for the third time, I realize I've lost myself in the labyrinth that is Minerva *again*. Backing up, I pause, overhearing a teacher whispering fiercely outside the Year office to the sour-faced girl who sits next to Liam in English.

'This is the second time this term you've turned up to class in this state! You promised this year would be different. You know I can't keep sending you to the library,' hisses the Head of Year.

'Won't happen again.' The girl giggles, her speech oddly slurred.

'It's not funny!' sniffs the teacher.

'Sorry. Guess I'm still high.'

I cover my mouth, wondering who'd admit a thing like that so casually to a teacher. Man, is Minerva different.

'You're an excellent student but you've had four chances already. Any more of this and we can't accommodate you any. . .' The teacher falls silent then is suddenly right in my eavesdropping face. 'Can I help you?'

'Yes, please,' I say, beaming even though I'm crapping my pants. Hastily admitting I'm lost, she gives me directions and I'm out of there at light-speed.

'Dua!'

I turn round, trying to balance my physics and bio textbooks.

'Did you write that article for *Bodley Voices*?' asks Josiah, pulling out an airpod. 'The piss-take one?'

'Co-wrote with Morowa. It was supposed to be a lot more vanilla but Morowa kept coming up with all these killer lines.' I bite my lip. 'You think we took it too far?'

'Nah, man. It's jokes!' he says, chuckling, walking further down the corridor. 'Besides, one of their players literally just called me a "roadman" cos I kicked the goalpost after he fouled me. This feels like payback. It felt real.'

Harrison walks past and thumps me on the back, his ginger spikes quivering with enthusiasm. Unfortunately, my textbooks go flying.

'Here, let me do that,' he says, dropping down and picking up my books. 'I always thought you were weird but you're actually pretty chill.'

'Thanks. I think . . .' I say, backing away and bumping into Huda. 'Sorry.'

'Hi, Dua,' she says, blue satin daisies circling her hijab in a boho crown. 'I want to write for the paper too. Here, these are a couple of articles I wrote.' She thrusts a wodge of sheets into my hand, giving me a paper cut.

'Er, thanks. I'll get back to you.' I step away and bump into Keira. When did the school corridor turn into dodgems? I think I have concussion. 'Sorry.'

'You will be,' she says icily. 'So I'm a Journo who prints last year's news?'

'Um. It was a joke?' I say, dipping my eyebrows, wondering who told her about our paper.

'Let's see how funny you find it when you and your chavvy mates get excluded.'

With those chilling words, she vanishes into the crowd just as Liam emerges.

'This is surreal!' Liam says, his cheeks rosy with excitement. 'Mo was just telling me how much he liked my review of the best free events in Enley.' He shakes his head. 'All our lives we're nobodies. Two weeks and one issue later, everyone knows who we are and exactly what we stand for. Say what you like about Roshni, but that girl has more influence than PewDiePie.' I shake off Keira's threat and focus on Liam.

'Yep. Think I fractured a knuckle from all the fist bumping,' I agree, rubbing the back of my hand.

'Think it was a fluke?'

'Mate, issue two will be even better,' I blag.

'*If* there is an issue two!' says Mr Aden, materializing behind me.

Liam and I both about-turn, our eyes bugging. 'What do you mean, sir? The paper is a hit,' I say.

'Let's find an office to discuss it. I'll write you both notes to explain the delay to your next lessons.'

Liam and I resign ourselves to following Aden to the interview rooms at the front of the school. Denial is more than a river in Egypt. It's a lie that makes you feel invincible till reality sets back in. I know I've brought this on us.

'Let's start with the positives,' Aden suggests. '*Bodley Voices* is certainly professional-looking, has a nice range of articles, and good photos.'

'Also no profanity, nudity, slander or fake news,' I point out, trying to soften the blow of Aden's so-obviously-coming reprimand.

'Ye-es . . .' Aden allows, though he doesn't look the least bit impressed. 'I did, however, spend quite a bit of time Googling the meaning of some of your more colourful phrases. I'd always assumed tea was an aromatic beverage one enjoyed with biscuits, but apparently it's slang for *gossip*.'

'There you go! Bodley is all about putting learning first,' I yammer.

'Everybody's been mad complimentary about it!' Liam says, jumping on the enthusiasm bandwagon. 'Bare people have been asking if they can join the paper too. Even a Minerva student — this kid called Tristan.'

I snap my head toward Liam in surprise, before realizing Aden is waiting for us to shut up. 'I find that hard to believe after the appalling article comparing the unification to war on a battlefield,' he says.

'That was just jokes!' Liam explains.

'Joke or not, it was inappropriate. You took a pop at Minerva students, characterizing them as snobbish toffs — what would their parents say if they were to read your article?'

I sigh inwardly. I knew some of it was going too far, but Morowa convinced me that jokes and parody got a free pass. We egged each other on. Still, as editor, it was my responsibility to put my foot down, and I lapsed.

'With all due respect, sir,' I begin, my hijab steaming like a sauna. 'It's a newspaper for Bodley students, not a newsletter for parents.'

'Have you already forgotten the terms of our agreement? Come on, remind me what they were.'

I ball my fists at being patronized. 'We were supposed to submit every article for your approval before uploading to the website.'

'But we did that, didn't we?' Liam asks, looking from me to Aden and back again.

'Yes, you did,' Aden concedes. 'Just not *that* one.'

And just like that, my terrible executive decision is laid bare. Liam and Aden are both unimpressed.

'It was a last-minute addition,' I say calmly. 'I honestly thought it was pretty harmless and would give people a bit of a laugh. Everybody's proper stressed with the shift, you know?'

Aden strokes his beard, sighing. 'I understand, Dua. I wasn't born without a sense of humour. But Minerva has been very amenable in allowing us to use their facilities. Would you have preferred being taught on Bodley premises in a Portakabin like a refrigerator in the winter and a furnace in the summer? We simply cannot risk offending them. Do you both understand?'

'Yes, sir,' we say in unison like a funeral dirge.

'If anything like this should happen again, I will be forced to revoke your privileges and *Bodley Voices* will be over.'

CHAPTER 9

Summer is defeated for another year as autumn saps the blue from the sky, turning it into a featureless cold, grey void. Glancing at the clock, I wonder why Mum hasn't come down for breakfast and decide to take it up to her on a tray. Knocking on her door gently, I peek round. The curtains are still drawn, casting the room in a pessimistic gloom. A human-shaped lump hides under the duvet, her back turned to me.

'Mum?' I say gently, tiptoeing in. Her face is screwed-up, worry lines etched into her forehead. Even in sleep Mum cannot find peace. I don't have the heart to wake her, so I leave the tray on the stand. I'd hoped getting signed off from work would bring relief but now all she does is lie in bed all day.

Back downstairs, I spot the local paper and have a quick flick through while I boil the kettle. Same old, same old . . .

I back up, certain I saw mention of Minerva College somewhere. Skimming and scanning, I finally spot it on the letters page.

I would like to draw your readers' attention to some of the many problems that have arisen from the recent Minerva-Bodley Learning Trust partnership. The public consultation was far too short to establish any meaningful dialogue, and criticism was largely ignored. These two schools couldn't be further apart in outlook! Minerva has a proud history of catering to the borough's most able students, whereas Bodley does a good job of helping the less academically minded. The latter school caters to predominantly BAME students, which

*is reflected in curriculum choices and their annual celebration
of Black History Month and Bollywood-themed school
productions. Neither of these are of particular relevance to
Minerva students, whose extracurricular activities include
rugby, archery, rowing, scholarly debates and organizing
charitable dinners. I do not say this as a slight on character.
Both schools have noble and lofty aims for their respective
communities. However, their needs are quite disparate and
unique, and in throwing them together we are failing both.*

*My concern arises from having found drugs on my
daughter last week. One does not like to cast aspersions, but
this sort of problem did not arise until the Learning Trust
was formed. Draw your own conclusions! Rather than
Minerva being a shining beacon to guide Bodley students, it
appears our children have fallen astray!*

'The nerve of that parent!' I say, gripping the rail on the bus
fifteen minutes later. Having already told Liam about the conversation I overheard between his English partner, who was clearly
high, and the Head of Year, I'm spitting teeth.

'I feel you,' Liam says, handing the paper back. 'Insane that
someone thought they could blame us for their daughter's drug
problem – and even more insane that the paper printed it!'

'Look at how it makes out like Minerva kids are some shining
beacon of perfection. Remember how disgusting they were being
when Dr York left the classroom? Makes me wonder what the
heck goes on at their Rumbals,' I snap, waving the rolled-up
newspaper like a club.

'That paper is trash.'

'Exactly! Like why would they mention race at all? It's the
racist stereotype that we're all a bunch of low-achieving
smackheads.'

'Someone should report them to the press watchdog.'

I briefly consider doing it myself but the idea of adding even one more thing to my to-do list makes me feel physically sick.

'Could that someone be you?'

Liam covers his face. 'Love to, but I'm taking Nan to the doctor's after my speech and language session.'

'Is it getting worse?' I ask sympathetically.

He peers over his fingers, his eyes red as he nods. 'She left the stove on again. Coulda burned down the whole estate.'

Instead of asking him why the batteries in the smoke alarms still haven't been replaced, I tell him everything's going to be OK. I decide I'll fire an email off to the press watchdog during lunch, after checking up on Mum, of course.

I send a silent prayer up to the gloomy sky for me to discover a long-lost twin or something that meant there'd be two of me: one to stay at home and keep an eye on Mum, while the other goes to school.

'Silence!' snaps Miss Rowntree as I add another label to my diagram of a bacteria cell during tutor period. 'We have an assembly with Mr Aden this morning.' Between researching how to help a depressed parent and facts for my next news article, homework sort of got bumped to the bottom of the pile. Lucky for me, biology's never been a problem, so I should have this sorted in the next two minutes before we have to go to the hall.

'Dua!' she suddenly shouts. I jerk, raking my pencil through my painstaking work. 'Why are you out of your seat?!'

Glancing round I realize she is having a go at Huda, who is comforting a distraught girl at the back of the classroom. 'Miss, she's upset cos some guy on a moped thieved her phone,' Huda explains.

'Well, that's what you get for waving expensive phones around on the way to school!'

That is harsh, even by Rowntree's standards. Harrison points this out to her and gets slapped with a detention. It's at this point I notice Rowntree's bugging eyes and sickly pallor. The woman is stressed and I'm guessing Aden's coming assembly might have something to do with it.

By the time we're silently seated in the hall, it's obvious this will be no regular assembly. For one thing, the Blue Bloods have been left off the invites. For another, Aden is wearing a black tie. We've had patterns, colours, even anime characters – but never monotone.

'Good morning, Year Eleven,' he says cursorily. 'At the start of the year, we explained why we had chosen you, our precious Year Eleven, to study at Minerva. I also made my expectations about your behaviour and attitude exceptionally clear. You are in your exam year, I said, and there is no room for a lapse in focus. But you have let me down.' He pauses, swallowing us all in a disappointed stare that consumes me with guilt for every bad thing I ever did since the day I was born.

'*Drugs.*' It explodes from his lips like the filthiest swear word. 'Specifically, the misuse of them for recreation. Yesterday, I had to permanently exclude two students for engaging in this filthy habit.'

A ripple of shock runs through the crowd.

'Some of you seem to think that since Minerva College has opened its doors to you, you can abuse their hospitality. I am *deeply* ashamed. Sir Reginald brought it to my attention after a number of parents complained. The students in question have brought the entire Bodley community into disrepute! The same rules have *always* applied: if any one of you indulges in the buying, selling or sharing of drugs – no questions asked, you will be excluded! You will be saying goodbye to your education and the chance of A levels at any reputable school.

'I was going to involve the police, but Sir Reginald graciously said he'd prefer to have us deal with the matter internally. So my message to you is this: end the nonsense now so we can hold our heads high and achieve our best GCSE results. It's *your* future.'

'This is bollocks, man!' Josiah says once we've been dismissed. 'Two players from the school team? How are we supposed to win without Mo and Joe?'

'Do you know what happened?' I ask, still reeling.

He shrugs. 'Yesterday during PE, someone tipped a teacher off and Mo and Joe had their bags searched. They found weed but I'm telling you it must've been planted. I bet that racist Sir Reg pushed Aden into excluding them!' He kicks a fire extinguisher and slopes off, leaving me in shocked silence.

A sombre procession of Bodley kids glides past to their next lessons. Among them I spot Huda, her face flushed and contorted. Just when I realize she's doing her best not to cry, she ducks out of the line. I finally catch up to her on the stairs.

'Huda, don't cry, hun,' I say gently, sitting down and handing her my pack of tissues.

Taking one, she dabs at her eyes, eventually descending into some good old-fashioned ugly-crying. Eyeshadow and eyeliner run together, forming glittering black streaks down her cheeks. I wrap my arms around her and tell her everything's gonna be fine.

'No it won't!' she snaps, drawing back. 'My fiancé got excluded, for flip's sake!'

'You mean your boyfriend, Mo?' I ask, a little surprised.

'Boyfriends are haram,' she says, giving me a dirty look. 'Our families know each other so Mo and me are tying the knot when we're both sixteen. Or at least we were gonna before he got excluded for *nothing*.'

'He had weed,' I say sadly.

'Bullshit!' she cries. 'We've been together nearly two years. If he was a druggie, don't you think I'd know?'

Mo doing drugs doesn't gel with the kid who used to come to our house for tuition, but I *guess* people can change?

Huda stares at the damp, multicoloured tissue in her hand. 'Mo's into football, PlayStation and helping with the Sunday madrassa at Enley mosque. That's it. He literally has no interest in drugs. Plus, Joe is my next-door neighbour. He cuts our hedges for free and politely listens to Dad banging on about cricket. That boy is a saint!'

Hiding in the shade of an elm, I dial the number Huda gave me. He answers on the fourth ring.

'Who is this?' Mo's voice is strangely dull.

'HeythisisDuafromschool!' It shoots out of my mouth all at once like projectile vomit. 'I need to ask you something.'

'Sorry, I don't feel like talk—'

'Wait! I believe you were set-up but I've got to know the truth.'

A quivering sigh echoes in my ear, 'There was this guy at the school gates, acting all friendly and stuff. Gave me and Joe a bag of weed each and wouldn't take them back. Called them free samples and said if we didn't want them, we could sell them on or give them to a mate. Then the bell went for PE so I just sorta stuffed it in my bag. It doesn't matter that I was going to chuck it later cos someone grassed us up.

'Look I gotta go. I'm sorry.'

'Thanks for coming here on such short notice,' I tell the news team at lunchtime after commandeering an empty classroom from a bunch of Year Sevens playing swapsies with their *Fortnite* stickers.

'Is this about the letter from that vile parent in the *Enley Post*?' Morowa asks, using her phone as a mirror as she tries to reattach a slippery silver cuff to a braid.

'My girlfriend showed me that!' Jenny says, slamming her fist down. Her pink pixie cut is looking particularly prickly. 'Coward had her name and address withheld.'

'Just as well,' Abdi says matter-of-factly. 'Or "someone" might've smashed up her windows. Know what I mean?'

'Interesting you both assume it was a *she*,' Max fairly points out.

'Assumptions!' I say, pointing an accusing finger at no one in particular. 'That's what we're here to talk about. Two of our own were excluded for possession. I've had two independent character witnesses corroborate that neither Mo or Joe have ever done drugs or are likely to. Abdi, can you help me hack into SIMs so we can check their records to verify this?'

Abdi shrugs. 'Sure thing. Gotta go in and delete a detention I got in maths anyway.'

'Woah! When did we start breaking into private school records?' Liam asks in horror.

'When shit got serious,' Jenny says glibly.

I tell them about my call with Mo. 'The problem is we don't know who the guy handing out weed was. Secondly, it's been suggested that Sir Reg is a racist who pushed Aden to exclude,' I continue.

'I saw Harrison and Josiah both walking down the corridor in their trainers,' says Morowa. 'Sir Reg stopped them but all his telling off was aimed at Josiah, like Harrison must have been dragged into it. Coincidence? I think not.'

'An exclusion can seriously affect someone's future,' I say. 'Sir Reg was wrong to pressure Aden, and Aden was wrong to roll over. Those boys did not deserve to have their final year messed up for a first offence, especially when it was a mistake.' Swallowing thickly, I tell the crew about witnessing the Minerva Head of Year sending a girl to the library for getting high at school. 'Apparently this was her *second time this term*.'

'So one rule for them and another for us?' Abdi snaps.

Liam flexes his jaw thoughtfully. 'You want us to write an article?'

I nod.

'Are you people mad?' Roshni asks, stabbing the table with a nail. 'You nearly got cancelled for just *joking* about this school. Aden will crucify you for sure if you publicly challenge him.'

I rub my temples, feeling the throb of an impending headache. My mind swirls then spits out an unpleasant memory: *GROSS MISCONDUCT*.

'What's the point in having a platform if you don't use it to help others?' I say wrathfully.

'We already know that parent in the *Enley Post* was scapegoating us for her daughter's habit.' Morowa points out.

'How long before another Bodley kid gets set up and this happens again?' Jenny asks.

'Know what I think?' Liam asks. 'Too many unanswered questions. We ain't ready to run with this article. Not yet – but we should start collecting evidence: figure out who's dealing, who's buying, see if there is an actual problem.'

'From both schools,' Morowa adds. 'That way we'll know if it's the "Bodley problem" they're trying to frame it as or if Minerva are projecting. We need to make people care about it enough to investigate.'

'Apparently they hold exclusive parties called Rumbals,' I tell her meaningfully.

Morowa notes it down. 'I'll see if I can finesse an invite or sneak in.'

Abdi shakes his head. 'Mo was a great striker. Arsenal came sniffing when they saw him in Sunday football league. Josiah's gonna have to carry the team alone now and for what reason?'

'I'm telling you, if you use *Bodley Voices*, it'll be the last thing you print,' Roshni warns. And though it pains me to admit, the girl's not wrong.

'Then we'll just have to use something else,' I say, refusing to let it go. Somewhere in my mind Sir Reg and David, Mum's head of department, have just become the same person: a combined entity of prejudicial wickedness. My conscience demands justice. 'Snapchat, maybe? We need to get everyone involved in a silent protest. Let Sir Reg know he's not shooting fish in a barrel. We're piranhas and we fight back.'

'How about sending a link round for an online petition?' Jenny suggests.

'Perfect!' I say, pointing at her. 'Maybe we could get everyone to wear badges in protest.'

Max shakes his bald head. 'Badges would cost too much and take too long to make. If you want to make a silent protest, get everyone to wear a black armband.'

'Those are for mourning death,' Morowa points out. 'My Uncle Elolo owns a printing shop. Maybe I could get him to do stickers on the cheap?'

'Everyone loves stickers.' Liam agrees.

'Great!' I say. 'Graphics-man-Abdi can help you create an eye-catching design. Roshni, if I come up with a message, can you get word out to all your Bodley contacts?'

Roshni sighs, looking at all our pleading faces. 'Fine. It's your funeral.'

#JUSTICE4MO&JOE

   2 Bodley kids have been permanently excluded for a crime they did not commit.

   The boys maintain their innocence claiming the weed was planted. This allegation should have been properly investigated. Aside from just being good people, they were in their final GCSE year and getting booted will damage their futures. A first offence should not trigger a death sentence.

   THESE BOYS MUST BE RE-ENROLLED AT ONCE!

   Show your support for the cause by wearing a sticker this Thursday and signing the online petition which will be handed to Sir Reg and Mr Aden on Friday.

The next day at break, I walk to the rendezvous point by the lockers. My palms are clammy and my lungs feel shrunken. 'Special delivery for Ms Iqbal,' Morowa murmurs from the corner of her mouth like a CIA agent, slipping a plastic wallet to me. Inside are several glossy sheets of custom-made stickers. #Justice4Mo&Joe printed in blood red on a black background.

'Uncle Elolo is a lifesaver,' I mutter.

'Then why do you look like you're on Death Row?' Abdi asks me. I ignore him.

'Roshni, did you put the word out?' I ask, licking my dry lips cos Abdi is right: I am scared. If this goes spectacularly wrong, I might be looking at my own exclusion.

'Did my part. Now I wash my hands of it. It was nice knowing you.' Roshni wrinkles her brow. 'Scratch that.'

Her snub sets off an electrical storm in my already fraught nerves. I'm praying she means she doesn't want to be part of the protest. If she's leaving the paper, we're dead.

'We really doing this?' Liam asks nervously. 'I put the table out there in the playground but if we don't move fast, someone's gonna move it back.'

Trepidation stands out on each of my friends' faces. But if we don't make a stand today, Bodley students will be easy pickings for the rest of the year.

Tucking the wallet under an arm, I march out into the playground, feeling strangely empowered by every step I take. Soon my friends are flanking me and we move as one towards the desk under the flagpole with so much gritty determination people stare at us like they can sense something big is going down. Abdi throws open his blazer, whipping out a pair of tablets like twin guns, ready to add signatures to the petition. Jenny and Max unfurl a banner like a pair of rhythmic ribbon gymnasts, attaching it to the front of the desk, making our cause clear. Me, Liam, and Morowa split the stickers between us, ready to slap them on supporters and spread the word.

The response is unlike anything we could've imagined. Within minutes there's a mad rush for the stickers and people queueing up to sign the petition on the tablets.

Hugo, singing Drake's 'One Dance', is walking past with his mates when he suddenly makes eye contact with me. My heart skips a beat. Flustered, I end up giving somebody two stickers. When I look up again, Hugo is in my face.

'You're the girl-with-the-Kobes!' he says cheerily. 'I'd like to donate to the cause.' He reaches inside his blazer and pulls out a twenty.

'It's not that sort of cause,' I say with irritation. 'Two Bodley kids got excluded for drugs without a proper investigation.' I wonder why I'm wasting my breath. It's not like Blue Bloods – who never wanted us here in the first place – are going to care.

'There must've been evidence?' Oba says sceptically, stepping forward from behind Hugo.

'It was planted,' I say, bristling. 'They never took or sold drugs before. Anybody who knows them, knows they wouldn't.'

'That's so unfair!' Hugo says, frowning. 'Can *I* sign the petition?'

Dumbfounded, I swallow. 'Um, I guess so?' I hand him a tablet and he signs, then shouts to his jock mates, telling them to get their arses over and sign the petition too.

Giving them room, he moves a little closer to me, sending involuntary chills down my arm. I cringe and suppress an eye-roll at my own damn self. Being taken in by Minerva's MVP is Not. Part. Of. The. Plan.

'So you gonna tell me your name or am I going to have to keep calling you girl-with-the-Kobe's?'

'Dua,'

'Can I get one of those cool stickers please, Dua?' he asks with a cheeky grin.

'Sure,' I say, grabbing a sheet and peeling off a sticker. 'Where do you want it?'

'On his dick!' one of his friends says, making me blush.

'On my tie, please,' Hugo says, puffing his chest out. Maybe I'm thinking too hard about it, but there is something horribly intimate about grabbing his tie and placing a sticker on it. His aftershave slips inside my nostrils like an aphrodisiac. Why can't the boy wear bog-standard Lynx like everyone else?

'Thanks for your support,' I say brusquely, grabbing Huda like a shield as she's walking past, a slice of pizza dangling limply from her lips. I tell her to sign the petition, laying out all the benefits in graphic detail until I'm sure the jocks have gone.

'I already signed it!' she sniffs.

We clock up tons of signatures before the shit hits the fan.

The agent of our downfall comes in the sleek form of a Minerva teacher in a black roll-neck sweater, twisting her pearls like a garrotte. 'Do you have permission for all of this?' She waves a disparaging hand at our table.

'Justice for Mo-Joe!' shouts Harrison from behind her in answer, pumping his fist.

'MO-JOE! MO-JOE!' bellows Josiah and some other Bodley kids, joining in.

'Strike a pose!' Max sings, voguing to the chant. 'Joe was innocent, Mo was too. Mo-Joe Mo-Joe, We love you! They were us, they were Yute. They were excluded with faked proof!'

'I beg your pardon?' shouts the teacher, drawing herself up to her full height.

The impromptu madness and mayhem provides us with much-needed cover. Grabbing our things, we bounce. We don't stop running till we've safely made it across the grounds, through two sets of fire doors, and to a part of the school we've never even seen before. We collapse on the floor, laughing insanely.

'We did it!' Abdi says, raising a tablet like a torch. 'One hundred and seventy-three verified signatures. That's more than the whole year group!'

'Yeah, there were some Minerva kids getting involved,' Jenny says in surprise, making me blush.

'Those stickers went *fast*!' Liam confirms.

Result! When Aden sees the united front Year Eleven have put forward, he'll have no option but to re-enrol Mo and Joe, or at least investigate the allegations properly. Of course we'll need to send him the petition from a dummy email account to avoid a bollocking, unless that Minerva teacher reports us, but I seriously doubt she'd be able to pick us out in a police line-up. The fact that all of Year Eleven are wearing stickers will demonstrate how far-reaching the silent support is. Bottom line: we can't be ignored.

It comes as a total surprise when Aden turns up on the courts in the last fifteen minutes of the day. Our PE teachers hush us into silence.

'I won't keep you long,' he promises, looking tired, frustrated, and volatile. His tie is tombstone grey. 'I am going to say this only once. You are here, at Minerva College, to complete your GCSEs without disruption. You are not here to form protest groups or challenge decisions that I or the governors have made. If we see any more silly stickers, playground protests or petitions, I will be contacting your parents. Consider this your only warning.' His gaze pierces my heart like a flaming arrow. *He knows.*

'The two students who were excluded for drugs were not dealt an unfair hand. Their parents were part of the exclusion process and accepted that Bodley operates a no-nonsense policy when it comes to drugs. Since some of you do not seem to understand the importance of this, all PSHE lessons for the rest of term will be about the many dangers of drugs.'

Everybody is stunned.

'It's very simple: if you do not wish to be excluded, stay away from drugs, keep your heads down for the rest of the year, and focus all your attention on your studies. That is all.'

CHAPTER 10

'Hey, boss,' Morowa says. 'Wanna walk home together? The buses are running super late.'

She's clutching a folder with a picture of Harry Potter and friends, each one reimagined as a Black kid.

'Cool folder,' I say, pointing at Black Hermione rocking criss-cross goddess braids.

Morowa glances down at her folder as if she'd forgotten it exists. 'Ugh! A "new term" gift from Auntie Tameka. I think it's crap.' She chuckles when she sees my expression. 'Don't look so surprised. I'm not a fan of race-bending characters. It's lazy and desperate. Give us the space to make our own original Black characters and really have something to celebrate. I mean, would you be satisfied if they put out a . . . I don't know . . . Muslim Dora the Explorer?'

I consider her question carefully as we walk up the street. 'A knock-off? Hell, no. But it's kinda comforting to see people who look like you doing cool things.'

'I only stan real people who deserve it: like Assata Shakur and Alicia Garza.'

'Framed and called a terrorist,' I say, shaking my head. 'They did Assata dirty.'

'Hey, girls!' Max trills, hooking his arms round our necks as he catches up. 'Mind if I tag along? I'm on a hair-rescue mission.' He pulls out a bottle of argan oil and a tub of hair mask from his satchel.

'The plot thickens . . .' Morowa says, raising her eyebrows at Max's bald head.

He rolls his eyes expressively. 'My dumbass boyfriend fried his hair in a sensational peroxide fail. Crazy TikTok challenge – don't ask. Yours truly has been summoned to repair the literal hot mess.' He pushes his phone into my hand and Morowa ducks her head for a look. There's a picture of a frowny man with amazing cheekbones but hair that looks like dried pampas grass.

'How old is your boyfriend?' I ask, thinking he looks about twenty.

'He's a sixth former,' Max says, stuffing the phone in his pocket. 'Matteo looks older cos he's had a hard life. But at least he's still got a full head of hair, which sadly I have no claim to. Mother Nature cursed me with premature balding so I shaved the leftovers. That witch may have stolen my follicles, but she will never take away my fierceness!'

I clap with glee. 'I pity the balding man who doesn't share your aerodynamic skull.'

'Girl! My dad tried it and looks like Mr Potato Head. Honestly, it's *so* embarrassing.'

My smile fades as my mind turns to other matters. 'Do you guys think there's any chance Mo and Joe might be allowed back in?'

Morowa shakes her head. 'But we gave it our best shot.'

'You'll never believe this,' Max says, like he's about to drop some juicy gossip, 'but I literally just overheard Harrison asking a girl if she'd like to "go blackbirding". Apparently it's slang for doing drugs.'

'No way!' I say in shock. What has the shift to Minerva awoken in us? Harrison is such a chill guy.

'Why do bad things always have to be black?' Morowa asks tetchily. 'Blackmail, black heart, black magic, black-listed.'

'Black cats being a sign of bad luck,' I add.

We walk together for a while, brainstorming article ideas,

until Morowa comes to a stop, hitching her bag higher. 'My guys, it's been real, but unless you want to come home and meet my Ghanaian granny who is guaranteed to feed you three helpings of *kelewele* then get you to explain every app on her new phone, this is where we say goodbye.'

'She sounds fun!' I say a little too enthusiastically, wishing I had a grandma who doted on me enough to force-feed me helpings of anything.

'I've gotta run too,' Max says.

'Good luck rescuing Matteo's hair! Give my love to Granny!' I call after them. Then suddenly I'm walking home alone. I wonder how Liam's nan is doing with her dementia assessment. Pretty sure he won't put it on his stories but I check my phone for text updates anyway.

When I look up again, I find I've wandered into unfamiliar territory.

Glancing round, I try to get my bearings. There are park gates to my right and a workshop to my left. One of the mechanics wolf-whistles as some Minerva girls walk past. I stare open-mouthed at the park sign:

ROOKE PARK

Under the name is a map and to the right, a dramatic image of a crow glaring over its shoulder.

'Blackbirding . . .' I mutter. Could this be what Harrison meant? Rather than a euphemism for taking drugs, could it be the location kids go to score? There's almost no way it would be this coded . . .

Taking a photo of the sign on my phone, I pass through the gates with grim determination. This warrants investigating. What do I have to lose?

Wet from the rain, the tarmac path glistens like crushed black diamonds beneath my boots. Conkers as glossy as marbles and pine cones like delicate sculptures are strewn about. I snap a picture of them and suppressed memories rise like ghosts:

Dad showing me how to drill a hole in a giant conker and threading it through with a bootlace – Shattering a boy's conker in the playground with such force, a fragment strikes him in the eye – A dinner lady calling me a 'little terror', saying conkers isn't a game for good little girls.

Exactly one term later, I would be told the same thing about basketball – another game Dad got me into. I went home and cried and Dad comforted me. He told me to stay true to myself because all my life people will knock me down, not because I can't do something, but because I can do it better than them.

The sound of a snapping twig cuts through my reverie. Craning my neck round, I spy a tall figure in a black parka behind me, the grey fur-edged hood zipped up over his face serving Nazgûl.

Scanning the area, I'm slightly freaked out by how isolated I am right now. So much for this park being a possible hotspot for contraband. It's basically deserted. Slipping my phone back inside my pocket, I pick up the pace. Like an echo, the Nazgûl's footsteps quicken, crunching through pine cones, scattering conkers. Am I being paranoid or is this guy following me? Far away, under a plum tree, sits a decrepit old man with a shopping trolley, nursing a beer can. The only other potential witnesses are a couple of seagulls trying to bully a raven out of a bit of chicken.

Not caring how pathetic it looks, I bolt to the right, streaking across wet grass. The Nazgûl becomes my shadow and all doubts go up in smoke. *He's after me.* I run faster, my left boot sending a fox turd arcing through the air.

'Hey!' the guy calls, gaining on me. 'Is this yours?'

Nice try, weirdo . . .

Ahead, the tarmac sweeps to the left, leading towards the exit. *Too goddam far*. In that moment, I realize I'm screwed and reach for the very thing he's probably after. That's when I discover that dialling a number even as simple as 999 is virtually impossible when running for your life. I punch two out of three nines before my coat is yanked and my wrist grabbed. 'Gerroff!' I yell as the Nazgûl snatches my phone. Fighting back, I rip his hood off, revealing the emaciated face of a middle-aged man, matted hair like oily feathers. He grimaces, trying to knock me down. Dodging the blow, I twist sharply, landing a right hook in his kisser. His lip bursts, and his eyes fly open in surprise.

'You're dead!'

My stomach contracts but I ball my fists, ready to fight him for my phone.

Then something completely unexpected happens. A blur in maroon, gold and charcoal grey comes shooting from the right, ploughing into my mugger like a locomotive, knocking him to the ground. My phone slips out of his hand, skipping across the wet grass. Pouncing for it, my finger finds the missing nine, my thumb engaging the call.

'Emergency, what service do you require? Fire, police or ambulance?' asks the voice calmly on the other end.

'Police!' I shout, watching the large blond boy and the man grapple with each other. I almost drop my phone when I realize . . .

It's *Hugo*.

'Stop making hoax calls!' the man shouts at me, trapping Hugo in a headlock. I gasp as Hugo twists and slugs the guy in the belly. Pushing home the advantage, Hugo's powerful arms trap the man in a chokehold, his weight yanking him back to the ground.

'Just to confirm: this isn't a hoax?' the woman on the line unbelievably asks. 'Wasting police time is a criminal offence.'

'I've just been attacked!' I yell. 'I'm at Rooke Park! Hurry!'

Clicks and beeps as my call gets transferred. I manage to give the call handler my name, number and location before the mugger slithers free and grips my ankle. Reflexively I kick out, my foot striking his nose. The mugger shrieks and Hugo restrains him once more.

'Oh, shit!' Hugo yells, his once-pristine uniform stained with mud and grass. 'I think you broke his nose!'

I cover my mouth with both hands, shocked at the sight of the too-bright blood gushing from the mugger's snout. Clearly I don't know my own strength.

'No worries,' Hugo says through clenched teeth. 'You acted in self-defence.'

I shake my head and straighten my hijab, 'Whose story do you think the cops are gonna believe?'

'I was filming my speech for tomorrow's presentation when I spotted this guy tailing you. Got it all on camera. If the cops don't believe us, we have footage to back it up,' he says between heavy breaths.

Gratitude floods my heart. Maybe the Blue Bloods aren't all complete arseholes? At least this one isn't. A silver blister pack on the grass catches my eye. I pick it up and shake the tablets. 'Yours?'

Hugo looks relieved. 'You're a lifesaver. Need my painkillers.'

'Are you sick?' I ask, a little confused as I stick them in his jacket pocket.

He blushes. 'No, I bench. Gotta make those gains.'

Man, how I wish he'd stop drawing attention to his muscles. We get it: you're buff – but I will *not* let you threaten my single life.

'So I'm Hugo, by the way,' he says, dimples appearing in his cheeks as he dazzles me with a smile.

I look at the deactivated mugger lying on top of him and laugh.

Could the situation get any more surreal? 'I know who you are.'

'Oh gosh! Don't listen to anything people say about me,' he grunts, tightening his legs round the mugger.

We've been waiting for over an hour before two police officers finally show and I wave them over. As if a switch has been flipped, the mugger starts howling, whipping his head left and right. One of his flailing hands hits Hugo in the face.

The cops start sprinting, the female wielding an ASP baton like a lightsabre, the male whipping out some handcuffs. Taking a page out of Hugo's book, I surreptitiously start filming on my phone. The past has taught me you can never be too careful. Within minutes the officers are reading the cuffed mugger the riot act.

'Nah, man! You got it wrong, like.' The mugger fabricates a story in which we were attacking him for *his* phone. He's escorted away by the male cop, while the other stays with us.

'I'm Officer Baozhai Lu,' she tells us, scratching her impressive jawline. 'We're going to have to take statements from you both. We can do it down at the station or here, but the station would be easiest.'

'No problem,' Hugo says, swiping at clumps of mud and grass clinging to his uniform.

'I'll come down to your station if you answer me this,' I say, rather forcefully, sensing an opportunity. 'There are rumours that Rooke Park is *the* place to score drugs.' OK, there are precisely *zero* rumours of this, but why not embellish what you know to get more information? I push on. 'From the looks of him, I'd say the guy who tried to steal my phone has first-hand knowledge. It doesn't take a genius to figure out stolen phones pay for a habit. So why aren't the police on it?'

Both Hugo and the officer look at me in surprise. But I'm an editor on a mission.

'Look, I understand you're upset but we came as fast as we could. We're very understaffed,' she says.

My ears perk up. 'So are you saying the local police force is underfunded or that there's a recruitment problem?'

'That's a question for Councillor Briggs,' the officer says diplomatically, though she doesn't look too happy about it. 'Now if you'll follow me, we can take a statement down at the station.'

'But public trust in the police force is at an all-time low,' I persist, thinking of the girl from my tutor. 'I'm the second schoolgirl to be mugged since the start of term that I know of.'

'I know and I'm sorry,' she says. 'Everybody's feeling the pinch with budget cuts at the moment. But we're bound to adhere to the priorities the governing body set for us. Come on, I'll drive you down to the station.'

She seems as miffed about it as I am. A good journalist always looks for the story behind the story, knows that the words left unspoken are usually the meatiest part. *So what don't you want to tell me, Officer Lu?*

As she leads us to her vehicle, I stealthily stop recording.

'Were you filming her?' Hugo whispers, smirking.

'Maybe,' I say non-committally.

'Woah. You just battled a mugger and you're conducting secret interviews?'

I blush. 'Guess that makes me some kind of monster, right?'

He gives me a dazzling smile. 'Actually, it makes you pretty amazing.'

My heart flutters. Not just from the blinding smile, but this is the first time anyone's said anything like that to me – besides Liam of course. People are always calling me 'tenacious', 'headstrong', or (my personal worst) 'feisty'. Even Mum's on at me to dial it down a notch. But not this guy.

'You don't work for the *Chronicle*, do you?' he asks.

I shake my head, still nursing the bruise from the rejection.

'Didn't think so. That paper's a snoozefest. Your name is Dua, right?'

He remembered.

'Yeah.'

'Like the artist? Cool. Better than Hugo. I get called Huge Ego too often for my liking.'

'Scooby Dua, DooDoo Head, Dua-Thinkisaurus. Think I win,' I say grimly. 'Hey . . . thanks,' I add.

'For what?' Hugo asks.

'For the . . . assist.'

'I'll take it but you really didn't need me. You had the mugger on the defensive before I rode in like some uninvited white knight. Your battle instincts and height point to one immutable truth: you're an Amazon.'

I search for the mockery in this compliment but his placid eyes are a sarcasm-free zone. A surge of confused feelings flood my chest, threatening to cast me adrift in an ocean of teenage crushdom. These unexplored waters scare me.

'I'm just spatially aware,' I say off-handedly. 'You have to be on the basketball court.'

He snaps his fingers. 'So that's why you were wearing those trainers! Minerva girls are all damsels in distress. They wouldn't even begin to know what to do with a basketball let alone square up to a mugger.'

'Well, that's a huge generalization and even if it's remotely true, it's not exactly their fault,' I say, instinctively defending the sisterhood. 'They got netball and that's pretty much it. Sir Reg or whoever makes the rules is a chauvinist pig who thinks a Y chromosome is a basic requirement in sport.'

Hugo booms with laughter. 'That's my dad you're dissing.'

The blood rushes to my face. 'Your dad?! I'm so sorry!'

'Don't be. He *is* a bit of dick.'

The cop opens the rear door of the car and Hugo climbs in.

But I *can't*.

My heartbeat echoes in my ears with the intensity of a snare drum, remembering all the terrible things I've heard about the police dealing with the Muslim community. Uncle Khalid once went to report an arson attack on a neighbour's car and ended up getting arrested under suspicion of terrorism. It was a week before they let him go *without charge*. He lost his job and reputation.

'Don't worry,' Lu says gently. 'We'll contact your parents down at the station. I give you my word: no harm will come to you.'

From one woman of colour to another, her words carry weight.

'You'll be fine,' Hugo says soothingly, bizarrely seeming to understand my fears. 'Got it all filmed, remember?' A sly smile sweeps across his face. 'Give me your number, I'll forward it to you.'

I raise an eyebrow. 'Really? At a time like this?'

He laughs, his cheeks going pink. So the King of Jocks isn't above making a fool of himself in front of a girl from the other side of town?

Against my better judgement, I climb in and give it to him.

CHAPTER 11

At the station, we're left in a waiting room while our parents are contacted. Officer Lu returns looking confused. 'Are you sure your mother's at home? I've tried about five times and nobody's picking up.'

'Can I try?' I say, holding up my mobile. She nods and I speed-dial Mum. With each unanswered ring, my heart beats a little faster. 'I-I don't understand.'

'How about your dad?' she asks.

'He doesn't live with us,' I murmur, dropping my eyes. Even after all these years, it still hurts.

'But can we call him? We can't interview you without a responsible adult present or at the very least parental consent.'

Why isn't Mum answering? I wrack my brains, trying to remember if she seemed worse this morning.

'Dua?' Hugo says, making me flinch. 'The officer asked if she can contact your dad.' The corners of his eyes crinkle sympathetically.

'Yeah. Sure. Sorry,' I mumble, giving the officer Dad's number.

'Don't worry,' Hugo says. 'Your dad will understand. It's not your fault you nearly got mugged.'

Twenty minutes later Dad arrives and, in spite of what Hugo said, I *am* worried – but not for the reason he thinks. I'm startled by how young Dad looks. When was the last time I saw him? I balk, realizing it was over three months ago when I iced him out. Dad's dressed in a black leather jacket and denim jeans. The officer is saying something to him but, seeing me, Dad rushes over.

'Dua,' he says, hugging me. 'You OK, princess? Came as soon as I heard.'

I'm not even sure why, but I burst into tears.

'Everything's gonna be all right,' he says, stroking the back of my head.

Sir Reg arrives a couple seconds later and, right in front of everyone, gives Hugo a clip round the ear. 'What have you got yourself into now, you stupid idiot? Your brothers weren't half as much trouble!'

Hugo blushes when he sees me watching. 'You're a hero, Dua. See you at school tomorrow.' Whether I needed it or not, Hugo helped and hasn't once acted like I owe him anything for it. He's not at all what I would've imagined from Minerva's future prom king.

Sir Reg turns accusatory eyes on me.

'Who is that man?' Dad asks, frowning at Hugo as the male officer leads him and Sir Reg to an adjacent interview room.

I wipe my eyes with a corner of my hijab. 'Just a boy I go to school with. He helped take down the mugger.'

'Boy?! Looks flipping twenty-five to me!'

Wish Dad would stop being extra. He hasn't really been around for two years and I don't need him putting in overtime now.

But I *am* grateful he's here.

I lead Dad to the room the officer indicated. Need to get this interview over quick so I can go home and find out what's up with Mum. Officer Lu comes in and takes my statement. It's quick and painless since the mugger confessed to everything under threat of the video.

'The perpetrator has confessed to being part of a gang that steals phones and sells them for drug money,' Officer Lu explains. 'His intel together with yours and your boyfriend's statements should go a long way to dismantling the gang.'

'Woah!' Dad says as I facepalm. 'Why you saying "boyfriend"? My daughter doesn't have a boyfriend, madam. We are religious people.'

Lu looks at me for confirmation.

'Hugo goes to the same school. That's literally it.'

'I see,' she says, noting something down. Shortly after, we're given the all-clear to leave.

'I hate this place,' Dad admits with a shudder as we head out. 'Too much bad blood.'

I look at Dad in surprise. 'You've been here before?'

He gives me a look. 'I just mean they haven't done enough to gain the trust of the community. Last week I got stopped and searched on my way to a comics convention in Birmingham. Me! Made me late because I "looked suspicious". All I was doing was driving!'

'That makes me so mad!' I growl, remembering what happened to Uncle Khalid.

'No.' He places his hands on my shoulders, looking me in the eye. 'The absolute worst thing to do is to get angry. Aside from being haram, it can land you in trouble.'

Out in the cool air, he places a hand on my back, walking me to his car. 'So, how you been? Still clocking up all them As?'

A flash of anger makes me shrug him off. 'Look, can you just stop now, please? Thanks for helping out and all but it's not like you're winning Father of the Year any time soon.'

He looks stunned, then dejected. 'Sure, whatever you want. I didn't mean to cramp your style.' My own eyes water, ashamed of my rage.

'My style? Dad, we haven't heard from you in *months*. Do you have any idea how difficult it's been for us lately?'

'I tried but you kept giving me the cold shoulder!' he cries.

I look at him, exasperated. 'You could've tried harder!'

He takes a steadying breath. 'I messed up. I'm sorry and I know that's not good enough. But I'm trying to be here for you now.'

'Just drop me home and go. I need to make sure Mum's OK.'

I clock the pained look that flashes across his face before he's able to hide it. The familiar pang of regret for my harsh words settles in my stomach. But I can't just welcome him back with open arms the way he wants.

We start walking up the road towards wherever he's parked the car, presumably. 'Why didn't Aisha show?' he asks after a while.

Blushing, I instantly feel defensive. 'She must've fallen asleep. Mum works extra hard to put food on the table without *your* childcare payments.'

He stops in his tracks. 'What you talking about?' The shock in his eyes is like a pinprick. 'I haven't missed a single payment in the last two years. I only missed them a few times at the beginning because I was starting up my business. Your mum knows this.'

I blink in surprise. Is Dad lying? He must be . . . because the only other option is that Mum lied. She wouldn't do that just to get me on her side, would she?

The encroaching darkness slips around our shoulders like cloaks as we walk up the road. Caught in the glare of a street lamp, I see a large Batman decal glowing on the bonnet of a sleek black car. I latch onto it, eager to turn my attention to something else. 'Oh my God, Dad! You are such a *geek*.'

He unlocks the car, holding open the passenger door for me with a flourish and a conspiratorial look in his eye. 'Know what they say? Always be yourself. Unless you can be Batman.'

Asian Batman – I can't help but laugh. But as soon as the easy moment began, it ends. *I don't want Batman*, I think. *Just a dad who's there*. We drive back to Mum's in silence.

*

As we pull up to the house, something feels wrong.

'Why are all the lights off?' I mutter. Thrusting open the car door before Dad's even had a chance to park, I pelt up the wet drive, fishing for my keys.

Throwing open the door, I call out to Mum, snapping on the lights as I go. Dad is soon beside me, echoing my calls. I know she'll be mad at me for letting Dad in on our problems, but I am so consumed with fear that nothing else matters. I hope she's OK. She *needs* to be OK.

We eventually find Mum cowering behind the sofa.

'Mum?' I ask, astonished, dropping to my knees.

She looks at me with haunted eyes, swollen from crying. Cocooned in a Sindhi shawl, she bleats, 'I'm so sorry!'

I hide my horror with a hug. 'What happened? You weren't answering the phone.'

She's as cold as ice. 'I tried. Really I did, but I just couldn't face it! My mind started inventing all these horrible reasons for why you hadn't come home. I couldn't bear to have them confirmed on the phone. Then I had an intense panic attack.'

Dad creeps forward and kneels down beside her.

'Aisha, this isn't you,' Dad whispers softly, taking her hand. 'Dua, go make your mum a nice cuppa, yeah?'

Glancing at Mum, I'm relieved to see her nod. I hurry to the kitchen, grateful to have Dad to comfort Mum. I pour milk and water into a pan and wait for them to boil, listening to the murmurs of my parents' voices coming from the front room. The sounds transport me to the past, back to when my parents still loved each other and the world didn't have muggers or posh cliques or drugs or newspapers at war. A time when Dad called me his *choti malka* (mini empress) and Mum oiled and braided my hair.

The pan hisses as a cloud of frothy milk bulges over the rim.

Lowering the flame, I toss in saffron, ginger, and cinnamon, imagining I'm making a potion that can undo the evil spell that has transformed Mum into a shivering mess.

By the time I carry a tray with two steaming mugs into the front room, Mum is sitting upright on the sofa. Was she ever really hiding behind it or was that a hallucination brought on by today's completely bonkers events? All I know for sure is that the behaviour was so un-Mum-like, that if I ever see it again, it'll break me.

'Thanks.' Dad winks at me, taking a mug and handing the other to Mum. 'Your mum and me have made a decision.'

Mum nods, looking exhausted. 'I'm not well, Dua. Haven't been for a while. I thought I could fight this sadness and get on with my life but I . . . I just can't. There are good days, but the bad ones creep up on me without warning like a great suffocating cloud and they're getting more frequent.'

'What are you saying?' I ask, praying silently.

Mum's light-brown eyes find mine, pleading for understanding, for forgiveness. 'I don't think I can look after you at the moment. I should have asked for help sooner . . .' A tear rolls down her cheek. 'You're going to have to live with your dad for a while.'

'Just till Mum's back on her feet,' Dad says soothingly. 'She needs space and time.'

Tears prick my eyes as a high-pitched whistling starts in my left ear.

Dad says he'll give us a moment to talk it over and goes out to the kitchen. For once, I'm at a loss for words.

How can I leave Mum by herself? We've always taken care of each other. Plus I barely know Dad any more. 'You can have all the space you need, Mum. I'll look after myself,' I promise. 'I won't be any trouble.'

'No, beyta,' Mum says, drawing her shawl round herself

with finality. 'You may not think it, but you need looking after. I wish I could do it, but today's made it abundantly clear that I can't – I wasn't there when you needed me most. Your dad's a good man. Let him look after you. Blood is thicker than water.'

That cliché. I glare, furious at them for springing this on me. 'But you said Dad was unreliable and immature and selfish . . .'

Mum nods, guilt making her eyes glisten. 'I said many bad things about Rashid because I was angry, not because they were necessarily true. My parents hated him. We were left alone in the world because of our union, and then we weren't together any more and the loneliness crept in . . . And then things at work began to spiral out of control. I began to blame your dad for *everything*. Even things he hadn't done . . .'

'So it's true what he said? Dad *was* paying child maintenance then?' I ask in shock.

She takes a deep breath. 'He was. He only took a break when he was struggling to set up his store.'

Before I can squash it, I burn Mum with a look of blazing anger. I thought he was abandoning us. I thought he was selfish and cruel. I believed every word *she* said. Mum flinches.

'This is what I mean, Dua,' she replies sheepishly, tapping her temple. 'I have so many issues up here that they're all tangled up and all I feel is pain. I'm sorry I lied about Rashid. He's not a bad man. He never was.' Her eyes close with dismay. 'I think I have depression . . . but today's shown me I have to seriously work through it with a psychologist. It'll take all of my focus and energy.'

Her words are a cluster of grenades. My proud Mum has never admitted needing anybody's help in her entire life, least of all from a professional. Not because mental health is generally seen as wishy-washy pseudoscience by a lot of the Desi community, but because she's always approached life with a firm belief that she can handle anything it throws at her.

'Can I still visit you?' I ask, my voice wavering as I fight back selfish tears.

'Oh, Dua!' Mum says, swallowing me up in her shawl. 'Of course! I will never give up on you. Not now, not ever. I want to get better so I can be the mum you deserve. You can visit me whenever you like. This will *always* be your home.'

'Fighting depression takes guts, you know?' Dad says, leaning in the doorway, looking at Mum with admiration. 'The psychologist will help, but Aisha's gotta confront her darkest fears alone and defeat them.'

Dad makes it sound like war, and maybe that's exactly what it is. Good vs Evil, a reclamation of Self from systemic oppression, a battle to see yourself as you really are instead of the way the haters see you. No, Mum can't be worrying about me while facing her demons.

'I'll go pack.' I pause, hoping Mum will say I can delay it to the weekend or even tomorrow, but she just stares into her mug. Dad squeezes my hand and . . . I don't brush him off. Tremors begin low in my stomach, creating sickening ripples as bitterness spreads up the back of my throat. With the last of my dignity, I walk out of the room. I've made it halfway up the stairs before the first sobs erupt.

Dad's house is compact but modern. He's always kept a spare room for me but I stopped using it back in Year Eight. My parents' relationship was worsening – angry phone calls, loaded words, an incessant need for them to ask me for a full report on what the other had said. Man, I felt so lonely in those early days, wishing for a younger brother or sister to share the burden. Just someone to reassure me that no, I hadn't been the one to rock the boat and cause the divorce. Someone I could look after so I wouldn't feel so completely useless. These last couple of years, Mum's anger grew into a living, breathing thing with horns and fangs. After her earlier admission, I'm left wondering how much of it was actually Dad's fault.

'Well, here we are,' Dad says, turning off the engine and giving me a dopey smile. It makes me mad. I don't want him to act like he has to walk on eggshells around me. 'What's wrong?'

'I'm fine,' I say through gritted teeth.

'Come on, you don't have to pretend with me. You stopped a mugging and found out you're switching homes all on the same night. That's a *lot*.'

'I'll be out of your way once Mum's better,' I say quickly.

A protracted silence makes me stew in my own juices. I'm being pricklier than a porcupine, I know. I just can't seem to find the OFF switch.

'It's OK to cry,' Dad says finally. 'Sometimes I wish *I* could, but the older you get, the less tears you have left.'

I narrow my eyes. 'Why would *you* cry?'

He slumps, resting his arms over the steering wheel, looking like a man carrying an elephant on his back. 'There's no manual for being a good dad after your marriage fails, you understand? I wanted to be someone who could provide for you, someone you could rely on and be proud of instead of the loser your grandparents painted me as. But cancelling all those weekends to get the business up and running only pushed you away . . .' He sighs and steels himself. 'But I can be there for you both now.'

I fold my arms tightly. 'Well, you're too late. Mum's gone crazy.'

'Don't say that! She just needs time.' He scrubs his buzzcut fiercely. 'Look, I don't expect you to forgive me overnight, but can we at least try to get along for your mum's sake?'

Flaring my nostrils, I nod, not trusting myself to say another word. I wish Mum wasn't so stubborn and I wish Dad had tried harder, but most of all I wish I could've been the glue that kept them together.

CHAPTER 12

Sir Reg stands behind the lectern for Monday morning assembly. He's in a brown herringbone suit instead of his official robes, but even his hair, glowing like a silver crown, does nothing to disguise his foul mood.

'I am sorry to be bringing this up, since it doesn't involve the vast majority of you.' His eyes swim over the bulk of Minerva students. 'But nonetheless, I must address it as completely as possible. Two students were excluded for breaking school rules. Some of their peers thought it would be a good idea to set up a petition to reverse the exclusion. This. Is. Completely. Unacceptable.' He pounds the lectern four times, driving the message home with a cacophony of feedback. Poor Liam rips out his hearing aids in shock. 'School rules, school decisions and school decorum are not up for debate. Anyone found aligning themselves with such a movement –' here his eyes seek out the jocks, finally resting on Hugo, right at the front – 'can expect the proper disciplinary procedures to be followed.'

Everybody simultaneously claws off the #Justice4Mo&Joe stickers on their blazers. Suppose I can't blame them.

I remove my own, even though I'm seething.

Sir Reg takes a sobering breath, breaking out into a disconcerting grin.

'Now, onto better things! It gives me tremendous pleasure to welcome an old school chum to the stage. A man with a great vision and big plans to transform our town. Please put your hands together for the hard-working leader of Enley Council: the Right

Honourable Councillor Ethan Briggs!'

A large man in a navy suit with chocolate-brown hair coiffured like an ice cream swirl ambles onto the stage. I've seen him a hundred times splashed all over the local newspapers and promotional leaflets during election time, but this is the first time I've seen him in person. Mum always wonders how the man keeps getting elected when he does sod all for Enley West. Five years ago she tried to get his help when campaigning to stop them from building a supermarket over West Enley Park, but he couldn't give a toss. It makes my blood boil to think someone as hard-working as Mum could be bullied into a state of depression while lazy idiots like this guy always seem to rise to the top.

A rumble of polite applause provides him a lacklustre sound-track as he clasps the lectern with gold-ringed fingers. Councillor Briggs grins like a cat who just discovered a nest of baby mice under a loose floorboard.

'Thank you, thank you!' he booms into the microphone, his moustache twitching. 'Your 'eadmaster is too kind. Course he weren't back in the day. Called me all sorts, I can tell you! Yorkshire man, like me, ending up at Cambridge. Cor, dear! Ruffled feathers enough to stuff a shedload of pillows, me.'

No one laughs.

'I'm here to speak to you about a scheme that's very close to me heart. Over the last year, we've spent money marking up cycling lanes so riders can feel safer knowing they won't be squashed like sardines by a rogue HGV. We've installed more cameras to act like little guardian angels. And best of all, we've made fitness affordable. That's right: we've opened up two outdoor gyms in local parks with brand-spanking-new equipment and lots of it. Research shows that if we're all engaged in healthy pursuits, there's less chance of us getting depressed, doing drugs, or getting involved in acts of vandalism.'

I raise my hand. Councillor Briggs looks over at me in surprise then looks away. I wave my hand like a metronome causing other students to chuckle.

'Er, did you want to ask summat?' the Councillor says, chuckling disingenuously as he catches Sir Reg's eye. Sir Reg is not amused.

'Yes, please,' I say politely. 'I don't know if you're aware but there's a major problem with students having phones stolen by muggers and moped gangs. The local police say they're underfunded. What are you doing about it?'

A surge of laughter spreads through the hall as the teachers try to quash it.

'Nothin' more beautiful than a young lass takin' an interest in the welfare of her local community!' Briggs says, his face suddenly shiny. 'It's a problem that we're working on with the police to resolve as soon as possible. The council is funnelling sufficient funds to our boys in blue. You can be sure of that! It's not a question of being underfunded, but rather a case of smarter policing. You can all help by making sure you're not waving yer fancy phones when you're out and about on the street.'

I wave my hand again.

'Put your hand down!' hisses Rowntree.

Liam grins then raises his own hand.

'Another question!' Briggs booms in surprise. 'My, my!'

Sir Reg signals to Liam to put his hand down.

'No, no, quite all right,' Briggs says, jamming his thumbs inside his waistband and rocking on his feet. 'Yes, young man?'

'My friend's got a question,' Liam says, tagging me. More laughter around the hall.

The venom in Briggs's eyes hits me like a laser pointer. The effect is amplified by a hundred pairs of staring eyes from curious students and vexed teachers.

'If there's no funding problem, please can you explain why the police station next to the library got closed down?' I say quickly, before I bottle it. 'Exercise equipment and painting lines on roads is all very nice, but people getting mugged to fund drug habits is surely more urgent?'

'That's another good question and no mistake, but this en't the proper time nor place forrit. Why don't ye come along to one of my drop-in surgeries and we can have us a good ol' chin-wag? I'll even throw in a sugar bun and a nice cuppa.' He swiftly moves on while Rowntree beckons me to sit on the end of the aisle next to her.

'Dude couldn't answer your question, though,' Liam whispers as I rise.

I glower at the stage. Men like Councillor Briggs and Sir Reg think they can do whatever they want and we should be grateful for the crumbs they toss our way. Someone needs to shake up the establishment. 'Can you text the news team to meet me in the library at lunch?' I whisper back.

Nodding, Liam pulls out his phone, shielding it between his lanky legs as his thumbs go to work.

'You're such an attention whore!' Indira hisses as I shuffle past. 'That's why I got to be on the *Chronicle* and you didn't.'

'I think you'll find that was *cronyism*.' I see her confusion. 'Look it up.'

I drag myself over to Rowntree, preparing to look remorseful as she gives me yet another unimaginative bollocking while calling me 'Huda'.

'Thanks for coming during your lunch break.'

'Can we eat?' Abdi asks, taking out a bag of crisps. Just behind his head are the library rules: number three says not.

I wink. 'Just be discreet.'

Abdi rips open the crisps and stuffs his face as a veritable feast is produced from everybody's bags.

'First on the agenda,' I begin, consulting Notes on my phone. '#Justice4Mo&Joe – sorry guys but we've gone as far as we ca—'

'We can't give up!' cries Jenny.

'We all heard Sir Reg's warning,' Liam points out.

'Let me finish. We've gone as far as we can *in public*. I can't put any of you in danger,' I say firmly. 'They hold all the power; we can't force them to undo an exclusion. But I want you to hang on to your research about drugs for now. I'm going to try to figure out a way we can get our information out there – *safely*.'

There's a sea of firm nods around the room.

'You were on point this morning, giving the Right Dishonourable Crapbag Briggs what for!' Morowa says, biting into a tuna sandwich.

'It's the least I could do. Every time Mum's campaigned for a better deal for our side of town, he blanks her. Plus, closing down that police station means slower response times.' I swallow, wondering if Mum has gone to get a referral to a psyche today. Maybe I should've taken the day off and gone with her? No. She wanted space; me and Dad have to respect that.

Max snaps his fingers, bringing me back. 'My dad's always pissed that he keeps raising council taxes yet the town looks shittier than ever!'

'Only on the west side,' Morowa says darkly. 'Of course he lives in a mansion on the Elysian East.'

'Some guy mugged Dua last night,' Liam announces, getting the meeting back on track. I send him a silent thank-you. He was beside himself this morning when I gave him the deets on the way to school. I ended up having to console *him* because he felt so guilty.

'You OK?' Max asks.

'No wonder you kept grilling that man in assembly,' says Roshni. 'I hope you had phone insurance.'

'Our editor fought the mugger for her phone – and *won*,' Liam continues proudly.

'I had help,' I admit. 'From a Minerva kid, actually.'

Everybody looks surprised.

'Which one?' Morowa persists.

'Read the report for details,' I say, feeling flustered. 'Which is why I'm holding this meeting. Strap in for our explosive next issue: Phone Muggings and Drug Gangs.'

'My phone got swiped in a drive-by just before the holidays and my auntie's a cop!' Jenny says grimly. 'Not only are police underfunded but they have none of the fancy equipment needed to tackle moped crime and drugs.'

'Which tallies up with what the cop who took my statement said,' I say reflectively.

'Some fool tried to take mine. I just booted his bike, alie!' Abdi says, doing a slow-motion re-enactment of a move probably stolen from a Bruce Lee movie. 'Seriously, though, if my phone got nicked mum would've given me licks!'

'I'm getting my phone surgically attached to my appendix,' Max promises. 'Oh wait, my phone's shit. If a mugger takes it, the joke's on *him*.' A smatter of laughter fills the room.

I tap my lips thoughtfully. 'We owe it to our readers to find out what's going on. Jenny, do you think you could ask your cop aunt for a favour?'

I finish handing out assignments and everyone's raring to go. 'Let's meet back here tomorrow for show and tell. Krispy Kreme doughnuts on me.'

There's a collective cheer, then we all go our separate ways. My phone vibrates and I feel my face flush when I realize it's a message from Hugo.

> So when do I get to see your fabled basketball
> skills in action? You free Saturday?

Hastily, I shove the phone back in my pocket. I don't have time for new emotions that I don't know how to deal with. *Bodley Voices* has to be my focus. Truth be told: I want Minerva kids to read our stuff too. Things could be a lot easier if the channels of communication were open and they could see where we're coming from.

Dad buys me a box of twelve delectable doughnuts, no questions asked, which go down a treat with the team at our next meeting. Jenny hands out her printouts.

'Prepare yourselves for *shade*,' she warns. 'I never would've found any of this if my aunt hadn't pointed me in the right direction. But we have to keep her name out of it.' We all nod in agreement.

Jenny's research articles paint a harrowing picture. Central government wrote local councils fat cheques. Part of it was to be spent on educating communities in how to avoid becoming victims of moped crime and muggings. The rest was supposed to make its way into the hands of the local police force for specialist training and to buy equipment like remote-controlled spikes to burst moped tyres and unwashable sprays to identify perps later. Jenny's aunt confirmed that this did not happen.

'So *potentially*, someone's been embezzling funds,' I say in disgust.

'I found something too,' Morowa says, handing out more printouts. 'This one's a story about when Enley Arcade opened.'

'LOVE shopping there!' Roshni says with glee. 'One time I got talent scouted.'

'So how comes we ain't seen you in no movies, Ariana Grande?' Max asks acerbically.

Roshni suddenly looks embarrassed. Not something I've ever seen before, and certainly not something I want to see again.

Morowa clears her throat, returning our attention to her research. 'The shopping centre used to be a disused multi-storey car park. Last year there was a big unveiling when Enley Arcade opened and they got that buff guy off *Love Island* to cut the ribbon shirtless. It was a really big deal – all the articles I read were surprised that the council had the budget for a renovation that big.'

'So keep Enley's shoppers happy and nobody cares that they've been short-changed in the safety department?' Liam summarizes. Jenny and Morowa nod ominously.

'Kind of like what the no-good councillor was saying about exercise equipment,' Max adds. 'Give us shiny new things to distract us from being denied the basics like having a well-equipped police force.'

'What are the odds Briggsy has shares in Enley Arcade?' I ask.

'It's worse,' Morowa says darkly. 'I did A LOT of digging. He's on the board of directors.'

My mouth drops open. There's the smoking gun.

'Okurrr, this is getting *House of Cards* deep!' Max says, fanning himself. 'So why haven't we heard any of this dirt before? There's no way we're the first people to be asking these questions.'

I consider this. We all know Briggsy is useless yet he's never lost his seat. 'I think Briggsy has control of the local press,' I surmise. 'It would defo explain why moped-related crimes and muggings are hushed up or brushed off as a "national phenomenon". It's still too small for national newspapers, so they get away with it.'

'Wait, back up a sec,' Abdi says, playing with a gimmicky

virtual-reality app on his phone for a toy he got out of a chocolate egg. 'We work on a school newspaper, right? What does local government corruption have to do with Bodley?'

'Are you serious?' I ask with annoyance. 'Every kid owns a phone and they don't come cheap. If our phones are being stolen to pay for drug habits, the school, police and local council should all work in tandem to protect us. You feel me?'

'I do,' Morowa says, consulting her notes. 'School-age kids have been victims a total of fifteen times since January. And that's just the *reported* cases.'

'The local press is failing to raise awareness, so we're going to show them how it's done,' Liam states.

'We're gonna do it and we're gonna do it big,' I agree. 'No blushes spared. Don't get me wrong: these gangs are scum, but they wouldn't be such a problem if Briggsy wasn't embezzling funds.'

'Allegedly,' Morowa says cautiously.

'You're seriously gonna take the fight all the way to Briggs?' Liam asks, looking a little green. 'He's massive, Dua, with the best lawyers money can buy. Forget Aden – if Briggs sues for libel, we're basically dead.'

'Not if we follow the National Journalism Code of Conduct,' I promise. 'No slander, no unsubstantiated facts. Anything we're not sure of, we'll put to him in a question, get his opinion. If he refuses to speak to us, that'll make him look messy. If he tells us lies, we'll fact-check and our readers get to be judge and jury.'

'You're framing the article around what happened to you though, right?' Morowa asks.

'Yes, that way Aden can't argue it's not Bodley-centric. I'll also add in Jenny and Abdi's run-ins and that girl from my tutor.' I pinch my nose, thinking. 'Jenny, I want you to call Briggs's office and set up an interview. Be upfront about what we're doing so they can't hold it against us later.'

'You want me to go there *alone*?' Jenny asks, lurching forwards in shock, the ends of her pixie cut trembling.

'If you get an appointment, I'd like Morowa to go with you.'

'Me?' Morowa says, nearly dropping her lotus biscoff, golden crumbs decorating her lips. 'I think the kind of back-up she needs is the Dora Milaje!'

I shake my head. 'Your minds work quicker than the rest of us. If anyone can cut through the BS, it's you two.'

Morowa and Jenny exchange glances, flattered by the compliment but daunted by the task. 'We'll give it our best shot,' Jenny promises.

'Excellent. We'll publish Friday.'

As everybody leaves with their appointed tasks, Roshni hangs back, studying me coolly. 'You really believe in those idiots, don't you?'

'How could you not? They've turned up two lunches in a row now, working their butts off for no reward other than helping people stay safe.' My heart expands, feeling so damn proud of my dedicated, fearless crew.

She smiles slightly, then quickly rearranges her face and shrugs half-heartedly. 'Anyway, I won't be able to promote your paper till Monday. I have a big fat Indian wedding this weekend. Prakash Chopra – as in *big Bollywood director sahib Chopra* – is heavily rumoured to be there. If I'm going to move up in the world, I need to cover that on all my socials.'

'I feel you,' I say. 'Weddings are a huge Desi deal but please can you make at least one post promoting the mugging story? Or no one's gonna read it.'

She throws her hair over her shoulder. 'I'm telling you I can't! The place is going to be crawling with other up-and-coming Asian influencers like that awful Shaista Mian. If I don't get in there and charm the pants off Mr Chopra first, I'll have lost my chance at moving up in the world. You know the deal with Asian weddings. I'll be dodging matchmaking aunties hungry to trap me in some sort of binding *rishta!* I can't stop a small sigh escaping my lips.

Roshni's expression shifts, examining my reaction. 'You OK?'

'I don't do Asian weddings any more. The invites started to get lost in the mail after mum and dad separated.' I try to keep my face neutral. 'You know, I actually prefer it. Kinda awkward when all the other girls are getting scouted for *rishtas* and you're the only one who's not. It's worse when you overhear the aunties saying your parents must've done something really bad for God to curse them with a dark-skinned child *and* a broken home. But yeah, I get you. Do what you have to do.'

Roshni gasps, flapping her false eyelashes like raven's wings, looking genuinely upset. 'I'm so sorry you have to deal with that. Colourism is such a problem in our community — it's racist and judgemental as hell. Especially after all the hate we get in this country just for being brown, to not be able to feel safe in our own spaces is ridiculous.' She takes in a breath. 'OK, look, I'll promote your story. Just don't expect the works.'

'You're a good person, Roshni,' Liam says, stepping out of the shadows, gently placing a hand on my back.

'Your hearing aids must be malfunctioning!' she replies tartly, and leaves.

Dr York is now officially my favourite teacher. Not only does he know his subject inside out but he wrote me a note to go to the toilet without a fuss.

Downstairs, I spot a PE teacher at twelve o'clock and prepare to repel him with Dr York's permission slip, but as he draws closer I'm surprised to see it's Hugo serving *Love Island* in his PE kit. Remembering my hijab means modesty in all things, I ignore the fluttering in my stomach and wrench my eyes away.

'You ignored my text,' he says, folding his bulky arms. My eyes drift to his soft lips before I come to my senses and regain control.

'I have a lot going on. My mum's—' Applying the brakes before oversharing, I remind myself that being hot AF is not the same as being trustworthy and I don't really owe him this truth. '. . . not well.'

'Oh, sorry. Hope she feels better soon. And she's got a really kickass daughter looking out for her, so I'm sure she'll recover quickly.' I swallow the wave of guilt that rises to the back of my throat, before realizing Hugo's waiting for my response.

'Sure, thanks. And now I'm not fighting off drugged-up muggers with you, I even have some kickass to spare for *Bodley Voices*.'

'Yeah, I got that from the way you were grilling Councillor Briggs yesterday,' he says, chuckling.

'He totally deserved it,' I say tetchily. 'How'd things go with your dad?'

He grimaces. 'No matter how many cups I bring home, I'm never going to be as good as my brothers in his eyes.'

'Winning approval is not something you can control, so why worry about it? Just live your best life.' I give him an upbeat smile.

'Wow. You're profound and you have the prettiest smile.' he says, making my insides squirm.

Without warning he thrusts a hand forward, attempting to snatch my permission slip. Pivoting out of reach, I defensively fling out an arm, fixing him with a scowl. He bursts out laughing. 'You really *do* have great reflexes. Meet me at Langley Park on Saturday at five o'clock. We can shoot some hoops together. And bring that smile.'

He walks off grinning, like it's a done deal.

'I can't!' I blurt – but he's already gone.

I stand in the silent corridor trying to slow my hammering heart, and just when I think I've got a handle on it, the bathroom door to my right is thrown open and Renée strides out.

'*Slut*.'

'Excuse me?'

'I said, you're a *slut*,' Renée spits. 'Hugo and Keira are everybody's one true pairing. Stop trying to seduce him, homewrecker.'

What?! Hugo and Keira are dating? How could I not know this? And why has Hugo been flirting with me . . . unless he never was? But then what the hell is he doing? Nausea warps my belly.

'I'm not trying to *seduce* anyone,' I say quietly, my cheeks smarting.

'For your sake I hope that's true. Remember: a good reporter has eyes and ears in all places.'

'Including the toilets, apparently,' I say, gesturing behind her. 'Hear any suspicious farts lately?'

She stalks towards me, a dangerous challenge in her eyes. Calmly, I hold her gaze until she snaps her fingers inches from my face, making me blink. She grins triumphantly and the bell goes. Screw the toilet break. Gripping my bag tightly, I run.

CHAPTER 13

Liam and I are heading towards the bus stop in the drizzle when a horn beeps at us. It's Dad with his Batmobile in the biggest PDF I've seen this year. I'm cringing so bad, I'm practically origami.

'That your dad?' Liam asks, smiling. I roll my eyes.

As if to confirm it, Dad lowers the window and bobs his head. Who wears sunglasses in the middle of autumn? It's official: Dad is having a mid-life crisis.

The rain switches up, coming down monsoon-style while the kids, unable to all cram under the bus shelter, scream and attempt to cover their heads. Liam and I race for the Batmobile.

'Dad, remember Liam? Can you drop him off at the Rosehip Estate?'

'Salami lick-em,' Liam says, posting his hand through the lowered window. 'Your wheels are sick, Mr Iqbal!'

Dad doesn't look impressed with his pronunciation but shakes his hand anyway. 'Thanks. Yeah, I can drop you off.'

We jump in the back, trying and failing not to make the seats soggy. Outside, some kids are snapping pics of the car. The Dad-Mobile is going to be all over everyone's stories tonight. Liam fills me in on what I missed from the last ten minutes of English. Through the rear-view mirror, I spot Dad's less-than-friendly stare burning a hole in my bestie.

'Look, my young friend, I might be old-fashioned but listening to music while talking to someone is disrespectful,' he says, making Liam blush.

'Dad! This is Liam, remember? Those are hearing aids, not earphones.'

'Oh-oh!' Dad says, his eyebrows hoicking up. 'Pardon me. So you're the skinny kid who couldn't shoot to save your life? Man, you got big! You got game now, son?'

'Nah, I got worse,' Liam says proudly. 'But Dua's *fire*. Shame she had to give up being captain of the basketball team to focus on exams this year.'

'Dua's not captain?' Dad's shades slip down his nose as he throws me a reproachful glance. I bite back on a nasty comment about him knowing if he'd bothered to keep in touch. Liam, sensing the tension, asks Dad about all the hideous modifications he's made to the car – Dad's only too happy to wax lyrical.

I smile gratefully at Liam, pull out my phone and stare at Hugo's messages as Dad drones on. An involuntary shudder rips through my body as the image of Hugo in his PE kit ambushes my mind – only in this version he empties a water bottle over his head and shakes his hair in slow motion. Unfortunately, Renée's '*slut*' rips through the fantasy like a wet fart. If Hugo and Keira really are an item, then why did he diss her paper and why have I never seen them together?

'Woah!' Dad says, staring out of the window at the block of flats that make up the Rosehip Estate. Along the side, some talented artist has painted a mural of a Syrian girl in a floral hijab, releasing a dove into the sky. Her smile is beatific, the vivid colours transforming the drab building into something both uplifting and hopeful.

'You know that kid that got a big comic-book deal a few years back?' Liam asks us.

'Ilyas Mian?' Dad replies. 'The one who created Big Bad Waf?'

'Yeah, him,' Liam says, pointing. 'He painted that over a *single night*, covert ops style.'

'Talented kid. Buys all his comics from *my* store,' Dad boasts.

'We've got to get him in for an interview,' I tell Liam as he gets out the car. 'Give your nan my love.' He gives me a thumbs up and clambers out, throwing Dad a grateful 'Thanks' and heading towards his flat.

As we pull away, Dad asks, 'Interview? Is that for the paper you set up?'

'It is, yeah.'

'Great! But . . . aren't you worried working on a paper will encroach on your study time?'

I tell Dad we have a whole team handling business. It feels so good to say it out loud, to remind myself that it's no small miracle that no matter how different we all are, we came together at the right time for a cause we all believe in.

'My daughter's a boss, mashallah!' Dad says, looking impressed.

I can't help the cheesy smile as I remember what it was like to be praised by my dad. Maybe it *is* time to let bygones be bygones. Mum and Dad both made mistakes and we all suffered, but that doesn't have to mean we can't move past it and heal. Right?

But healing is going to be hardest for poor Mum. Missing the signs that she was going under is unforgivable, especially since I was living under the same roof. I can't ever let that happen again. 'Dad, could you drop me off at Mum's?'

I ring the doorbell and wait, warming my hands in my pockets. I'm nervous as hell given the last time I saw her she was hiding behind the sofa like a lost child. Man, that image will haunt me till the day I die. What's taking so long? Dad made me call beforehand so she knew I was coming. Has she had a relapse?

The door opens. Even though Mum is beaming at me, she looks tired. Scraggles of hair are escaping from under her scarf and I notice her socks don't match. She hugs the life out of me.

Dad beeps his horn and Mum waves. 'What on earth is your dad driving?' she asks from the corner of her mouth.

'I think it's called the Male Menopause.'

She chuckles and it sounds real. Maybe knowing she's going to get all the support she needs is giving her the boost that's been missing for so long?

'Gosh, it's nippy. Come in, beyta, before you catch cold.'

Wiping my boots on the mat, I step inside, placing them on the shoe rack. We sit in the front room. She's got *Clueless* on in the background, and although everything looks the same, it feels like I'm in a doll's house version of home instead of the real thing. The uncomfortable silence is a chasm that threatens to swallow us.

'I'm really sorry about the other night . . .' Mum begins haltingly.

I wave a hand, though I'll never forget it. It was the night I found out my mum is not indestructible after all. Now I want to wrap her up in cotton wool and make sure nothing can harm her ever again. 'Don't apologize, Mum. It's not your fault.'

'I was so ashamed of myself. My poor little girl having to deal with a mugging all by herself and me having a meltdown!' The mask finally slips and I see how terrified she is by what happened. I try to imagine what it would be like to find yourself acting in a way you have no control over.

Reaching out for Mum's hands, I warm them between my own. 'Mum, stop expecting too much of yourself. I was completely fine. I *am* fine now. Just take this time to look after yourself. Me and Dad are rooting for you.'

She gives me a kiss on the head and smiles. 'When did you get so wise?'

'Right around the time I discovered Google was a thing,' I joke. She cracks up, the sound of her laugh warming me up and easing the tension. Before too long, we're chatting as if the last couple weeks never happened. I want to tell her so many things – mainly how proud of her I am, but in case it comes across as condescending or triggers her, I just focus on fun and gesture to the TV with a smirk. 'There are two girls at my new school who are just like Cher and Dionne, but evil.'

'I probably shouldn't be watching high-school movies,' she says sheepishly, 'but this one's a guilty pleasure. Owned it on VHS as a teen. How are you finding it at your dad's?'

Difficult? Weird? Emotionally draining? 'You don't need to worry about it. We both just want to help you feel more like yourself.'

Mum sighs, adding more sugar to her tea. 'I hope you and Rashid can use this time to patch things up. He really loves you.' She pauses, rolling her ring on her finger.

My mind spins, returning to my early childhood, remembering all the good times I shared with Mum and Dad without realizing what they were having to deal with in the background.

'I'm sorry, Mum,' I say, sniffling. 'I'm sorry for every time I slammed a door or threw a tantrum or told you I hated you. I wish I could've been a better daughter.'

Mum puts her cup down and scooches closer. 'You're perfect. Every child has their moments, beyta. The things that bind us aren't just the good things but also the bad. One day you'll look back at this and laugh or cringe or cry but these are the things that make you realize you lived.' She sighs. 'Like me and your dad. We were in love and that love hasn't gone, but the world changed it and it changed us, for better or worse. Though, of course, at the time it felt like the world was ending, and nothing would ever feel warm like the sun again.'

As I walk back to Dad's place, I think about everything Mum and Dad suffered just because they wanted to be together. TV lied: love doesn't conquer all. It never did and it never will. I guess it doesn't really matter whether Hugo is dating Keira or not. Pulling out my phone, I fire off a text saying something came up so I can't join him at the park, then delete his number.

That evening, as I'm running final checks on our next issue of *Bodley Voices*, I allow myself to dream big. The guys are fire. Every article feels like spending time with a different friend, listening to them talk about something they love or feel strongly about. I attach the files to an email addressed to Mr Aden. My mouse hovers over the article I wrote about Councillor Briggs based on Jenny and Morowa's research. Without a doubt, Aden's going to call for drastic cuts if not an outright ban. I glance at the Henry Grunwald quote on my wall:

'Journalism can never be silent: that is its greatest virtue and its greatest fault. It must speak, and speak immediately, while the echoes of wonder, the claims of triumph and the signs of horror are still in the air.'

Flaring my nostrils, I delete the email. Aden can read the article about Briggsy like everyone else when it's already been published.

CHAPTER 14

Saturday morning, I'm woken by a message from Roshni:

> Your article went viral. Congrats!

Too groggy to understand, I stumble into the shower to wake myself up. By the time I'm back in my bedroom, my phone is blowing up.

> OMG! Sis never said she had friends in high places!

Max texts.

> Our articles have gone NATIONAL!

says Morowa.

> Bet Briggs regrets not giving us an interview. Makes him look SKETCHY.

> WE! DID! IT!

shout-types Jenny, followed by approximately a thousand emojis.

All these crazy messages are linked to a single tweet. Opening it, my eyes pop out as a smile surfs across my face. Mega grime star ZayZay Ramos has only gone and retweeted my article about the attempted phone mugging to her 3.5 million followers with a comment.

> *What the actual fuck?! Why aren't the police being funded to protect us? Enley was ends. Sack corrupt councillor now! #BodleyVoices telling it like it is. #fromthemouthofbabes #sackbriggs*

Somehow ZayZay has got #BodleyVoices trending. Our tiny school paper – that Aden tried so hard to keep contained – has exploded onto the national stage.

Result!

Flipping open my laptop, I call up the *Bodley Voices* website and get a message saying the page isn't available right now due to high volumes of traffic. On a third refresh the website pops up and I beam with pride. Abdi is king. It looks more professional and perfect than I could ever have hoped.

My phone rings and I pounce on it. 'Liam, Roshni's got us trending on multiple platforms! We must have clocked up thousands of views.'

'Tens of thousands!' My heart flutters.

'Can't believe ZayZay came through for us. I don't even listen to her music,' I say, feeling a bit guilty.

'Well, maybe we should. Her army of fans have been checking out our paper and tweeting about it all morning. Man, I can't believe you finessed Aden into approving our articles. He's usually obsessed with not offending anyone.'

I bite my lip. 'Yeah, about that . . .'

'No . . . Bruh! You didn't!' Liam says with dread.

'Aden left me no choice! I had to use my initiative and publish before the whole thing turned into old news. Besides, it worked, didn't it? People are at'ing Briggsy like it's their job. The police will probably get their funding, phones will stop getting stolen, and the drugs business will take a hit. Mission accomplished.'

He sighs. 'Pray Aden sees it that way.'

I swallow thickly. Who am I kidding? Aden will throw the book at me. I just hope I can avoid an exclusion, which is a distinct possibility given the paper's gone viral.

OMG – suppose Mum finds out?

What have I done??

Dad knocks on my open bedroom door, making me jump. 'Look, I gotta go. My Dad's here,' I say, hanging up. He looks hilarious in a Batman apron, brandishing a spatula like a fairy wand. 'You smell like blueberry muffins.'

Dad grins. 'Must be the pancakes I rustled up. You hungry?'

I press my stomach and groan. 'In a bottomless pit sort of way. I'll be down in a couple of minutes.'

'That your newspaper?' Dad asks, squinting at my laptop. '"Phone-snatchers: Enough is Enough! by Dua Iqbal",' he reads. 'Go on, girl! You shame that wasteman councillor.'

'You approve?' I ask in hopeful surprise.

Dad gives me a funny look. 'Course I do. You're a chip off the old block.'

'Eh?' I ask, intrigued.

He shakes his head, looking a bit embarrassed. 'I was small fry. Back in the day I started a newsletter at my high school. It wasn't sanctioned but we used to sneak into the photocopy room and print copies to sell for ten p.'

'Who's we?'

'Me and my old mate, Jubba. Aw, man, we wrote everything we were told we couldn't say! About history being whitewashed, about police brutality, top ten movies starring Black and brown actors: basically anything about taking pride in your identity. Something to make us feel valued. I drew this comic, making caricatures of all the racist teachers. Like Mr Smith became Mr Spliff and I drew him getting high at a Klansman meeting. Mrs Lucas who was always picking her nose became Missus Mucus and I reimagined her as a skinhead with a National Front tattoo.' He gives a naughty schoolboy laugh.

'So I get the journalism bug from *you*.' A warm sensation envelops my heart. 'Did you sell a lot of newsletters?'

Dad smiles sadly, ducking his head. 'Nah. Someone grassed us up, the newsletter got shut down, and we got suspended for "racism".'

I glance at the front page of *Bodley Voices*, feeling a little guilty as I stare at Hugo's video of the mugging. Without it, the article wouldn't have had half as much impact. Since he's Keira's boyfriend, he couldn't possibly be looking for anything other than friendship, which is all I want. Besides, befriending a Minerva student would be proof that I genuinely have nothing against them. I just want equality, and from what I know about Hugo, so does he.

Of course, Dad wouldn't be happy about me becoming friends with another boy, but hey: a girl has to make her own decisions, right? Aden didn't think a Bodley paper was a good idea and it ended up *trending*. Briggsy thought he could come to his old mate's school and lie about being a good councillor. Fact-checking showed him. Grown-ups don't know everything. Sometimes you need to shake things up, and with my incredible news team, I'm not likely to make the wrong decisions.

I slip my hand inside Dad's. 'Come on, pops, let's go have us some pancakes.'

His delight is priceless.

CHAPTER 15

Monday morning is seriously weird. As Liam and I walk in, we're cheered and applauded like heroes by our Bodley brethren. It might be my imagination, but a number of the Blue Bloods seem to be smiling at us too.

'Hey, Dua,' says a Minerva boy I've never laid eyes on before in my life. He tousles his curly bob before giving me a friendly smile. 'I'm Tristan. I work for the *Chronicle* but I'd like to work for you instead.'

'On *Bodley Voices*?' I ask in surprise.

'Your articles are fearless and relevant to everyone. That's the future, not some preppy bullshit printed on glossy forest-destroying paper. I took the liberty of preparing a portfolio. I write mostly about environmental issues but I'm willing to give you whatever you need.'

Confused, I take his elegant portfolio. 'Are you sure? You guys get paid on the *Chronicle*, don't you?'

'Fifty a month,' he confirms.

My eyes nearly pop out. 'Well . . . we do it for the love.' I push his portfolio back at him but he refuses to take it.

'Which is why I want to jump ship. I've had enough of the cliques and the politics and the embargos on telling the truth just because it might offend someone "important". I've got more integrity than that.' He scratches his slightly patchy sideburns. 'Come on, give me a chance? What harm could it do?'

'We'll get back to you,' Liam says, snatching Tristan's folder and pulling me away.

'Did that really just happen?' I ask in a daze.

'We're the shit now and the flies have come buzzing,' Liam says darkly. 'Come on, we've got English and you'll be sitting next to the patron saint of the *Minerva Chronicle*. Best put your bulletproof vest on.'

My stomach lurches.

Dr York has us working on modern prose questions. In spite of the silence, I *still* can't concentrate. Poor Elspeth has a cold and every one of her infected breaths sounds like a death rattle, Harrison keeps scratching his crotch like he's got crabs, and the irritating squeak of Oba's new shoes might as well be nails on a blackboard. I glance at Dr York, who is gradually sliding off his chair as he reads an ancient copy of *The Necronomicon*. He's been reading it since the start of the year so I googled it. Apparently it's a book of dark magicks. I'm down if his endgame is to raise some giant octopus-headed monster from the Thames, so long as it means cancelling the mocks.

Keira, who's been blanking me all afternoon, taps her finger impatiently and it takes me a moment to realize she's trying to get me to read her note.

Let's talk after class.

I raise an eyebrow. Keira's cold, marble blues betray nothing. After a beat, I shrug and nod.

'Keira!' snaps Dr York. 'If you pass notes around during the exam you'll be disqualified.'

'I was just . . .' The whole room is staring at her. Her cheeks flush and she lowers her watery eyes. 'Sorry, sir.'

Placing *The Necronomicon* down on his desk, Dr York gets to his feet, stretches and begins to prowl the classroom, making sure everyone is on task. Not gonna lie, seeing Keira taken down a notch was kind of sweet. I can't help but wonder what Hugo sees in her . . . I mean aside from the fact that she's a total babe and probably a c-cup. Maybe that's all boys are interested in?

'Leave your papers on your desk for me to mark,' Dr York calls as the bell rings. 'Woe betide anyone who forgets to write their name at the top of every sheet.'

As I'm packing my stuff away, I become conscious of Keira hovering at my side. She's obviously going to take issue with my article so I better put my best clapbacks forward.

'OK, I'm done!' I say, smiling like an insane person. 'Where do you wanna do this?'

'There's an alcove at the top of the corridor,'

We cut through the mass of bodies heading down to lunch. At the end of the corridor, there's a dip and a large brightly lit window seat the size of a bench. Keira perches on it and gestures for me to join her.

'Have you ever read a book, thought it was decidedly average, but couldn't stop thinking about it, only to return to it later and realize its greatness?'

I study Keira's eyes, twenty per cent of my brain pondering her question, the rest trying to figure out the motivation behind it. 'Sure. Who hasn't?'

She seems relieved by my response. 'That's how I feel about your submission article. You were right. It made me feel uncomfortable and it's been bothering me. Since our schools are bonded through the Trust, there's no reason why Minerva can't take more than two new recruits this year.'

'Wait, you're asking me to join your paper?' I ask incredulously.

She sucks her lips in, swallowing. 'Yes. Yes, I am. I think you'd be an incredible asset.'

'You waited all this time to figure that out!' I say, laughing. 'In case you hadn't noticed I've got my own paper now. And I get to be *editor*.'

Keira bristles. 'I don't think you realize that starting a paper from scratch is an enormous task. The *Chronicle* isn't mine, anyway. It's been around almost as long as the school. You'd have all that wealth of knowledge and support to help you grow. We have an impressive list of industry contacts and, as I'm sure you already know, journalism is one of the most challenging industries to break into.'

I chuckle. 'Funny. I poured my heart and soul into that article because I wanted to be on the *Minerva Chronicle* so badly. You made me doubt myself so I showed it to Dr York. Know what he said? He called it a "profoundly thought-provoking piece cleverly written in contemporary colloquial language". If you couldn't immediately recognize that, you're just not the editor for me. Thanks, but no thanks.' I hop off the bench.

She catches my arm, her hand like a vice. 'You peaked with the article about the mugging. Think you'll ever get another story like that again? Interest will wane. Last chance: join the *Chronicle* or be forgotten.'

Turn her down a second time and Minerva's queen will probably go out of her way to make my life a living hell. But joining the *Chronicle* at this stage would mean abandoning my mates and everything we've built from the ground up. I don't want the voice I've just started to use to be used by someone else.

'Hard pass.' I flee, feeling her eyes burning into the back of my head.

'It's been mad!' Liam tells me as we head to the dinner hall at lunch. 'All morning people have been talking about nothing but phone muggings. Even my DT teacher told us some dude pinched his phone Friday night and how he doesn't think you should fight back because they've been known to launch acid attacks. We could maybe do some kind of follow-up about where they're getting the acid from?' He grabs a couple of rolls and before I can get a word in, he continues: 'Hey, did you get a chance to look at my *Fortnite* article? I was thinking of having a regular gaming column.'

'Loved it, but I think it's probably best as a one-off,' I say.

He blinks. 'I'm passionate about gaming and loads of people are into it.'

'I'm sorry, but there're tons of gaming review websites out there. Now we've had major success we have to keep focused on making us stand out from the competition . . .' I trail off. 'What's up?'

Liam goes as pale as a ghost. He's staring somewhere over my shoulder. 'Run!' he hisses.

Glancing round I see Aden, his jacket flapping like the sails of a Viking warship as he cuts through the ocean of kids milling around. My stomach drops anchor.

'Dua Iqbal!' Aden booms loud enough for everyone in the dinner hall to shut up and stare. 'Follow me.'

With all the dignity I can muster (which isn't very much since I'm bricking it) I hold my head high and follow. Indira snaps a picture on her phone. 'Breaking news: wannabe editor gets cancelled for smearing local councillor. Hashtag: fifteen minutes over!'

'Should've taken my deal,' Keira mutters.

'Good riddance to the gutter press,' Renée adds, waving.

'Haven't you three got a cauldron to chant over?' Tristan snarks. He catches my eye and winks.

'I'm sorry, did you hear something?' Renée asks.

'Just the sound of Judas hanging himself,' Keira replies, smirking.

Mr Aden glares across the desk at me in an interview room. Angry veins wriggle on his forehead like a nest of snakes. My polite smile flags in the face of blistering hostility.

'I trusted you,' he hisses. 'I gave you exactly what you asked for: a school newspaper with you at the helm.'

'And we delivered. It's only issue two and your paper has already gone viral. Congrats on being the coolest principal ever!' I say, masking my fear with false cheer.

'Dua!' he barks. 'The paper was only supposed to be for the Bodley community. You gave me your word you wouldn't publish until you had my approval.'

'Your secretary said you were at a conference so I had no choice but to wing it.' Though this is true, no force on earth could stop me from going public with the article on Briggs's corruption.

'You *winged it*,' he says with an unhealthy amount of sarcasm, making me want to duck and cover. 'Do you have any idea how much damage you've done? Do you realize how many rules you've broken? Both you *and* Liam. As your deputy, he is equally responsible.'

'No!' I say, raising a finger. 'He writes and edits. I'm the control freak. Let's leave him out of this.'

Aden frowns. 'You published without my approval *again*.'

'I thought you'd be proud of my independence.'

'You posted salacious allegations about the local councillor—'

'Every word fact-checked and backed up by evidence. We gave him the opportunity to give his side but he refused to speak to us!'

'A man who happens to be a very good friend of the headteacher of our partner school!'

'And? Nepotism should place a person above the legitimate scrutiny of the press?' My adrenalin spikes like a volley of javelins: I'm practically having an out-of-body experience.

'You're not the press, Dua. You're a rabble-rouser. You nearly started a riot with your Justice for Mo and Joe campaign. I was the one who had to deal with angry parents from both schools.'

'That's regrettable, but no more than those exclusions were.'

'Sir Reginald is absolutely *furious*, especially after your disgraceful performance in assembly last week. Be grateful I am the one having this conversation with you and not *him*.'

'He's not my headteacher, you are,' I huff in frustration. 'Why won't you stick up for us any more? You excluded Mo and Joe just because Sir Reg demanded it. They were both handed weed just before it was discovered in their bags. How is that right?'

Aden stares at me coldly. 'I don't take kindly to you questioning my integrity. Your reckless actions have put me in an impossible situation. *Bodley Voices* has run its last issue and I have no choice but to exclude you.'

My jaw drops. 'You're kicking me out for telling the truth?'

'The exclusion will be for a fixed period of four days.' He tosses a hastily scribbled note at me. 'Go and spend the rest of the day up in the library. When your mother arrives, I'll send for you and we will have a meeting.'

'You can't call my mum!' I cry. This is my worst nightmare. I can't let Mum down with all she's going through.

'I beg your pardon?' He looks at me like he thinks I might actually have taken leave of my senses. Who knows? I probably have.

'I mean: I'm living with my dad.'

'Then why haven't the records been updated?' he asks, blinking at the computer screen in exasperation.

I snatch his note and rise. 'At the start of the year, you said any school would be proud to have a student like me. Guess you didn't mean it.'

'I'm sorry it's come to this, Dua, but you've brought it on yourself.'

I snort, slamming the door on the way out.

*

En route to the library, my phone vibrates. It's a message from Liam.

> You OK? What happened?

> Aden cancelled the paper like the predictable lapdog he is.

> So it's over then.

> Did I mention my four-day exclusion?

> Dua, man, we went too far.
> What happened to taking it slow?

> Call a meeting.

> What!? Did Aden give you brain damage?

> In the library. Do this one thing for me. Trust.

No response. I make it all the way to the top of the stairs before my phone buzzes again.

> Done. Can't guarantee anyone will turn up tho.

As it happens, they all do.

'Thanks for coming on such short notice,' I tell them. 'I've called this meeting cos I need to come clean.'

'You mean you're a double agent hired by Sir Reg to expose all the Bodley troublemakers?' Jenny asks with a smile. *Enjoy that smile while it lasts,* I think. *In a moment the daggers will be out and they'll have every right.*

'If only,' I say glumly. 'An hour ago Aden cancelled *Bodley Voices* and it's all my fault.'

'Why would he do that? He's been OKing all our articles, right?' Max says, cottoning on.

I drop my eyes and give a diminutive shake of my head.

There is an explosion of groans and my name is used like a curse word. Jenny asks Liam if he knew about it, which of course he didn't. This mess belongs to me.

'Well, at least we don't have to pretend to like each other any more,' Roshni says, trying to cheer everyone up. 'Sorry, Dua, but you really should have put the paper before your own inflated ego.'

'She did right,' Morowa says unexpectedly. Everyone looks at her in mutinous surprise. 'Chill. She used our platform to warn people of a growing problem in our town. Aden would've blocked it. OK, so we have no paper now, but at least we went out with a bang.'

'Still better than anything the *Chronicle* put out in the last five years,' Tristan quips.

'Are you people coming down with an attack of cray?' Max demands. 'Dua's my girl and all, but this paper gave me purpose. I'm going to fail my GCSEs – that's what all my teachers say. But it was nice to come to school and be involved in something I'm actually good at.'

'Don't you get it?' I ask them in exasperation. '*Bodley Voices* was a hit because it dared to go where no paper had gone before.'

'And now it's over,' Jenny snarks. 'Gee, ya think maybe *that's* why no paper ever went there?'

'In Dua's defence, Mr Aden and Sir Reg are acting like pricks,'

Liam states honestly. 'We wait all these years to get a paper, literally do all the work ourselves, then have those two calling the shots? This ain't a freakin' dictatorship.'

Abdi nods. 'Innit tho'? Those two should focus on running their schools instead of bothering us.'

'Welcome to the real world!' Jenny says, throwing her arms wide. 'Where you can't poke a hornet's nest without getting stung. So Briggsy is a corrupt official – aren't they all?'

The room erupts into a frenzy of disagreement and arguments, each person shouting louder than the other to be heard. This can't be what we've come to. Not after everything we've been through, all the work we've put in to tell the truth.

Mum once told me evil people get to the top by climbing over the corpses of their colleagues. It's what David did to become the head of her department. Was Mum wrong to stand up to discrimination? Should she have kept her mouth shut and accepted that this is the way the world works and kept her job?

I will not accept that.

What we put out was well-researched and timely. There has to be at least one voice of truth in Enley, even if it is from a bunch of teenagers struggling at a new school.

I blink as an idea lands.

'We might be schoolkids, but we don't have to make a *school* paper,' I say triumphantly.

The room suddenly goes silent.

'What?' Roshni asks.

'*You* guys are *Bodley Voices* – not Aden,' I say with renewed vigour. 'People want to read what you have to say because it's the truth. They *need* you. I'm setting up a new paper – should've done it in the first place, but hey, you live and learn. It's going to be one hundred per cent independent and even more exciting because we won't have Aden, Sir Reg, or the ghosts of the parent-governors breathing down our necks.'

Whatever the guys were expecting me to say, it definitely wasn't this.

'Could you hook us up with a new website, please, Abdi?' I ask.

He wrinkles his nose, scratching his head. 'I guess . . .'

'Good,' I say, steamrollering over his opportunity to follow up with a 'but'. 'Roshni, could you use all available channels to alert our readers to our new, improved platform?'

'Obviously, but why would I bother?' she asks tartly.

'The same reason any of us bothered in the first place. We created a safe space for Bodley students after we got sent to this prison camp. And guess what? Even the Minerva kids are starting to listen.'

'Case in point,' Tristan says, making jazz hands.

'Yeah,' says Morowa, looking at him disapprovingly. 'I wondered what you were doing here.'

'I wanted to join a paper with integrity and fearlessness in every published word,' Tristan explains. 'When I saw you and Liam headed here, I thought I'd make my debut.'

Morowa glances at me and I nod, letting her know he's a talent we could definitely use.

'I might be deaf but even I heard tons of Minerva kids chatting about our paper,' Liam adds. 'There was this group of posh girls who really liked your article on cinema being taken over by comic-book movies, Jenny.'

'Really?' A questioning smile replaces her scowl. He nods and Jenny goes into high-beam mode. 'I actually heard a couple of those girls quoting Max in the toilets when they were doing their make-up. Something about a "soft glam glow-up".'

'For real?' Max says, clasping his face. 'Do you have any idea how many kids have bullied me since we got here? Not a day goes by I don't get laughed at or pushed in the corridor.'

'We all get it,' Morowa says. 'These Blue Bloods started a post-code war the day we arrived.'

'They don't like us but they don't like each other much either,' Abdi adds. 'One of their players missed a penalty and they were cussing him out, bruv! Saying stuff about his mum and how he was uninvited to some party. Shit got *nasty*.'

'Popularity is fickle,' Tristan explains. 'A lot of us are impressed by you guys because even when you have your differences, you still stick together.'

'Kinda like now . . .' Liam mutters.

'Exactly,' I chime. 'Your talent is bigger than Bodley or Minerva.' I look every one of them in the eye, showing my sincere appreciation for what they do. 'We'll rebrand. Do the paper bigger and better, with forty-two per cent more sass.'

A Year Nine Minerva kid knocks on the glass door then comes in. 'Sorry, is one of you Dua Iqbal?'

'I am. What'cha got for me?' I ask. He hands me a note from Aden telling me that Dad has arrived and they are waiting for me in interview room three. Doom zaps the happiness from my heart.

'This time we'll have to use aliases,' Liam says as I tuck the note away. 'Wouldn't put it past Sir Reg to force Aden to exclude the lot of us.'

Max scratches his jaw. 'Maybe we should all report under the same name?'

'How about something simple like . . . Nunya Byz?' Morowa asks.

'As in none-of-your-business?' Tristan asks, smiling at her. 'Genius!'

'From this point on we're all Nunya Byz so no one has to take a bullet for the team,' I agree.

'I know there's a lot more Minerva kids who want to work

for your paper too,' Tristan says.

'No,' Morowa says firmly. 'Like Max said, we have to put up with microaggressions every single day. In class, in the corridors, in the lunch hall, on the way home. Just because we got successful doesn't mean y'all get to leech off our success.'

'Hey,' Tristan says, raising his hands in submission. 'A lot of us aren't like that. It's a smaller-than-you-think group making the environment toxic for everyone. Us included.'

A quick glance at the clock reminds me Aden and Dad are waiting but I want to end this meeting right. I think about Dad's newsletter.

'Allies are useful and welcome,' I say gently. 'If Sir Reg tries to shut down our new paper, he'll have an even harder time if his own students are involved.'

'I'm sorry, guys,' Jenny says, getting up. 'It's been real but I can't risk getting excluded. And I can't put a secret paper on a sixth-form application.'

Morowa touches Jen's shoulder. 'Jen, please stay. We had so much fun trying to get Briggs to give us an interview!'

Jenny looks tearful. 'I love you, Mor, but school isn't supposed to be fun. Being a journalist right now is just too dangerous.'

There are more protests so I butt in: 'Jenny, you know how much I value your skills. But I also accept writing for this paper is a lot more trouble than we thought. I'm going to miss you if you go, but it has to be *your* choice. No pressure.'

Jenny looks at me, jaw muscles working, her face going red. Anyone can see the girl is torn. 'I'm sorry!' she says, blinking back tears before grabbing her bag and rushing out.

'Anyone else want to walk away?' I ask, trying to hide my shock. Instant regret. Roshni is the most likely to ditch the paper, and without her skills we'll be DOA.

There are some mutterings, Roshni tuts a few times, but

thankfully nobody speaks up. They must believe in the paper as much as I do. I hope they do.

'Good, now I better get my ass down to Aden's before I'm permanently excluded.'

'Wait!' Roshni calls as we're all rising to go. 'If we're going to rebrand the paper, then what is it going to be called?'

'*Lost Voices*,' Max suggests, snapping his fingers.

Liam shakes his head. 'Makes us sound like a home for strays.'

'That's kinda what we are on Minerva turf,' Morowa argues.

'We need to stop thinking like that,' I say. 'We have every right to be here and we're going to shake things up. Roshni, any ideas?'

'Hey, I'm comms gal, not ideas gal.'

'A good name should reflect who we are and what we're about,' I say, bouncing a pencil off my lower lip as I think aloud. 'We're kind of like WikiLeaks with the whole expose-the-truth vibe but for the TikTok generation. We spill the tea with no shade and we're Generation Z.'

'Got it: *TeaLeakZ*!' Morowa says, throwing open her arms.

Liam, Abdi and I are here for it. The others, not so much.

'I've got places to be and Dua needs to get shouted at by Mr Aden!' Roshni snipes, rising to her feet. 'The damn paper is called *TeaLeakZ*. End of.' And with that, she storms off.

'Watch your back, boss,' Abdi whispers, overdramatically. 'Looks like Roshni's after your crown.'

CHAPTER 16

Dad and I sit opposite Mr Aden in interview room three. Still shook by Jenny walking out on the movement, and worrying how Mum's recovery is going, it's all I can do not to start crying.

'Is Mrs Iqbal unwell?' Aden asks like a nosy bastard.

'We share responsibility for our daughter's care,' Dad replies tersely.

'I see. It is helpful if you could let us know which parent she is staying with. It's a legal requirement for school records to be kept up-to-date,' Aden says with a small smile.

'So you're handing my daughter a four-day exclusion for publishing an article raising awareness about mobile phone theft?' Dad asks, baffled.

'No, Mr Iqbal. Dua uploaded an article without receiving permission. I'm sure you can understand the importance of checking material for appropriateness before it is published under the school name? It's the second time she's done it, and she was warned clearly about the consequences of failing to abide by the rules. The tone of the article was also felt to be slanderous towards Councillor Briggs, who is a friend of the school.'

'My understanding is that the Minerva kids have a paper and all the support and resources they could want. My daughter showed enterprise in setting up a paper for your school and recruited a whole news team. Now you're taking that away from them?'

I look up in surprise. Did Dad just defend me even though he's being dragged for my reckless behaviour? Let's be real: though I stand by what I did, I know I broke rules.

Aden flinches, apparently as surprised as me. 'I'm afraid there must be consequences for incorrect behaviour. I'm having to make a report to the governors about the incident following a number of parental complaints.'

'Frankly, Mr Aden, I don't care about the governors or those parents. I think it was morally wrong for you as a school to put Bodley kids in this environment, where they are constantly reminded of what they don't have. Then when they try to bridge that gap, you punish them.'

I stifle a laugh. Dad is on fire, giving it to Aden with both barrels. This is the hands-on Dad I remember from before the separation, who always took the time to understand the reasoning behind every mistake I ever made but always expected me to do better.

'I'm sorry you feel that way, Mr Iqbal. I can only reiterate that I have nothing against Dua. She is one of our brightest and most able students.' WTF?! If I'm all that, then why the hell does he keep clipping my wings? The fricking school motto is 'Learn, Grow, Take Flight'! Live by it!

'Brother, you must see reason,' Dad says.

Eek!

'I can't imagine what life must be like for you as one of the only Muslim headteachers in the borough. But I'll say this, you should know better than to break the spirit of our children.'

Considering the hate he's had from within the community, reaching out to Aden from a place of religion is brave. Aden maintains a courteous silence.

'Dad, you were killing it!' I say, my chest swelling with pride as Dad unlocks his car. 'I thought Mum was good at winning arguments, but you held your own back there.'

Dad gives me a side glance and laughs. 'I wasn't arguing, Dua. I was doing what any other father would do, which is stick up for his little girl. That school is mad messing with you guys in Year Eleven. They've got no clue how to look after a smart kid like you.'

I think of my news team and how smart and talented they all are in their own special way. I definitely lucked out with them, though I can't help wondering what each of us could've become if we'd gone to a school like Minerva from the start, bathed in privilege and opportunity. Then I think of Jenny walking out on us and my heart sinks. She shouldn't have to decide between education and writing for the paper, since she's brilliant at both.

Stopping at the traffic lights, Dad turns on a recitation of the Qur'an. The Kuwaiti Sheikh is my favourite, his voice melodious and emotional. I sigh. 'You missing your mum?' Dad asks, his voice perfectly neutral.

'Course, but I know giving her space to heal is the best thing right now. Besides,' I say in a shy voice, 'it's nice having the chance to chill with *you*.'

He reaches out, intertwining his fingers with mine. 'I am blessed.'

Once I've rushed through the maths assignment, I check my emails. I'm gobsmacked to find three articles sent by Minerva students wanting in on our paper. I open up a really good one from Tristan giving the inside scoop on an Extinction Rebellion protest scheduled for the weekend and why everyone should care. I shoot him a thank-you email. Scrolling down, I see another email from someone called 'ThotWithAGun'. Curiosity gets the better of me and I open it.

Dear Ho-jab-Bitch,
Print bullshit about the right honourable councillor again and
we'll end you.

    PS Please hang yourself with your hijab. Be sure to tie the
knot extra tight.

My heart pounds like it's going to burst out of my chest. A suspension is one thing, but an actual death threat? This is next level. Do I tell Dad, call the police or inform the news team? Or all three? Or . . . none?

In the end, I do none of these things. Instead, I wrench back control by drawing up a list of suspects:

Keira – not crazy enough

Renée – the right amount of crazy

Indira – can totally imagine her coming up with the bit about hijabs

Cllr Briggs – doubtful. Plus he's unlikely to get his hands dirty even if he did want to scare me off.

Sir Reg – unbelievable

Could Briggsy have a kid at our school? Might be worth looking into . . . One thing is certain: from now on I am going to have to watch my back.

The next day, Dad takes me to work with him since I breezed through the assignments left for me on the school intranet. There's still some reading to do for English, but I take it with me.

'Ta-da!' he says, gesturing doubled-handed like a cartoon character. 'What do you think of your pop's store?'

Never having been to his shop before in protest over our cancelled weekends together, it comes as a bit of a surprise. Way bigger than I thought, the frontage is sunshine yellow with bold black and red accents. Through the large shop window I see intricate displays of busts, minifigures, games, statues and other collectables. The sign at the top reads '!KOMIC KINGDOM!' complete with a stylistic golden crown tipped at an angle.

'Mashallah!' I say, laughing. 'My dad is an actual twelve-year-old boy trapped in the body of a thirty-seven-year-old geek.'

He laughs, ushering me in. Stepping over the threshold, I'm surprised by the size of the shop. Long aisles of assorted merchandise travel deep inside.

'You want a frappé or anything?' Dad asks.

I shake my head.

'Sure you know how to work a till?' he asks, hand poised on the I'LL BE BACK! sign with a photo of the Terminator.

'Summer job at Agni's Cafe. I'll be fine. Go.'

Settling behind the counter, I open my laptop and bring up the *Enley Post*. Just as I thought, they've given Briggs the whole front page to pooh-pooh our investigation.

After a local school student became the victim of an attempted phone mugging, she alleged in her school newspaper that this was the fault of the local councillor. The article gained national attention when a celebrity grime artist took up her cause by retweeting to her 3.5 million followers. Cllr Briggs denounced the attack but refuted claims that the local police was insufficiently funded to tackle the growing problem. 'This is unfortunately a nationwide phenomena and you can be sure we're giving our all to support our bobbies. The shortage of equipment was due to a delay in delivery from the supplier. I'm glad the young student was unhurt in the mugging, something that must have been deeply traumatizing for her and her family, but "woke" celebrities should use their star power to highlight genuine causes rather than fan the flames of controversy. Even better, dig deep and help fund some of these noble causes!'

The Rt. Hon. Councillor was asked if he was going to pursue legal action against the student and school which allowed the false allegations to be published.

'Certainly not! I do encourage our young folk to get involved in local causes. After checking in with her and her family, I advised her of the ramifications of printing damaging articles even in something as innocent as a school paper. I'm assured she's a bright lass, so I'm delighted she has decided to focus on her GCSEs instead.'

Principal Mohamud Aden of Bodley High confirmed that he had been unaware of the article prior to publication. He has apologized unreservedly to Cllr Briggs and informed us that he and the parent-governors have decided to shut down the school paper permanently.

In recent years, the academy has struggled with poor exam results, student indiscipline and high staff turnover. A new Learning Trust was revealed at the start of this year in which Minerva College and Bodley High aimed to share best practice and improve student outcomes together. Minerva consistently ranks as one of London's top grammar schools with impressive Progress 8 scores. However, within the first few weeks of reopening for the new term, two Bodley students were excluded for drug possession. Several parents of Minerva students have been critical of the Trust and expressed fears that their children may be led astray.

'The world has gone PC mad!' one particularly distressed mother stated. 'Our children worked so hard to pass entrance tests to be educated at Minerva. Now they've thrown open their doors to all and sundry in the name of "diversity and inclusion"! It's lowered the tone and it's simply not fair.'

'Bollocks!' I shout at my laptop, punching the nearest thing, which happens to be a jumbo-size Hulk plushie.

'Hulk SMASH!' it growls back, vibrating like a plane hitting turbulence.

'Oh shut up, ya big green idiot,' I scoff, knocking it off the counter. Scrolling through the comments left beneath the article, my heart sinks. They range from subtle digs passed off as parental concerns to outright bigotry. The article completely glosses over what we uncovered about Briggs being on the board or directors of the company that owns Enley Arcade, having a family member own the company that was contracted to provide the exercise equipment, and the mysterious absence of council funds.

The electronic buzzer over the door beeps as a delivery man wheels in a stack of cardboard boxes on a sack truck. Another man shuffles in behind him, disappearing into the aisles at the back. I glance at Dad's computer screen, showing a range of security views. The South Asian man appears to be just standing there with his hands in his hoodie pockets.

'Morning!' says the delivery man in a gruff voice, his cheeks raw from the ski-perfect temperatures outside. 'Is Rashid in?'

'What you got for me, Dave?' Dad asks, returning with a steaming cup of coffee.

They talk about a shipment of limited-edition action figures which apparently are going to be huge. I tune out their conversation, focusing instead on the man hidden in the aisles. He's standing right by the children's comics but he's not looking at any of them – he's on his phone.

Weird.

I watch the delivery guy leave, then survey the screen once more. The man has vanished. My eyes widen, scanning in all directions before I pick him up again on camera two. Call me crazy, but I think he's following Dad around the store.

Thinking about how valiantly Dad fought my corner with Aden, I snag a heavy replica sword, leap over the counter, and sneak up behind the man. Before I have a chance to pounce, he suddenly pulls off his hood and announces himself to the store.

'Yo, Shido! What's the matter, cuz? Ain't got no love for bredrin?'

I slink further back in the aisle to remain hidden just as Dad turns to look at the man. A shadow falls over his face. 'Get lost, Jubba. I don't have time for people like you.'

Jubba? Where have I heard that name before . . .

'People like me?' Jubba's body language is flamboyant – but he's a bit old to be a roadman. I tighten my grip on the hilt of the sword. 'What? You too good for your ol' pals now?'

'Where's this going, Jubba?' Dad asks, starting to lose patience. 'I know you didn't come here for a catch-up.'

Jubba's grin is all enamel and gold. 'Nice place you got here, Richie. Classy. I came to—'

With the heavy fake sword resting on my shoulder, I shift my feet, accidentally tipping a Funko Pop. My hand flies out, blocking its fall, and in the process setting off an avalanche – I *might* have forgotten about the rest of the vinyl collectables.

Jubba notices me and raises his brow in surprise as he eyeballs the ridiculous plastic sword. 'Who's this? Xena: Warrior Princess?'

'I'm Dua,' I say, placing the sword in the pile of fallen boxes like Excalibur wedged in stone. 'And you *must* be Uncle Jubba. Didn't you used to print a newsletter with Dad back in the day?'

Jubba guffaws, his mouth a veritable treasure chest. 'You tell her about that? Oh yeah, man, me and your dad were proper rebels. We said stuff that made the white man tremble.'

'We don't need to hear this,' Dad interjects sternly.

Jubba barely bats an eyelid, all his attention squarely on me. 'Somebody needed to teach them a lesson, so one day we smashed up their wing—'

'Jubba!' Dad snaps, cutting him off. *Is Jubba saying he and Dad were once violent protestors? My gentle dad could never . . .* 'What do you want? Money?!'

Jubba looks at me. 'You hearing this, kid? Your old man's disrespecting me.' He turns to dad, who glowers at him in silence.

I look from one angry face to the other. 'Um, feel free to tell me to butt out, but—'

Dad interrupts me. 'You got caught stealing again, didn't you, Jubba? You work for dangerous men, rob them and then expect me to bail you out?'

'I ain't stolen from nobody, cuz!' Jubba shouts. 'I'm a father and a businessman, just like you. I come to you asking for help and you bad-mouth me in front of your daughter like I'm some homeless smackhead.'

'Then talk. Tell me why you're really here?' Dad asks, folding his arms sceptically.

Jubba drops his eyes, slouching. 'Auntie Ismat died, innit?'

'Oh. Sorry to hear that,' Dad says, caught off guard. He runs a hand through his hair and sighs. 'Good woman. Used to give us iced buns when we came back from football practice.'

'The best!' Jubba says, knocking his heart with a fist. A moment of silence passes as both men stare at the ground remembering her. 'Look, I'm gonna level with you. I said I'd pay for the funeral cos she never had no kids, but it's left me in a bind.' Dad raises a brow. 'What do you say, Shido? You wanna help a brother out? Swear I'll pay you back.'

Dad says nothing. I watch him in complete disbelief.

'What, you don't believe me? Don't trust me?' Jubba shouts indignantly.

'You know damn well why I can't trust you!' Dad barks.

Jubba shrugs his bony shoulders. 'W-o-w. You still mad cos I told Auntie Kauther you was getting married? That was sixteen years ago, cuz! A mother has a right to know!'

'I was *going* to tell her, but you snatched the opportunity out of my hands, like you snatch everything! You sticking a firecracker in the headmistress's exhaust pipe got me expelled.'

Jubba rolls his eyes and retorts, 'They woulda expelled us anyway. What you complaining about? You still went uni and got your own business, didn't ya?'

'You were expelled?' I ask in surprise, looking at Dad. Sounds like Dad and I have a *lot* more in common than I thought.

'Is Auntie Ismat even dead?' Dad asks.

I gasp.

Jubba looks murderous, then flips Dad off and storms out.

'Dad!' I berate, unable to understand how the kind and patient man I've been reconnecting with these past few days could be so brazenly cruel.

'The man is a liar. You don't know him,' he says, folding his arms.

I shake my head with disappointment.

'Dua, come bac—' I hear Dad shout as I close the door on him.

I run down the street after Jubba. 'Uncle Jubba!'

He stops. 'Go back, kid. He won't like you coming after me.'

'Look, I'm sorry. Dad's just wound real tight. I'm sure he'd be happy to contribute towards funeral costs. Look, let me have a word with him when he's had a chance to calm down a bit. Seeing you seems to have brought up some difficult memories. How much do you need?' I pull out my wallet and have a look inside.

'Coupla grand. Three, actually, but that ain't happening,' he says, lighting up.

I hand him a twenty which he happily takes. 'I can't promise anything, but I'll see what I can do.'

He nods. 'Thanks, kid. I hope you're right. You know, you

grow up, you make money, but you should never forget your roots or the people you left behind. Your dad used to know that.'

I sigh, my thoughts involuntarily turning to the discrimination that triggered Mum's depression. None of the other members of the science department even tried to help her when they knew what was going on. Every one of them just looked the other way, forgetting all the times she'd helped them out by fielding difficult parental phone calls, helping to mark their papers during her frees and being a shoulder to cry on on more than one occasion. If Mum didn't have me and Dad, what might have become of her?

Poor Auntie Ismat, a little old Asian lady who had loved to treat Dad and Jubba, and didn't even have enough for her own funeral.

'You remind me of my daughter, Sarah.' His sigh is so heavy it summons a stone in my throat.

'Yeah? What school does she go to?'

He shakes his head. 'Her mum don't let me see her . . . You better get back, or your old man'll think I kidnapped you or something.'

'I'm sorry for your loss.' I offer him a sympathetic smile. 'I'll get Dad to give you a call later.'

He smiles sadly and lopes off.

I bring up the subject of the funeral again at dinner.

'Dad, you are going Auntie Ismat's funeral, yeah?'

'Dua, I honestly have no idea whether she's actually dead or not. I could check with my mum, but I can't deal with her "you're damned" bull right now.'

Dad got married sixteen years ago without her blessing. Why can't Nani just let it go? 'I honestly think Jubba needs your help.'

'Nope, it's my wallet he's after,' he says, scooping some daal in a tender piece of roti and guiding it to his mouth.

'How can you keep knocking him like that?' I ask, exasperated. 'You were once mates. He's clearly fallen on hard times, so why won't you help him?'

'Dua, you've only just met the man! Why do you care so much?' he asks with indignation.

'Because I don't have a proper family!' I blurt, embarrassed by how rude and childish it sounds. 'I only have you and Mum, and right now I don't even have her. The only other person who doesn't look at me like I'm an abomination is Auntie Irum, and she's halfway across the planet in Lahore.'

Dad's face shows pain and he squeezes my wrist. 'I'm sorry, Princess. When your mum and me got married, we didn't realize the entire community would turn their backs on us. We thought our parents might grow to accept it instead of trying to pull us apart. I don't ever want you to think any of it is your fault.'

'Whether it's my fault or not, I'm lonely, Dad. I want the support of a big fat Desi community just like Roshni and Huda from school have. I like the idea of having an Uncle Jubba. You were on the come up and he wasn't. Doesn't Islam teach us that no one gets left behind? Like even sinners? Isn't Jubba still part of the community?'

Dad shakes his head, frowning. 'If he cared about the community, he wouldn't be infecting it with drugs.'

I fall silent.

Jubba is *dealing*.

Dad squeezes the bridge of his nose, exhaling. 'A few bad eggs can spoil an entire community. Back in the nineties, someone murdered Auntie Ismat's husband and the cops didn't even bother investigating. They called it suicide. Then Jubba's mum spread gossip about Auntie murdering him herself and cut her off. That poor woman went through hell. If she's dead, of course I'll help with funeral costs. But trust me: Jubba is bad news, and you can't believe a word he says.'

CHAPTER 17

> Hey, what's up?

A sassy reply sizzles at my fingertips. Liam and I have so much work to do to launch *TeaLeakZ* and I'm absolutely buzzing to get started . . . as soon as I finish my stupid chemistry work.

I start to tap out my response before realizing that the message is not from Liam.

Not to be *that person*, but who is this?

> Ouch! You deleted my number?

My stomach flips. Hugo.

Sorry, have a lot going on atm.

> I heard you got excluded. Really sorry. ☹

Thanks. I'm sorry about cancelling our match.

> No worries. Wanna shoot a few hoops after school?

Can't. I have a thing.

> . . . Are you avoiding me?

What the hell do I say to that?! Of course I'm avoiding the two-timing Romeo. Fooling around isn't my thing.

> Ppl are gonna see us together and get the wrong idea then it'll get back to Keira.

> Who cares? We broke up over the summer.

I sit up. If Hugo's a free agent then why was Renée warning me off? Like that girl needs a reason . . . But it doesn't mean I want to get involved with him beyond friendship. Still, the journalist within has to *know*.

> Not that it's any of my business . . . but who broke it off?

Silence.

I realize that it's really not my place to ask that and start typing an apology, then stop when the three little pulsing dots come up.

> Meet me at Langley Park in twenty.
> I'll tell you everything.

> But you're in school?

> Not any more! Haha.

He pings me a photo of him giving a thumbs up just outside the school gates. Must have vaulted over. I shake my head, but a smile is undeniably tweaking my lips.

He's skipping school for me.

But can I go? Rowntree has completely failed to prepare me for the upcoming chemistry test, but Mum did say she could help me when she gets back from her CBT session this evening . . . I unclench my jaw. Playing some one-on-one sounds like the perfect distraction.

But it can't be too distracting – this doesn't mean anything.

Pairing up grey fleece joggers with a red zip hoodie, I pull on a fresh sports hijab then examine my tired-looking face in the mirror.

Maybe a little make-up would help—

I check myself. I don't own any make-up because I have literally *never* wanted to, and I'm not about to change that for someone else.

Making it as far as the front door, I double back, applying a double coat of rose lip balm.

Fast-walking along the Cromwell Road, I hug myself as a chill wind buffets me. Dark clouds gather overhead, seemingly in judgement, rumbling angrily as they turn the day into night.

Dates are haram! hisses the voice in my head, which sounds suspiciously like Huda.

'It's *not* a date,' I tell it, breaking into a jog.

The wind roars against my hijab, drowning out the voice as I pelt towards the park. Shooting through the forest-green gates, I make a beeline for the basketball court as guilt sloshes around in my stomach, telling me this little link-up is a bad idea.

What if he wants to be your boyfriend? asks Mind-Huda. I ignore her.

Floodlights bleach the court an effervescent white. A figure darts forward, pounding an amber ball into the glittering tarmac, thundering towards the hoop. Hugo: dressed in a baggy grey hoodie, three-quarter-length tights framing his muscular legs. Brow low, eyes focused like lasers, he races up to take the shot. He leaps, he shoots, he scores – a perfect layup. I cannot help but clap.

Hugo whirls round in surprise, raking back his golden hair. 'Dua! You made it!' Coming over, he gives me a side hug. I stiffen – Hugo is a little too familiar for my liking. Punching the ball through the loop of his arm, I snigger, intercept it, then dribble up the court.

'Oh, like that, is it?' He chases after me. 'Shit, you're fast!'

'Thought I was on the team to fill some diversity quota? Jokes on *you*.'

Instead of cringing at my joke like I would expect him to, he chuckles and says simply, 'Fair dos. You're good.' He thrusts his hand out, trying to steal the ball, but I dance out of his way, whirling the ball around with some fancy footwork. Then, streaking across the court, working up a solid tempo, I breach the scoring zone. Hugo gasps in surprise as I try a hook shot, sending the ball curving straight down through the hoop.

'No freaking way!' he cries.

'Swish,' I announce nonchalantly (though I had no clue the gamble would pay off).

Bounding over, he high-fives me, then takes a knee, looking up at me with his deep-set eyes. 'Marry me.'

I chuck the ball at his face.

He holds his nose, eyes watering. 'I can't believe you just did that!'

I laugh. '*I* can't believe you made me come all the way here to hear your story, but couldn't even bring your A game? Where is the promised tea?'

He stands. 'I'll play you for it.'

I smile – challenge accepted. 'Yoink!' I cry, plucking the ball from his hands. Turning my back on his penetrating gaze, I dribble towards the opposite basket. This time he doesn't hold back and uses his longer legs to race ahead of me and block my shot. I twist and turn, but each time his long limbs find me out, blocking my way, forming a great moving barrier between the ball and the basket. Running out of options, I bounce the ball between his legs, swerve round to claim it and attempt the shot. We both leap into the air at the same time and suddenly it feels like someone hit slow motion on the world. Hugo's huge palm slaps the ball away, but we just keep rising like gravity gave up on us and we're heading to the moon. Mid-air, our bodies crash into each other. Shockwaves and vibrations blast through me and I recoil sharply. Then the ground is racing up to meet us.

'Woah!' Hugo cries, his ears going pink.

Embarrassment sears my face. 'Let's call it a tie.'

Holding the ball between us, he looks into my eyes with a disarming intensity. 'Finish what you started.' The ball flies into the air. We both reach for it, but the height advantage is his. I watch him rush forwards, moving on from the faux pas like it never happened, pulling off a reverberating bank shot.

And just like that, I'm back in the game, leaping for the ball.

Going toe-to-toe, trading move for move, we play hard and fast till we're both sweating rivers and perfectly tied. His aftershave fails to mask the metallic smell of his sweat.

Making a time-out signal, he holds onto his knees, panting. Turning away, I wipe my sweaty brow, sweeping a coil of hair back inside my hijab. When I turn back, the witty one-liner I was about to dazzle him with dies on my tongue. His hoodie is pulled up over his face, exposing a glistening torso that is so acutely shredded it's practically an ice sculpture.

I look away, coughing. 'Well, this is a bust – neither one of us are winning anytime soon and I've got work to do . . . I'm gonna go.'

'Wait.' Dropping his hoodie back down again, he looks at me with pleading eyes. The lint hooked onto his golden-brown stubble makes me smile. 'I'll tell you everything.'

I suck my cheeks in, thoughtfully. 'OK.' We take a seat on the bench at the side of the court.

'Basically, Keira and I were totally wrong for each other. Two blondes don't make a right.' He folds his arms, frowning at the memory. 'I don't like being used.'

I stay silent, knowing from experience that people are more likely to talk if you give them space. Hugo is interesting, maybe even fascinating, but none of that means a damn if his motivations are messed-up. I can't help but want to know more.

He runs a hand through his sweaty hair. 'Look, I don't like to say bad things about exes, but *only* because you're asking . . . Keira is obsessed with status. Everything she does is engineered to make her look good.' I could've told him that.

'Wait,' I say, my lip curling. 'Are you saying dating *you* makes a girl "look good"?'

He has the decency to look ashamed. 'I'm captain of the rugby team. I'm the head's son. I get invited to the best parties. I'm not saying it's right or fair but it's the kind of thing Keira loves.'

'Why'd you date her in the first place?' I ask, trying not to feel jealous.

'I'm . . . not always the sharpest tool in the box. Keira's hot and she seemed really sweet. But all the pictures and the updates documenting every moment of our relationship for her Insta . . . she wasn't interested in me.'

'Yeah, well, as a fellow journalist, I kinda get why she'd want to document stuff. Some people bite their nails, we file stuff for posterity. It's a basic instinct.' I crack a smile, wondering why I'm sticking up for my tormentor.

He studies me, making me blush. 'You've not reached for your phone once.'

'Don't give me too much credit,' I say, having always struggled with compliments. 'It's only because I don't want you to laugh at how cracked my phone is after the run-in with the mugger.'

He laughs, then sighs with contentment. 'You just do your thing and rise to the top. That's what I like about you.'

The compliment makes my foot twitch nervously.

'Dad and Keira are both manipulative control freaks. You have no idea how stressful it is having your dad at school watching your every move.' He rolls his eyes.

I shudder, feeling sorry for him. 'Even though my mum is lovely, I thank goodness every day that she didn't take a job at Bodley.'

He cocks an eyebrow. 'Your mum's a teacher?'

'Yes. No. I . . . it's complicated.'

'You don't, uh, want to talk about it, do you? Because these big ears aren't just for comic relief.'

I glance up at his ears and chuckle, his charming lack of arrogance disarming me. 'My mum is the most *amazing* chem teacher. Ask her anything science-y and she can help, like on the spot, without textbooks or Google. But right now she's not much help with anything.'

'How comes? Hey . . .' He places a hand on my back as a tear runs down my cheek, making me look like an emotional wreck. Where has this come from? *Stop crying.*

I look up at him and something in me tells me to ignore my brain for once and to share.

When I'm done Hugo half hugs me, shaking his head. 'Arse-holes. All the clique clashes at Minerva are pretty shit, but the more I hear about the adult world, the more I think it's probably the same. Your mum's too good for that scum.'

'They're the worst! I just hate seeing her like this.'

'Tough times don't last forever. Soon enough, your mum will be the same amazing teacher you knew and you'll forget this ever happened.'

I can't explain it but with Hugo's warm hand on my back I feel so . . . *protected*. Maybe it's just because he's huge. Or maybe it's because he's actually listening, and really doesn't have to. Either way, I find myself wanting the moment to go on forever as I lean against him, staring into the distance. There's a rumble in the darkening sky and a flicker of lightning.

'I hope you're right.'

CHAPTER 18

'Where you been?' Dad asks before I've even had a chance to stick my key in the lock.

'To the park,' I say, stepping out of the rain. 'Playing some basketball.'

'Your mum called. Said you were supposed to go over to get some help with a chemistry test.'

'Noooooo!' I cover my mouth. I completely lost track of time. How could I do that to mum?

'You also turned your phone off.'

'No, I didn't . . .' I pull out my phone and am surprised to see I actually did. 'I don't understand.'

'You're not a forgetful girl. You wanna tell me why my spidey-sense is tingling?'

I feel myself wither under Dad's interrogative eyes. 'I already did! I needed some exercise so I went to the park. I don't remember turning my phone off but the game was intense, so . . .' I trail off, hoping he'll let it go.

'I hate to ask you this,' Dad says, stroking his beard. 'But I promised Aisha I'd look after you. So lay it on the line for me: do you have a boyfriend?'

'Oh, my days!' I say in exasperation. 'No! I've *never* had a boyfriend. You vanish for years and now suddenly you get to ask me personal questions?'

'Not fair. You keep throwing that in my face every time things get uncomfortable. I've already admitted I made mistakes and apologized to both you and Aisha. But here I am today, stepping up to the plate and being your dad. You can make all the sarcastic comments you want, but by Allah I'm doing my best. Are you?'

Shame clings to my face like a self-heating face mask, and I can no longer look him in the eye.

'Look, there's nothing wrong with being attracted to someone just so long as you remember the rules,' he says gently. 'Some day me and your mum want you to marry a pious brother that treats you like a queen.'

My feelings are complicated enough without having to have this conversation. The idea of being in love with Hugo makes me cringe, but in the moments I am actually with him – without the labels and the analysing – I *do* feel like a queen.

'You better call your mum. She's worried,' he says. 'And then you can join me in the kitchen for some leftovers.'

Saturday hails the return of a rare treat: a golden October sun blazing brightly in an Alice in Wonderland-worthy blue sky. The perfect day for a picnic, but I've already arranged to meet Max and Morowa at the local library.

'Hey, boss!' they chorus as I find their table by the biographies.

They catch me up on everything that's gone down at school since I got suspended. Apparently, the *Chronicle* girls were allowed to hold an assembly in which they announced that they've decided to go one hundred per cent digital. Keira gave her best Greta Thunberg impression and announced fifty per cent of proceeds from next month's special final print edition will go to the Wildlife Trusts.

'So Sir Reg gave them a platform to steal our thunder,' I say, scowling.

'You had your supporters,' Max says gleefully. 'Tristan actually shouted "fakes" and "rip-offs" and was escorted out of assembly. You shoulda seen that kid go!'

'I was surprised!' Morowa admits. 'One of the popular Minerva boys shouted your name in support too.'

'Which one?' I ask.

'Girl, it was the blond Adonis!' Max says, lolling his tongue.

Hugo publicly supported me against Keira? And in front of his *dad*?

'Also,' Morowa says, biting her lip, 'don't shoot the messenger, but I've identified a potential problem.' She holds up her phone and plays a video.

At first the camera is facing a pale grey wall, bobbing gently in tandem with the sound of Morowa's gale-force breathing. Then two voices are suddenly picked up – one I recognize immediately: I'd know Liam's subtle slurred speech anywhere, but whoever he's talking to is an enigma. Soft as velvet, the second voice almost coils around the first with invisible tendrils.

The video comes into focus.

'– you should,' says Keira, holding court on her familiar window seat. 'I mean, *I* would.'

'Really?' Liam says doubtfully, seated uncomfortably beside her with his gangly limbs akimbo and his cheeks pink.

'My little brother went crazy for your article about *Fortnite*, so naturally I had to take a look. It was really interesting – this from a non-gamer. You have a gift, Liam. I could use someone like you on the team.'

'Nah, I'm not interested in joining the *Chronicle*.' Liam's voice cracks in the middle, a shrill squeak escaping his lips.

'How come there weren't more pieces on gaming in *Bodley Voices*?' Keira has traded in her Thunberg impression for a phone sex operator. No wonder I didn't recognize her voice.

'Dua didn't think there was a big enough fanbase,' Liam stutters.

'Really? That's mad! You could have a section in the *Chronicle* every month. How does seventy-five sound?'

So Keira thinks everyone has a price? Unbelievable.

'Oh, my days! Are you serious?' Liam asks in surprise.

'Pleeease,' she moans, squeezing his thigh – the little sket. 'At least think about it. What's your number?'

I listen to them exchange numbers, my insides set ablaze, then Keira's ears perk up.

'Did you just hear something?'

On the recording, I hear Morowa swear under her breath then hotfoot it out of there before the video cuts out.

'Bitch, please! Asking a deaf boy if he heard something!' Max says askance, folding his arms.

'You OK?' Morowa asks, touching my shoulder. 'We just thought you should know.'

'Sabotage,' I say slowly, the word as corrosive as battery acid. 'Keira waited till I was suspended before going to work. In a twisted way, I kind of admire her ruthless military strategy.'

'I admire her nude shellac but I'd still slap the skank,' Max says hotly.

'What are we going to do about Liam?' Morowa asks. 'No tea, no shade, but if he's Keira's man on the inside now, just think of the damage he could do to *TeaLeakZ*.'

'No,' I say vehemently. 'Liam would never betray us.'

'Hate to say it, Dua, but thirst can be a powerful motivator,' Max says darkly.

'How many people know about this?'

Max and Morowa exchange guilty looks. 'Everyone on the team,' Morowa confirms. 'That's the thing with journalists: sniffing out secrets is what we do.'

'So when you gonna sack his two-timing ass?' Max asks.

I'm stunned. I can't sack Liam. He's my best friend. My partner in crime. I can't push him out. Can I?

He's always had a weakness for romance, but this time he's not only compromised himself but the whole paper. For sure this requires a higher level of damage control.

'If we're going to continue beating the Chroniclers, we're going to need to lead with something big,' I say thoughtfully.

'But the launch issue is going to be our Black History Month Special, right,' Morowa says. 'I've been working on articles for weeks.'

'The BHM special is a given,' I promise, 'but we need to lead on something bigger – a scoop that's going to appeal to a wide audience.'

Morowa looks at me scornfully. 'Since when do we care about a wide audience? I thought this was supposed to be our safe space to talk about the things that matter to us?'

'Totally, but if we rally the troops, we might be able to get another issue out before then. We have to launch *TeaLeakZ* quickly so that it remains at the front of everyone's minds.'

'So a follow-up to the mugging story?' Morowa suggests.

I shake my head. 'And tell everyone exactly who we are? The anonymity of Nunya Byz is key.'

'So what's the big lead story going to be?' Max asks. 'And what are you gonna do about Liam?'

Glancing at my friends with a confidence I don't have, I tap my temple meaningfully. 'Leave it with me.'

In the afternoon, after helping with chemistry, Mum agrees to go for a walk with me. This is a huge deal, since she's become a little people-phobic in her recovery, but I try not to make a thing out of it. Every time I see her now, she's sounding more and more like herself, and I can't help but hope I might be able to come home soon. Though I'm not sure I want to leave Dad just yet.

Mum pauses outside the entrance to Enley Market, staring up at the red-and-white marquee fluttering listlessly in the wind. I give her hand a squeeze and link my arm through hers. She smiles nervously as we venture into the hustle and bustle.

'It's changed so much!' Mum says.

'Really?' I ask, furrowing my brow.

'I used to come here a lot with your Nani to buy cloth for shalwar kameezes. It was our ritual. Every year she'd bring me to pick out something special for Eid. Then she'd cut it and sew it, and on Eid I'd wear it to the mosque.'

'Mum . . . do you think there's any way you could ever reconnect with Nani-Ji?'

She rethreads a hijab pin. 'I've tried for years, beyta. Time to heal and move on.' Mum takes us over towards a coffee shop. 'Now let's get you a knickerbocker glory. This place – Uncle Steadman's – makes the absolute best— Oh no, look!'

On the coffee shop door is a sad-looking A4 piece of paper: 'Closing for Business on Friday. Drop by for One Final Cuppa.'

'What happened?' Mum asks after we make our way inside.

An old Jamaican man in a tattered apron who must be Uncle Steadman himself turns to us and sighs. 'Man, what happened to any of us? There was a police raid last week. Came in with their sniffer dogs, slobbering all over me ginger cake! There was about ten of them. No, Mister Policeman, I ain't got no drugs here, just cake and tea. Honest! I been running this business now for forty year!'

'Did they find something on the premises?' I ask, bewildered.

He looks from me to Mum, heartbreak reflected in his watery eyes. 'I've got health problems, so my young friend got me painkillers and they work a treat! Police confiscated them – said they weren't legal medicine – then reported me to the market manager. They cancelled my licence!'

'Oh no!' Mum says in despair. 'Did you explain what happened?'

'What's the use? My friend is a young man. They find out he's involved and they'll be locking him up and throwing away the key!' He sighs and takes a seat wearily. 'It's not been the same here for a while . . . Rent keeps going up, up and these new shop owners don't like us. They always complaining they see lots of young, Black men coming to my shop to buy drugs. I told them I've been serving tea and cakes to Black men, white men, brown men since their mothers were wiping their bottoms! Why would a respectable old man involve himself in illegal rubbish? Anyway, enough of me complaining,' he says, drawing a breath to steady himself. 'What can I get you?'

'Poor man,' Mum says, once we find a table. 'Uncle Steadman's the last of the old guard. It's all changed so much. Over there was Maira Fabrics, where Nani used to buy her cloth, and that was the samosa wala.'

I glance over at the flash sushi bar. 'It's the flipping east side of town pushing us out!'

'I suppose they call it "progress",' Mum says pensively. 'Time and tide wait for no man.'

'If we don't preserve the old ways, Mum, we'll lose our culture. History will forget us.'

'That's what my dad was forever saying. There were so many Asian shops back then . . .'

'Mum, if you like this place so much, how comes you haven't been back before now?' I reach across the table, taking her hand.

'I think . . . I didn't want to ruin my old memories of my parents with the more recent ones. I guess I wasn't brave enough.'

'Mum, you're the bravest person I know. After every crazy thing life's thrown at you, you're still standing. I'm so glad Dad and I are patching things up, but you will always be my first hero.' My voice hitches as my eyes start watering.

Mum leans forward and kisses my forehead, sending more love than words ever could. Then she looks at the coffee shop sadly.

'Enley Market will never be the same.'

'Regenerate, Don't Gentrificate' by Nunya Byz

Last weekend my mother took me to Enley Market to sample a fabled coconut knickerbocker glory (YUM!). Since the 1960s, this place has developed a unique character as the Windrush generation and South Asian immigrants brought their own influences, bestowing a cultural glow-up to a part of town that had long been abandoned to post-war decline. Buzzing with activity, it soon became the backbone of the community.

On Saturday, my mum's sense of nostalgia took a hit when she discovered most of the shops she'd fallen in love with as a kid had been replaced with corporate enterprises, high-end restaurants, and hipster-laden coffee houses. The very part of town built by the blood, sweat and tears of our communities has caught the eye of greedy developers who are transforming it into a soulless money-making machine. Make no mistake, this is a particularly aggressive form of social cleansing: gentrification.

Prejudice has led to a high number of police drug raids on ethnic traders. Many sold up and moved out rather than endure the relentless intimidation. This was a golden generation of traders who poured love into each of their products, knew the community inside out, and placed customers' well-being above profits.

TeaLeakZ heard one particularly heartbreaking story about a shopkeeper in his eighties who was taking alternative medicine for chronic pain. The poor man had no idea it contained anything illegal and, after being scared half to death by a brutal interrogation (including slobbering sniffer dogs), immediately had his licence revoked. This is no way to treat a senior who, come rain or shine, has served this community for decades.

Just as sites of historical significance and natural beauty are preserved for posterity, so too should the small parts of town that keep alive the stories and achievements of immigrant and working-class communities in the face of adversity. Enley East has always been prosperous. With gentrification forced on Enley West, our histories, our communities, and our very character are under attack.

TeaLeakZ calls on Councillor Briggs and other decision-makers to stop the madness. Pump taxpayer money into regenerating run-down parts of town while respecting the character that made them so great in the first place.

Do you have any special memories of Enley Market? Are you for or against gentrification? Sound off in the comment section below!

CHAPTER 19

I am totally dreading going back to school on Monday, but Dad isn't interested in any of my excuses. Who knows what's waiting for me there? I nervously pack my bag over and over again, trying to prepare for all eventualities. *Hopefully*, I think, *the Nunya Byz article is far enough away from Minerva to avoid suspicion.*

At least for now.

Liam sends me a message about waiting at the bus stop. I blow him off with something about not being sure if I'm going to make it today. What else am I supposed to do? I'm just not ready to confront him about Morowa's video. The question is, how long can I keep avoiding him?

Arriving at school, I head into the playground to find my friends. I turn in a full circle before seeing Renée and Indira marching towards me. My heart tells me to bounce but my head tells me to stand my ground. Might as well get it over with . . .

'Oh look, it's Dua!' Indira says, laughing.

'Be nice, Indira. The poor thing's mother got fired for going mental. It probably runs in the family,' says Renée, smirking.

The rug is pulled from under my feet.

The terrible sadness I've been holding back for weeks is wrenched to the surface, and to my shame, I feel humiliated to have Mum's business broadcast to the whole playground. How do they even know? I didn't tell Hugo everything. Literally nobody else knew except me, Dad and . . .

Liam.

He betrayed *TeaLeakZ* and sold me out for *seventy-five quid*. I nearly collapse, blinking back tears. The world turns as I realize just how alone I am.

'Aw! Don't be embarrassed,' Renée leers. 'I'm sure she looks fabulous modelling the latest couture in straitjackets. Best of luck for the lobotomy.'

'Careful, babe,' Indira warns darkly. 'In Dua's mental state, I wouldn't be surprised if she's strapped explosives to her flat chest to blow us to kingdom come.'

'You lot are sick!' Roshni spits, suddenly standing shoulder to shoulder with me. 'I can't *believe* I just heard those words come out your mouths. Who even *are* you people?'

Renée looks coolly at Roshni. 'I've no problem with you. Jog on.'

'Well, I have a problem with *you*!' Roshni snaps. Indira rounds on her, but I push her away from Roshni. 'Your beef is with *me*. So come out and say whatever it is you need to say to make yourselves feel better.'

'Yes, say it so we can let the world know,' Tristan says, emerging from the crowd, filming everything on his phone.

Renée glares at Tristan. 'Traitor.' She then turns to me with a hideously sweet smile on her face. 'So sad about your mum. Thoughts and prayers.'

I watch them vanish.

'Thanks,' I tell Tristan and Roshni.

'We have to protect each other,' he says.

'Girl, I thought you were going to destroy her on the spot!' Max says, joining us.

I can't believe I felt truly alone, even for a second.

Over their heads, I spot a lone figure observing everything from a safe distance.

Liam. He calls out to me.

I can't deal with him right now. We head in the opposite direction.

'It's great to have you back, boss,' Max whispers to me. 'We missed you.'

At lunchtime, as I'm heading to the library to print off an assignment, I see Hugo shaking hands with Harrison from my English class. I can't help but smile. See, this is why I like the man – he's chill with everyone. I walk up to them and smile. 'Harrison, do you have last week's worksheet from Dr York?'

Harrison blushes so deeply, his freckles vanish.

'Dua,' Hugo says, nodding as he heads out.

'Did I just interrupt something?' I ask Harrison, looking baffled. I'd hoped Hugo might be happy to see me but he couldn't even look at me.

Has something happened?

'What? No. Just man talk, innit,' he says, unzipping his bag and rifling through for the worksheet. 'There ya go. Keep it.'

What?

I spot Abdi at a workstation and push whatever the hell that was out of my mind. I sneak up behind him and my mouth drops open in horror. 'Abdi – are you streaming a film?'

At the click of a button, he makes it vanish. '*Astagfirullah!* Accusing a brother of ignoring his education. Shame on you. Go make *tawbah*.'

'Not judging,' I leave him to it then do a quick one-eighty. 'You must have overridden the school's firewall to access . . . forbidden content?'

'Say less about forbidden content and I might be willing to help you,' he says, sweat glistening on his brow. 'That is where you're going with this, right?'

'Thinking out loud here,' I warn. 'Aden wouldn't be so militant with the permanent exclusions unless there was more to it than just Sir Reg pushing him. Do you think you could maybe take a trip into their emails and find out?'

The first good sign is that Abdi neither freaks nor kicks me to the kerb. Instead, he leans back in his seat, his forehead taking on the appearance of a walnut. 'Hack into a coupla headteachers' emails? *Eh*, it's doable.'

I grin.

'I get caught, I'm telling everyone *you* made me do it.'

'Do not rest on your laurels!' Dr York warns us, spreading his hands theatrically. 'The mock exams may seem distant and unobtrusive, but they will be upon you in the blink of an eye, and failing to prepare would be a real Shakespearian tragedy. The results will contribute to your A-level applications. Class dismissed!'

As I leave York's room, thanking him for the third teabag I won, I'm accosted by Keira.

'Why are you doing this to me?' she demands.

I wrack my brains for what she might be referring to. 'What, winning the teabag?'

She presses her lips together in frustration. 'Look, I might not like it, but I respect you for setting up your own paper.'

'*Bodley Voices* got cancelled. You won.'

'Don't insult my intelligence. *Bodley Voices* gets cancelled: *TeaLeakZ* springs up out of nowhere?' The bottom of my stomach drops out, my eyes searching for a sneaky phone. Does she need a recorded confession to get Sir Reg to exclude me once and for all? 'Everyone knows it's you guys. It was a smart move, I'll give you that.'

Whatever happens, I must deny everything. Avoid the topic if I can. 'Why did you send your minions to give me a public roasting in the playground?'

'I didn't!' she insists. 'I heard what Renée and Indira said, and for what it's worth, I think they were completely out of order.'

'So then, what's the problem?' I ask tartly.

'Leave Hugo alone.'

My cheeks smart under her fierce glare but I fight it. 'Is he your boyfriend?'

She drops her eyes, pouting. 'We're working through some issues. But we'll never get there if you keep *seducing* him.' If I were seducing him, he wouldn't have just iced me back in the corridor . . . I force myself to focus on Keira.

'What, like you *seduced* Liam onto your paper?' I clap back. How dare she take the moral high ground when she made Liam commit bestie-cide? He would never have voluntarily told anyone about Mum's personal problems. God knows what she did to force it out of him. Plus, Hugo said they broke up ages ago. She needs to move on.

I notice, for the first time, that I don't want to deny something between Hugo and me.

'Liam is tired of having you veto his articles,' she trills. 'You claim he's your deputy but make all the decisions yourself and override all his suggestions.'

I blush. I can't help but admit that there's truth to her poison. I *have* been a bit Kim Jong-un . . . but that's only because someone needs to be in charge and keep the paper going! Otherwise it would've been dead in the water ages ago or just another *Chronicle*. 'Liam understands you have to publish the kind of articles people want to read.'

'Sir Reginald is gonna know you're behind *TeaLeakZ*. One smidge of evidence and you'll be permanently excluded.'

It takes every ounce of my being not to freak out.

'If you want to stay in school, stay the hell away from Hugo!' She walks off in such a huff she even forgets to strut. *How dare she—*

I notice Huda lurking by the lockers. Hiding my embarrassment and rage, I offer her a smile. She doesn't even attempt to return it.

'You should, you know,' she advises.

'I'm sorry?'

'Leave Hugo alone. I saw you guys at Langley Park.'

My vital organs drop like overripe fruit, trying to recall if anything happened between us which might've looked wrong. 'That's right. We were playing basketball,' I say levelly.

'Three words: full body contact. It's *haram*. But I shouldn't be surprised, with your parents. You guys do things *differently*.'

She clicks her locker shut and walks off.

I slump to the ground, completely exhausted. I knew coming back here would be hard, but I didn't think I'd be getting attacked from every angle of my life.

I'm checking my phone for Mum-updates when a message pops up from Hugo.

> Heard about your run- in with Renée. You OK?

Maybe I made up him blanking me earlier today?

> I'll be fine.

> Is your mum OK? I remember you said she wasn't well.

> She's better.

> Good, good. What happened to your mum was unfair. Anytime you need to talk or shoot a few hoops I'm here for you. Whatever you need. ☺

> Thanks. I really appreciate it.

'Dua!'

My smile drops as I hastily put away my phone. Sooner or later, I was going to have to face Liam. Mum was forever telling me that growing up sucks; guess this must be what she was referring to. Fixing a civil smile to my face, I turn around and nod.

'Are you avoiding me?' Liam asks, never one to mince words.

With too much traffic in the corridor, I direct him towards the toilets.

'Revision in this school is crazy-mad!' Harrison says coming out of the toilets, sniffing.

'True, but better to be over-prepared than underprepared, right?' I say, trying to make it obvious that I want to have a private convo with Liam.

'Still, stress sucks like a mother. I got something that could take the edge off . . .' He looks from one to the other, eyebrows waggling. 'Mates' rates.'

I scowl at Harrison. 'Are you tripping? Come to think of it: you probably are. Bodley doesn't need your drugs. You're the reason we have to do those stupid substance abuse lessons in PSHE!'

'Shut up – that was Mo and Joe! Plus, it ain't like I'm the only one dealing!' Harrison retorts, his freckles like crushed chillies. He rounds on me. 'You know what happens to rats – keep your mouth shut.'

He slips into the crowd.

'Man, that gets me mad!' I say, catching a fist. 'Mo and Joe were duped. This guy's doing it for real.'

'Enough about that. We got lessons in five. Why are you ignoring me?' Liam insists.

We've had our ups and downs over the years but this feels

terminal. In the end, I can't find the right words so I just show him the video of his clandestine meeting with Keira.

'I-I-I was going to tell you, but things happened fast,' he babbles.

'What things?'

He drops his head, gently pressing his eyes. 'When you got excluded last week, Dr York made me sit next to Keira. You don't know her, Dua. She's actually really nice.'

I actually can't believe what I'm hearing. 'So you *betrayed* me?'

'Betray *you*? *TeaLeakZ* isn't you, Dua. It belongs to everyone on the news team.' He gives me a reproachful look. 'At least it's supposed to.'

'So you're secretly submitting articles to the enemy while making make-or-break decisions for our paper?'

'Come off it! You didn't even want my articles, so why shouldn't I publish them elsewhere? Besides, Keira's not the enemy. She's just looking out for her school paper – and it's not like they weren't there first. You was the one who said on the first day the Minerva lot had a right to defend their territory!'

'You never could say no to a pretty face, even when that face is attached to a psychopath who wants to ruin your best mate's life!'

'Here we go! You live for drama. But the world doesn't revolve around you.'

His words hit me like a club, and despite my best efforts, my anger rises up like a wave. 'Working on two rival papers is so obviously a conflict of interest. We're competing for the same readership. We set this up because the *Chronicle* wasn't telling the truth, Liam, think about that. You need to make a choice. Come back to *TeaLeakZ* exclusively and I'll smooth things over with the guys, who by the way, think you're a traitor. Or choose *her*.'

He grabs fistfuls of his waves in exasperation. 'Oh, my days!

Why are you doing this? Surely you understand that I have my reasons? I'm your best friend, Dua. Think about what *you're* doing.'

I can barely hear him over the adrenalin pumping in my ears. There's no possible reason why that would make sense to me.

I stare him down. 'Pick. Me or her.'

'It's not about—'

'Me or her!' I yell.

'You all right, babe?' Keira asks Liam, appearing out of nowhere. Grabbing the back of his head, she draws him into a *kiss*.

She looks up at me in smug satisfaction. They pull apart.

'So you're not worried about Hugo any more, then?' I say indignantly, trying to keep the shock out of my voice.

Keira's china blues blink back innocently. 'What ever gave you that impression?' She winks at Liam. 'Wagamama after school. Noodles and canoodling. Don't be late.'

My eyes water from the betrayal but I refuse to cry in front of these arseholes. I turn around and head down the corridor. Liam calls after me but I just keep moving.

On the way to our meeting, Roshni stops me in the stairwell.

'Huda told me you're dating Hugo,' she says.

'That girl!' I say angrily. 'Why does everybody at this school always know my business? I write the news, not make it.'

'Easy. It's no one's business. Just that last night I saw Hugo's Insta and wondered if you'd seen this video?'

I glance at her phone. On the screen, Hugo is slouched in a chair, giggling as he tries to lift his sweaty head.

'Come on, sing it one more time!' the boy filming says.

Hugo's head pitches forwards. A hand reaches out and slaps his cheek. 'One more time!'

Hugo lifts his head, struggling to keep his blinks synchronized. Suddenly he leaps up and sings about being a 'Barbie Girl', dancing like an electrocuted go-go dancer before collapsing in a heap to hysterical howls of laughter from his friends.

'Shall we give "Barbie" another pill?' asks a friend.

'Piss off, you'll kill him!' responds another, chuckling.

What? No . . .

Could Hugo be . . . is this a one-off? I jump on the time stamp in triumph. 'This is Year Ten!'

'True,' Roshni says, studying my expression. 'But it's real. Just thought you had a right to know.'

It seems like every corner we turn, illicit substances are being traded about like candy. Something this pervasive doesn't just happen. Someone is behind it. And a person can be caught.

'Let's get started,' I tell the assembled crew.

It's 3.15 and we're meeting in 15C rather than our usual spot thanks to Keira's warning about Sir Reg. Tucked between a cleaning cupboard and a cellar housing what might be a nuclear reactor (judging by the loud thrumming), it's about as off-the-grid as you can get while technically still on school premises.

'Are we waiting for the traitor?' Morowa asks, icily. We all know she means Liam.

'He's working for the *Chronicle* now,' I say, keeping the emotion out of my voice.

Morowa nods with approval. 'Take note, people: a true boss makes tough decisions for the greater good.'

'This place stinks!' Abdi complains, pinching his nose.

'I'm counting on the stink to keep the authorities away,' I explain.

'Why can't we meet in the library, though?' Roshni moans, adjusting her Swarovski crystal-studded hair claw.

'Cos the librarian is a grass,' Abdi says spitefully. 'She'll go spill her guts to Sir Reg.'

'We have to protect *TeaLeakZ* at all costs,' I say fiercely. 'If they ever catch us, we'll all be excluded.'

'Previously, that might've seemed like a joke,' Tristan says, studying a disturbing pamphlet about the Canadian Seal Hunt. How anyone could kill a fluffy white cloud with large, dark eyes is beyond me.

Max is unusually quiet, staring gloomily at a whorl on the desk. I make a mental note to speak to him privately at the end.

'Thank you for your BHM articles,' I say, pulling out the wodge of print-outs I spent forever covering in red ink. 'I really appreciate the range of topics you were working with . . . but, I did have to do a *lot* of editing and frankly I'm not happy with the standard. My notes should be self-explanatory but let's all take five to make sure we're on the same page.'

As the minutes tick by, the expressions round the table shift between hurt, exasperation, outrage, and anger.

'Dua, you TL;DRed my article on misogynoir!' Morowa says in surprise.

'What?' Abdi asks.

'Too long; didn't read,' Tristan explains.

I consult my notes. 'Yeah, could you trim it down to five hundred words?'

'Are you serious?' Morowa asks, fuming. 'This isn't some throwaway tweet. We need to dismantle the systems that oppress Black women. It's not like we're fighting over printing space – it's online!'

'It won't dismantle anything if people don't even bother reading it because it's too long,' I hit back, trying to keep things moving.

But Morowa still isn't on board. 'Black girls will read it. Those who respect their culture and take pride in their roots will read it.'

'And what about white people?' I find myself saying before I can question the words leaving my mouth.

'Who gives a shit? They own everything anyway,' Abdi snarks.

'Um, sitting right here,' Tristan says, waving a hand. 'Can we tone down the racism, please?'

'Without power, it's called *prejudice* not racism,' Morowa states. 'I'm not going to apologize for not considering white peoples' feelings when writing an article to empower Black girls during Black History Month.'

I hold my hands up. 'Morowa's right: it's only racism when the people doing it hold all the power. But that's not what I—'

'But that's like saying it's open season on white people!' Tristan argues, shaking his shaggy head in disbelief. 'It's not our fault we have power.'

'It's not? I'm sorry, was that not white people chaining up my ancestors and forcing them onto overcrowded ships?' Max interjects.

'You didn't let me finish,' I retort. I don't have time to deal with white fragility. '*TeaLeakZ* has to appeal to everyone, and if white readers aren't engaging with the material too then sadly nothing's going to change.'

'It's a BHM issue, Dua,' Abdi states, tapping the table.

'*TeaLeakZ* is about brave voices telling the truth no matter who it offends. Don't wimp out on me now.' Morowa looks at me pleadingly.

Am I failing our Black readers? I close my eyes, struggling to think objectively. Why do I keep seeing Keira handcuffing Liam to a bedpost, Hugo snorting cocaine through a straw, Mum crying in a corner and Huda throwing me out of the mosque? I try to purge the nightmare visions but they just start to spin and strobe like I'm stuck on a mind-flaying merry-go-round.

I've got to get a grip.

'Fine, just trim it down a bit, lose some of the spicier clapbacks and we'll publish,' I say. Morowa looks mutinous so I quickly move on. 'Max, I'm living for your piece on make-up to compliment darker skin tones but can it be half as long?'

Max mumbles something which I doubt was a compliment.

'And Tristan, we don't want a history lesson on how the slave trade affected Enley. It's the opposite of empowering,' I snap.

'Why not?' he asks. 'We're doomed to make the same mistakes if we cover up our shady past.'

I struggle to be civil, feeling a headache taking hold. What happened to 'the boss has to make tough decisions'? Man, how I wish I was shooting a few hoops with Hugo instead of chairing this minefield of a meeting. 'Trauma porn, ain't it. And someone will inevitably read it as a commentary on the two schools.'

Wait, did I just wish to be with Hugo?

'Come off it!' Roshni says. 'Knowledge is power. And I know Renée was a bitch-faced-cow to you, but most Minerva kids are OK. Like Tristan, for example. What parallels are there to draw?'

'We're not treated as equals, Roshni,' I say, the headache sprouting electric fishing lines, one hooking into my left eyeball. I can't remember what we're even fighting about or what my point is or even if I'm actually right or not. 'I feel like we constantly have to be grateful just for being here. And who the hell do they think they are telling us to keep our hands off—'

'Keep our hands off?' Roshni asks confused.

My cheeks tingle, realizing I'm talking about Hugo. Have I become just another stereotypical brown girl with white-boy fever? Is the real reason I wanted Morowa to tone down her article so it wouldn't offend *him*?

'That's just Aden and Sir Reg though,' Abdi says. 'Everyone else is pretty chill. I actually like being here. They've got software and hardware I ain't never seen outside of the internet.' The headache turns into a pounding. In a moment I may vomit all over my notes.

'So has anyone found any more evidence of Minerva kids doing drugs?' I suddenly ask.

'Woah! When did this become a witch hunt?' Tristan says. 'Of course there are kids here doing drugs. But grassing them up won't bring Mo or Joe back.'

I shake my head. 'Nobody's hunting. It's about equality.'

'The only kids I found offering pills or weed were a couple of our own,' Morowa says morosely. 'If I didn't know better, I'd say the numbers of kids dabbling has gone up ever since those boring PSHE lessons. Way to go, Bodley.'

I frown, casting my mind back. 'That *is* seriously weird . . .'

The addict at Rooke Park.

The letter in the local paper from a parent blaming Bodley kids for coercing their daughter into taking drugs.

#Justice 4Mo&Joe.

Uncle Steadman losing his licence over drugs.

Harrison dealing.

What is going on here? What am I not seeing?

'OK, so while you guys fix up your BHM articles, keep an eye out for drugs and keep asking questions. We still need to uncover the source.'

'Are you acting like this because Liam defected to the *Chronicle*?' Tristan asks.

Abdi starts laughing which prompts a multitude of smirks. Sweat pools under my eyes, and in a moment I think my head may actually explode.

'Please! I know how to separate my emotions from my work,' I say.

'Coulda fooled me,' Roshni says, getting up.

'I'm here for us using our voices for good,' Morowa says, also rising to her feet, 'but you run the paper with an iron fist. I didn't sign up for that.'

My heart sinks as the rest follow suit, walking out on me.

All except Max, who is staring out of the window, lost in thought. I quickly slide into the seat beside him. Up close I can see he's been crying. 'Oh, Max, I'm so sorry – I didn't mean—'

He shakes his head, pulling on his jacket. 'No, it's not you, don't worry. It's . . . allergies.'

I raise a sceptical brow. 'Come on, hun.'

'Honestly, Dua, I appreciate it and all, but—'

'No judgements,' I promise.

His bleary eyes cut into my soul before his chin sinks. 'Matteo dumped me.' His eyes start to water.

'What!?' I gasp.

He nods, the dome of his head glistening in the dusk sunlight. 'By text.'

'Who breaks up by text?!' I shout, about to launch into a defamatory speech, but Max has become a blubbering mess. Pulling out my trusty pack of tissues, I dab at his eyes.

'He said he's into straight-acting guys and I couldn't serve Butch Queen if my life depended on it.' He flushes burgundy. 'Even in certain parts of the community, femme guys get slated.'

'Gay guys get judged by a heteronormative standard?' I ask in confusion. Maybe it's similar to girls of colour sometimes being judged by a European standard of beauty? Either way it sucks. Max is one of the nicest people I know.

'I should've known!' he wails, grabbing a further two tissues.

'I fail in school; I fail at relationships. Might as well strap a big L to my head!'

It's difficult to watch Max break down like this. 'You've just had some bad luck. You'll cry, you'll over-analyse, have "Irreplaceable" on repeat, but then you'll realize what I already know: that you are just too real for him.'

Max laughs, showering the table with spittle. 'You're just saying that.'

I hold his hand. 'It takes guts to be unapologetically different. Do you know how many people our age are out there pretending to be someone else just to fit in? Most of us, probably. You're stronger and more special than you realize and that, my friend, is the essence of beautiful. Matteo is a fool to let you go.'

'Ya think?' he says, hopefully.

'Only one of you, Boo.'

He blows me a kiss as my phone beeps. I ignore it, but as Max wipes the tears from his eyes he tells me to go ahead and read it.

> You free this Saturday? There's a Rumbal on. x

I stare at Hugo's message, at the kiss, and feel the earth shift beneath my feet. At the start of term, the Blue Bloods in my English class were brutal about their secret parties – their 'Rumbals' – being only for the crème de la crème.

My inner journo cannot refuse. Morowa tried and failed to infiltrate. Maybe this would be a way to bring the news team back onside?

> Is that a party?

I type, playing dumb.

> Dialled up to eleven. Dates back to when druids worshipped the moon goddess Minerva. Only we did away with the human sacrifices. Bummer, huh?

'I just got invited to a Rumbal,' I tell Max, a little shocked. 'An actual exclusive Minerva party.'

Max's eyes pop out on stalks. 'You got asked by Hugo?!'

My mind swims. Hugo is asking me to go out with him in public. This is *huge*. We have chemistry, for sure, but texting and basketball is a little different to attempting to enter his world as his equal. Despite all the low-key flirting and sharing, I'm still not sure about the guy or if I even want to be in a relationship. Maybe the party would help me decide?

Then Roshni's stupid video of Hugo pops into my head, making me frown. All that video proves is that one time last year Hugo got high. I know I'm not the same person I was back in Year Ten, so is it fair to judge him? Not without evidence. And something tells me that seeing the Blue Bloods in their natural habitat will reveal at least some of the answers we're after.

> Send over the deets.

He provides a time and an address.

> Steampunk attire is mandatory. See you there! X

'Crap! It's costumed,' I cry. 'I have the wardrobe of a nun.'

'You put me in charge of fashion and beauty for a reason. I got you,' Max says.

CHAPTER 20

On Saturday, while me and Dad are tucking into our scrambled eggs, my mind dances with thoughts of my first Rumbal. If Liam hadn't turned into such a traitor, I'd be sharing my excitement/terror with him. I tried to tell Morowa but she's still not taking my calls. Defo can't tell Dad. If Hollywood has taught my parents anything, it's that Teen Party = Sex Fest. As if *I'd* be going, if that was the case. But parents are always doing the most, and with Dad making up for lost time, he wins the prize for Most Extra Dad Ever.

My phone beeps as I receive a ten-second, self-destructing picture of Beyoncé. My jaw drops when I realize it's *MAX* in drag.

> When life gives you lemons, make LEMONADE!

> OMG!!! 🔥🔥🔥 You look HOT!

> I've got skills. When you coming over for your makeover?

> 1 p.m. sound good?

'We need to talk,' says Dad.

Pushing my phone away, I glance up. Those are like the four most ominous words any parent can ever utter. His expression is doing zero to change my mind.

'You wanna tell me what's going on here?' He places his

slimline phone down in front of me. It's all I can do not to choke. Papped on the basketball court with Hugo, the angle making the action look nasty.

'Looks like me playing a game of basketball with Liam,' I lie with such composure I disgust myself. 'Who's the paparazzo?'

'This is Liam?' Dad asks, scrutinizing his phone. 'I thought he was thinner.'

'The camera always adds ten pounds.' I'm really pushing it . . .

Dad studies me, making me sweat. 'One of the brothers at the mosque sent me this picture. He said his daughter saw you with this boy and thought I should know.'

'*Huda.*' I seethe. After all I did to try to get Mo's exclusion revoked. I have half a mind to show Dad her thirst trap TikToks but I won't sink to her level.

'Mobeen's a good brother,' he says.

'Well, his daughter's not!' I cry. 'They don't know jack about my commitment to Allah!' I bite back on telling him how Huda thinks my parents are bad Muslims because their marriage didn't work out.

'Dua!' Dad snaps. 'It doesn't matter what people say. Only God can judge, and actions are judged by intentions.' He glances at the picture on his phone. 'If there's ever a boyfriend in the picture, I want you to promise you'll tell me about him and I'll promise not to lose it. Deal?'

'Sure, whatever,' I say just to shut him up. Why can't the world just let me figure things out for myself? It's been one obstacle after another since I came to Minerva and met Hugo and I am so done with it.

The porch in front of me is white uPVC, just like every other house on the west side of town. Also like the rest of them, it's serving as extra storage space for the homeowners. I spot a broom, recycling boxes, a shoe rack and an old sewing machine. I ring the bell and wait.

The inner door opens and a sullen woman in her twenties with peachy-pink tight curls steps out in leopard-print pyjamas. One bare foot lands on a cotton reel and she yowls. 'Max! How many times has Mum told you not to leave your trash in the porch?'

'Hi, you must be Chris,' I say, delivering a smile that is all sugar and spice.

'I know who I am. Who are you?'

'She's Dua,' a disembodied voice hollers from somewhere upstairs. 'Come on up!'

Chris's animosity vanishes. 'You're the girl who runs *TeaLeakZ*? It's so good! That gossip column sends me. Love when you diss Councillor Briggs. Thanks for giving Max a focus. Now Mum doesn't keep getting calls from school about him bunking.'

Max scurries down the stairs and grabs my hand. 'Chris, can you drop Dua off at the party at seven? Great, thanks!' Like a glittering tornado, he sucks me into his slipstream and sweeps me up the stairs.

'Mate, check out your curves!' I say, taking in his Beyoncé tribute drag. OK, so in person? Not quite as mind-blowing as the picture he messaged earlier but who doesn't use a cheeky filter every now and then?

Splitting his thighs, he slut drops. 'Ya like?'

I laugh. 'You could totally catfish Jay-Z.'

'Ew! Not even for his billions.' Throwing open his bedroom door, he announces in a dramatic voice, 'Welcome to chez Maximillian Benítez.'

His bedroom is not at all what I was expecting. Serving Forties vibes, it's seriously mature and understated. The wallpaper is black and gold art deco, every piece of furniture ebony, and dancing across a wall is a panoramic decal of the Manhattan skyline at dawn. Two framed prints float above his bed in black and white: the decadence of queens from the city of dreams in *Paris is Burning* and a sparkling black sports car.

'Is that the Batmobile?' I ask in surprise.

'Bugatti Chiron,' he explains proudly. Gesturing to a table displaying a whole bunch of model cars, he adds: 'Someday I hope to sit behind the wheel, if I ever manage to afford the three million pound price tag.'

'You're like my dad.' I say, poking at his models. 'He has an insane collection of scale models. Ferrari, Maserati . . . but his favourite is the Batmobile.'

Max yanks open the door of his wardrobe. 'Feast your eyes on these one-of-a-kind creations, designed by the fabulous Oshuna.' He throws a wink over his shoulder. 'That's my drag name.'

Reverentially, I pass a hand over the line of dresses and gowns covered with diamante, feathers and brocade. 'You're telling me you made all of these?!'

He chuckles. 'Some. Most I picked up at charity shops and reworked using my trusty sewing machine and a li'l glitter.'

'Oshuna, this is amazing! *TeaLeakZ* has to do a feature on you—'

But he's shaking his head so fiercely his wig nearly pops off. 'I get bullied just for being me. Can you imagine what'd happen if word got out about my dresses? No. I'm not ready to handle that yet.'

I place a hand on his shoulder. 'School isn't for ever, hun. Some day you're gonna be up there with the likes of Louis Vuitton, Versace and Rihanna. You'll be driving a Bugatti, wearing a ballgown, and all the arseholes will be forgotten.'

So here I am, standing in front of a full-length mirror, staring at the vampish being inside, wondering how she and I could possibly share the same body. Her brazen lips are the colour of black cherries, her eyes twice as large as mine. A miniature top hat with a golden clock face grows out of the side of her head, glittering with rhinestones, and a waterfall of midnight ink cascades down her body in rivulets of satin.

Real talk: feathery false eyes cloud my vision, gloss makes my lips feel like I kissed a glue stick, and the foundation feels cakey. I realize the people who wear make-up every day are martyrs. Everything's super-weird but one part of this get-up is more alien to me than a trip to Mars: the forty-inch Kimani-lace front wig in bouncy, buttery blonde waves.

Max presented me with a black lace scarf before I told him I wanted a wig like his. This is deep. Wearing my hijab is a private act of worship based on the concept of modesty. It's literally nobody's choice but my own. My problem is that rocking up to the party like that could screw up my plans. My whole MO is to go stealth, slip in, mingle with the Blue Bloods, find out what they really get up to . . . and maybe figure out some romantic stuff with Hugo too.

So tonight, I've decided to bend the rules twice over: wear a wig and go out with a boy I have feelings for. Mind-Huda is glaring at me. Don't get it twisted: I love my hijab but I'd be lying if I said I hadn't wondered what it'd be like not to wear it. Covering my real hair under a wig may be a bit of a cheat but it'll also be a new experience. Every instinct in my body is telling me it's going to be a wild evening and that I'm not nearly prepared enough, but that's how I felt setting up *Bodley Voices* and *TeaLeakZ*. I've been breaking rules all year and thriving. I take a deep breath to steady myself and try and own the wig.

'Iconic!' Max trills, snapping his fingers. 'And now for the pièce de résistance.' He feeds my arms through elastic straps, attaching large, iridescent gossamer wings to my back. 'What do you think?'

'You sure I don't look—?' I ask nervously.

'Babe, you look gorge!' Max crows, pleased with his handiwork. 'Besides, as Mama RuPaul says, "We're all born naked and the rest is drag".'

The costume is definitely hard to miss but I'm guessing the wearer will fade into the background standing next to Renée, Keira, Indira or any of the Minervan goddesses. It's fine. I remind myself I'm not there to play Cinderella; I am Sherlock Holmes in drag.

'Hugo will think you're a princess,' Max says, beaming with pride.

Aunties have always shaded me at weddings, thinking a dark-skinned girl was the height of ugliness. Maybe it's all Max's make-up, but I do look pretty. 'I'm there for the cause,' I say firmly. 'The Bodley massacre has to end.'

'Watch yourself!' Max repeats. He still thinks I'm playing with fire.

Taking one more look in the mirror, I clutch onto his hand and shake my head furiously. 'I can't do this alone. You have to come with me.'

He smiles sadly and shakes his head. 'Nobody's ever heard about a fairy godmother crashing the ball! They're not ready for me yet – and I don't quite think I'm ready for them.'

'I would protect you to the end,' I say loyally.

He smiles. 'I know you would . . . but it's not my time yet.'

Chris appears in the doorway, dangling her car keys. 'Aw, you both look snatched!'

Max curtsies dramatically and forces me to follow suit, ending with us both collapsing in laughter on the floor. He helps me stand up and smooths out my dress.

'May the spirits of queens past, present and future guide you,'

Max says, giving me a long, twisted wand of ebony before whispering, 'Now, any of those preppy boys come onto you, just shove this baby where the sun don't shine and we'll come bust you outta there!'

CHAPTER 21

Half an hour later, Chris's car turns onto a sweeping gravel drive on the east side. We all stare out of the window. Projected on the front of the house, which is about three times the size of mine, is an animation of spinning cogwheels and clicking hammers, like it's a giant pocket watch. Music blares into the night, a deep bass sending tremors into the earth, vibrating the marrow in my bones and rattling Chris's old Corsa.

I climb out, the cool air making me nearly grateful for the layer of make-up on my face. Two doors are open. From the one closest to us, light strobes out in a spectrum of colours.

''Fess up time,' I blubber, turning around to talk to Max through the car window. 'I've never been to a party before except the kind where you play pass-the-parcel and eat cake . . . I'm scared!'

Max takes my hand. 'You've got this, Boo.'

'Thanks, Max,' I say, squeezing his hand. 'For the dress, the wig, the pep talk and for standing by me when the rest of the team walked out. I know things haven't been great lately . . .'

He smiles. 'You've been there for me. I know what it's like to have to act fierce when you're under pressure. I think you know what you said went too far, but come Monday, the guys will be ready to make peace. You're a good editor. But a great editor is never too proud to admit when she's wrong.'

His words are hard to swallow but he's serving so much truth, and if I want to be the editor they deserve, I have to grow.

Chris and Max drive off and I am suddenly aware of how alone

I am. As I walk up the drive, ghostly silhouettes dance in and out of the lights like figures in a zoetrope. I make it to the front door without another PDF but then nearly stumble over the threshold, not at all used to walking in heels. My heart palpitates, my mind rushing between thoughts of feeling like a fraud and being a sell-out by removing my hijab.

My eyes travel up a sweeping staircase, taking in a sparkling chandelier and people dotted about dressed like pirates, inventors and vampires. The sheer splendour and mystery sparks my curiosity, subduing my fears. I'm a badass journalist. I'm here for a reason. I don't need to be afraid.

'So this is a Rumbal,' I whisper.

A behemoth dressed in a leather kilt with a green tartan waistcoat accosts me. 'A beautiful lady shouldn't be without a drink.'

He thrusts a cup in my hand, the sharp fruity smell telling me it's booze. The guy introduces himself as Tom and I suddenly recognize him from the day the rugby team commandeered the bus ride home.

'Hugo invited me,' I say, deciding not to give him my name.

'I've not seen Hugo yet,' he says, checking out a couple of giggly girls who've just arrived in costumes that look like lace bodystockings. Mesmerized, Tom wanders off to join them.

Alone again, I watch the Blue Bloods cavorting and writhing. The grime beats pulse through me, and I stifle a laugh watching the mega-posh white kids attempt the lyrics. Tipping my cup into a rubber plant, I text Hugo.

Arrived. Where are you?

Putting my phone away, I run my finger over the tiny spy-cam I picked up on eBay which I've integrated into my costume. No one's gonna believe my report unless there's evidence.

I look down at my phone expectantly and notice my message has been read, but there's no sign of a reply.

I move off into the front room where a bunch of kids are playing spin the bottle. Pounding out a drumroll, the focus of their attention is Indira. A vivid lamb-to-the-slaughter look is in her eye, which I'm guessing means she's caught in a dare. She laughs uncomfortably to a torrent of catcalls. Oba is sitting among them, giggling uncontrollably. I'm struck by a wave of guilt – I've pretty much ignored him since the start of term. He probably doesn't want to chat. Indira closes her eyes and flares her nostrils as they give her a second drumroll, their voices rising in crescendo.

Suddenly she pulls open her bodice, flashing them. There are explosive cheers and some of the boys snap pictures as Indira quickly covers herself up. I walk out of the room, feeling sick to my stomach.

'Sorry,' a guy says, bumping into me.

I'm about to say 'no big deal' when I realize it's Liam, his hair slicked back, wearing a suit he's clearly outgrown as the trouser cuffs are almost three inches above his ankles. Hanging onto his arm, apparently bored, is Keira, wearing a criss-cross bandage dress, looking like she walked straight out of the Victoria's Secret Halloween collection. Liam clocks me with a double take. Quick as a flash, I flutter past, beelining for the kitchen. A rush of thunderous anger chokes me before I get a grip. Liam's made it clear whose side he's chosen. His life is none of my business any more. He might even help Keira grow into a better person? Lord knows he used to be the calming Yin to my raging Yang.

Where is Hugo?

In the large kitchen, I help myself to a cupcake – chocolate usually makes everything better.

'Hey, gorgeous!'

I turn round expecting to see Hugo. Instead there's a guy who seems to have left half of his costume at home. He's wearing a leather aviator hat, chunky boots, and plastic shorts that are so tight they're practically a biology lesson in male anatomy. Repulsed, I step backwards.

'Naughty angel, eh? *Shek-shee!*' He closes the gap between us, twanging one of my wings.

'Fairy,' I correct, brandishing my wand. 'Exceptionally evil.' Even in the dim lighting of the kitchen, I can see that his pupils are dilated and his speech seems slurred. The question is: is this dude drunk or high?

'Love the sound of that!' he purrs. 'I'm Marlon.'

'Hey, hardon— I mean, *Marlon.*' Flustered, I look for an escape route.

'Don't tell anyone . . .' He cups a hand to my ear, whispering hot breath into it. 'But I only date brown girls.' He puffs his chest out as if he's waiting for a medal to be pinned on it.

'Er . . . I think you might've had a little too much to drink?'

He bounces his eyebrows. 'Who would drink when you've got the good stuff?'

In spite of my fear, my ears perk up, hoping I'm getting everything on camera. 'What good stuff?'

He slings an arm around me and licks my cheek. 'You're a caramel queen. Let's go to the toilets. I want to worship you.'

'Ew!' I say, bashing him with my wand. 'Not interested. Ever.'

He winks then pulls out some kind of small, cherry-red pill with '$€x¥' imprinted on it. The strange spelling catches my eye before he cracks it in half and places one half on the tip of his tongue.

There's your smoking gun. Smile for the camera, I think. *Now get out before things turn nasty* . . . Marlon grips my upper arms with such force I drop my wand in surprise. Tongue lolling, he comes in low. I see him. The fool is looking to push both tongue and pill inside my mouth. Panicking, I drive my fist into his stomach.

'AAAGH!' he screams, clutching his belly as I flee the kitchen.

A new track comes on, pumping out seemingly indecipherable lyrics. Bodies come alive as if electrocuted, shout-rapping, stabbing the air with vicious dance moves. The volume is so loud I can almost feel my brain melting out of my ears. Desperate for escape, I totter out of a side door. Cool air shoots up my nostrils, drying my sweaty face and soothing my throbbing ears.

A sleek car pulls into the drive. I watch a man in a hoodie hop out holding a small box the same size as a shoe box. Wondering if this is Hugo's idea of arriving 'fashionably late', I draw closer. He pulls out a phone and I try to see his face in the light of the screen, but his hood forms a solid shield. Heels clickety-clack down stone steps as a girl appears from the other door. She's wearing a long red wig with brass goggles perched on top of her head, thigh-high boots and a gossamer gown that looks like a negligee. 'Have you got our order?' she demands. I'd know that voice anywhere: it's Renée.

'Where's the big man?' says the guy. Not Hugo, then. I try not to feel too abandoned. Then, my curiosity is piqued.

'He's busy. Just hand over the box, take your money and get lost.'

He does a furtive sweep of the area, forcing me to duck behind some rhododendrons.

'Show me,' he orders, snorting mucus up his nose.

'Ew!' Renée says, then, huffing, pulls out a bundle of notes.

He snatches it. 'Tell him I ain't doing business with no bimbo next time. Understand?'

Renée launches into a tirade of insults but he just flips her off, gets back in his car, and drives away. She holds the package to her ear and gives it a shake. Pleased with what she hears, she gives a squeal before vanishing back inside.

I text Hugo again but there's still no reply. Frustrated, I decide I'll pop to the loo, then head out. I have all the evidence I need and this place is way too intense. Figuring out how I feel about Hugo will have to wait for a time when the world isn't a drug-addled, sweaty mess.

Passing through the throngs of drunk and/or high kids, I spot Indira in a corner, smoking something with Tom and Marlon. Taking a toke, Tom kisses her, then passes her what smells like a spliff, while Marlon rests his hand on her bum. She looks so tiny pressed between those giants.

Unfortunately, the downstairs toilet is occupied and upstairs is no better, with a Conga-length queue trailing along the upper landing. Frustrated, I turn back when Keira and Renée come scurrying up the stairs.

Pulling a blinding one-eighty, I steal inside a bedroom, not wanting to deal with them here. Their voices grow louder and I wait for them to pass. Suddenly the door pops opens and I freeze, a deer in the headlights. With only seconds to spare, I throw myself to the floor, rolling under the bed. Max may kill me – I think I just mashed-up his fairy wings.

'I am so done with Liam!' spits Keira, snapping on the light and stomping inside. 'He talks far too much for a supposedly deaf boy and dresses like a homeless person.'

'He's deaf, Keira, not dumb,' replies Renée. 'It's your fault for inviting him. They're all charity cases. What were you thinking?'

'That Hugo might be jealous?'

I clench my fists, furious that Liam has been used in this way, then I wonder why I even still care. I look down and realize that my secret camera is probably too pressed into the floor to pick up what's happening. Biting my lip, I pull out my phone and start recording.

'Ugh! I didn't come all this way to hear you pine over Hugo,' Renée says with all of her usual tact. 'I mean, God, get a life already! He's moved on, why can't you?'

'What? By snorting that crap? I'm hurt, not suicidal,' Keira snaps. I detect a shudder to her voice, the kind that usually follows a spell of crying.

'Oh, like the great Keira Walsingham hasn't been off her tits before! Seriously, why did you even come if you were going to act all Mother Teresa? No one gives a shit about your paper any more and your boyfriend dumped you. Get over it!' I suppress an eye-roll.

'Harsh!' Keira says, her voice brittle. 'Look, I have trust issues. OK? And yelling isn't helping.' She takes a couple of deep breaths. 'Everything started going wrong from the moment that bitch showed up with her stupid little articles and her YA-worthy gang of misfits!'

Is she talking about *me*? Is that how they see us? Wow. Going to Minerva really must blind them to what the real world looks like outside their privileged walls. It's vibrant and diverse and messy, and thinking about the fight we had this afternoon, we're a true reflection of that.

Renée sneers. 'Screw her and her tick-box friends. Seriously, who does she think she's impressing with all that virtue signalling?'

'Well, *Hugo*, apparently!' Keira cries. 'He can't seem to get enough of her paper. Did you know he was the one who saved her from that phone mugging?'

Erm. Hugo and I *both* took down that mugger, but I guess in her warped mind every girl needs a white knight.

Suddenly the mattress bulges, nearly crushing my head like a grape. In the mirrored surface of the wardrobe across the room, I see Renée join Keira on the bed. And just inches below, my phone pointed at them. Man, I hope to God they don't look at the reflection. 'Urgh!' Keira groans in exasperation. 'How *dare* he make me feel like this?'

'Want to get even, babes? I've got the perfect pick-me-up.' In the mirror, I see Renée place the box on her knees and slice open the tape with a well-manicured nail. She pulls out a blister pack of pills as shiny as cherries. 'Ta-da! $€x¥ time.'

'$€x¥?' Keira gasps. 'Isn't that a bit extreme?'

'The best things in life always are. I'll join you. Then we'll apply a fresh coat of lippy, zhush our hair, and shake our gorgeous booties on the dance floor. If Hugo does finally turn up tonight, he'll be kicking himself for ditching you. You might even end up making that sex tape!'

Wait – what?

'What about Liam?' Keira asks. *Yes, Keira, what about Liam? Wait, no – I don't care.*

'We'll slip him a little sumpin-sumpin and knock the lanky chav out for the night.' They howl with laughter.

How can they joke about drugging Liam? Ex-bestie or not, he's a human being and what they're talking about is so incredibly messed-up. It's all I can do not to flip the bed over in rage and squash the two like flies. I have to warn him.

'You're so bad!' Keira chastises belatedly.

'Ready, gorgeous?'

'Are you sure we're not going to die?'

'Looking this good? Even the gods wouldn't *dare*.'

My mortal enemies are about to do hardcore drugs and I'm here stuck under their bed. Does that make me an accessory?

They give themselves a countdown, my throat constricting with every beat.

'Um, nothing's happening?' Keira says disappointedly.

'It will, trust me. They don't call them $€x¥ for nothing.'

Renée gasps then lets rip with a storm of expletives. Keira starts giggling. They both drop back on the bed and gurgle with pleasure.

That does it. I can't be in the same room as this madness. Hiding my phone, I roll out from under the bed, sick to my stomach at what I've just witnessed.

'Oh look! It's Bellatrix Lestrange!' Renée cries, pointing at me.

'Shared hallucination!' Keira enthuses. 'Trippy!'

Their screams of laughter chase me out of the room. I try the bathroom door again: no joy.

I squeeze myself into a corner of the corridor and calm my breathing, feeling the party atmosphere pressing at my skin. Without my hijab I feel horribly exposed even if my real hair is hidden beneath a wig. What was I thinking? I've got to get out of here. First things first: Liam. I send him a text marked **URGENT!!!** For some reason the video I captured from under the bed won't send. Frustrated, I leave him a voice message instead. With the ball in his court, I feel I've done my duty.

Lifting my skirt above my ankles, I head down the stairs. Ravers have spilled out of the front room, into the hall, and are dancing like extras from some perverted dance video. Among them I spot Indira, Marlon, and Tom, the three of them gyrating like some dirty love sandwich. *You shouldn't be here*, my mind tells me and I know it's right. Time to head back to—

'Hey, beautiful!'

Fluttering my feathery eyelashes in confusion, the world chops between negatives and pop art in the strobing light. The broad shoulders and height tell me I'm looking at Hugo. He's decked out in a burgundy tailcoat jacket, ripped skinny jeans, and a bowler hat covered in an array of gold and silver cogs. His skin glistens like a pearl; his eyes are cobalt. A beautiful smile spreads above his chiselled jaw.

'Sorry I'm late. My dad was being a bastard – more than usual, I mean. So, how are you finding your first Rumbal so far?' he asks, placing an arm round me.

'Honestly?' I shove his arm off me. 'I'm not loving it.'

'Are you upset?' he asks, rather uselessly.

'Check your phone and you tell me,' I reply tersely.

His eyebrows twitch as he pulls out his phone and sees my messages. 'Dua, I am SO sorry. I got held up and I should've messaged but—'

'I'm sick of this place. If people aren't acting like total arseholes they're trying to jump my bones.' Abandoning me in this hellhole without so much as a text to explain the hold-up is unforgivable.

'Can't say I blame them. You are so goddam beautiful!'

'If this is what beautiful feels like, I want no part.' I turn and start to walk away.

He catches my hand and his ears perk up. 'I love this song! C'mon.' My protests are drowned out by the thumping speakers and he drags me to the front room.

Clearing a space for us, Hugo starts dancing at me. He's so goofy, my anger unexpectedly thaws, and I even crack an uncomfortable smile. Bumped and buffeted by the people surrounding us, somehow I end up dancing too. And as mad as I am at Hugo, I can't deny that part of me would love to cut loose and have a good time. Stressing over Mum's health, Bodley exclusions, drugs, and the *TeaLeakZ* impending mutiny have all taken their toll. Closing my eyes, I give in to the rhythm, feeling the excitement of the beat pulsing through my veins. Something warm brushes my lips. I open my eyes – why is Hugo standing so close?

Then, too late, I realize he's *kissing me*.

No!

I jump back.

'What did I do?' he asks, surprised by the horror displayed on my face.

'You kissed me!' I gasp, blinking in shock. 'How *dare* you?'

His eyebrows furrow. 'But we were vibing! Weren't we vibing?' he asks, like I'm the one with a problem.

What is *wrong* with him?

'*I didn't give you consent!*' I shout, stepping back further.

'Consent?' he laughs. 'It's only a kiss!'

He did *not* just say that.

He sees the look on my face and grabs my arm, changing tack. 'OK, I jumped the gun. I'm sorry. But this is a thing, right: you and me?'

Is it? I try to calm my breathing.

'Dua? You do want to be my girlfriend, right? I know you're Muslim, and I totally respect that, but you have to give me something to work with here.'

The lighting surrounds Hugo in a shimmering nimbus. He's so heart-achingly beautiful, and basking in his golden glow does make me feel special, even if I don't want to admit it. I never thought I'd need this kind of recognition, never wanted to feel like somebody's Chosen One, but right here, right now, I feel like I could maybe be living my best life.

Except . . .

Fact: Hugo has brought me to an opium den.

Fact: he turned up late with a crap excuse.

Fact: he stole my first kiss.

This *can't* be my best life. All I've seen tonight is entitled kids abusing each other and themselves. And Hugo is one of them. On the surface he might be one of the hottest, most interesting guys I've ever laid eyes on, but underneath lies something else.

'Dua?' Hugo presses. I swallow, knowing I've run the clock down. I owe him an answer. I owe *me* an answer.

On the verge of a decision, I glance across the room and fall silent. Out in the corridor, Tom and Marlon are manhandling Indira. The mood has switched up and they're tearing off her clothes.

'Stop it!' Indira squeals, clutching at her half-unbuttoned top. 'It's not funny, you guys. I mean it!'

'Sure you do,' Marlon says, locking her arms behind her back. 'That's why you were bumping and grinding on *two* guys.'

Hugo's hand snaps around my upper arm, preventing me from entering the fray. 'Dua, don't.' I look at his hand, then back into his deep-set eyes. 'I *mean* it.'

At first I think he's worried about my safety. But it takes me a second to work out that he's actually talking about social suicide. Tom is one of the most popular kids at Minerva and whether I like it or not, tonight I have inadvertently joined the ranks of the East Enley elite, where reputations are everything . . . and *he thinks I care.*

I yank my arm free.

He just made my choice for me.

Using my imposing fairy wings, I jostle through the ravers into the hallway just in time to see Tom pull open Indira's blouse, but I'm not close enough to be able to help – there's a crowd forming. As I push forward, I pull out my phone like a gun above the crowd and start recording.

Indira swears at Tom, but the two boys laugh as if sexual harassment is all a big joke. She calls out to Renée, who's slumped on the stairs. 'Oh no, sweetie!' Renée sings, still tripping from her pill-popping episode. 'You got yourself into this mess, you'll have to get yourself out.' I can't believe it. Is this really happening? I push forward desperately, trying to call Indira's name, but my voice is drowned out from the cheering crowd.

'Gerroff!' gasps Indira, slipping free of Marlon's grasp and slapping Tom's hands away from her bra straps.

'Told you we should've given her something,' Marlon says, cupping Indira's breasts from behind.

I finally break through.

Beyond disgusted, I pull Tom off Indira. 'She. Said. *No*. Touch her again and I'll call the police and hand over this video as proof.' I point to my filming phone.

All three are startled by my bold and reckless interruption. Without missing a beat, I yank Indira free of Marlon, snatching her top up off the floor.

'Mind your own business!' Tom spits.

'I believe the caramel cutie wants to play!' Marlon says, making a grab for me.

'PISS OFF, YOU DISGUSTING PIG!' I yell, stamping on his foot.

Tom throws up his large hands – each one the size of a shovel – and for one frightening moment I think he's going to hit me instead of gesturing. 'Who the fuck let Bodley kids in? I've seen about four of the freaks here tonight!'

There are sounds of agreement.

Tom makes a grab for my phone which I just manage to dodge. Renée bursts out laughing like a crackhead.

'Get the fuck out of my house, you MeToo witch!' Tom snarls. 'Or I'll throw you out myself.'

'We're leaving,' I announce, tugging Indira. Still shell-shocked, she wordlessly totters alongside me.

Scathing eyes chase us to the door but none of it means anything until Hugo's eyes burn into mine. He's disappointed me so much but for some reason, he's looking at me as if I've failed to make the cut! I've let my parents down by being here, but more importantly I've let myself down. The fact that I've compromised myself and my religion to get dressed up twists round my throat like a ligature.

Someone hurls a cup which I just manage to bat away. A spray of beer flies wide, drawing curses.

Outside in the cold night air, exhaustion overtakes me and I sag. Indira is crying. 'Why wouldn't they stop? I told them to stop!' Mascara dribbles down her cheeks like tar.

'I know. I'm sorry this happened to you. They're so fricking entitled they think they can do whatever they want,' I say, thinking about Hugo's uninvited kiss. 'I filmed it, so if you want you could press charges or even report it to Mr Aden?'

'I don't understand!' Indira wails hysterically. 'They're supposed to be my *friends*. Renée just laughed at me.'

I'm about to tell her I think she needs to choose better friends when her eyes bug out and she starts hyperventilating. Having seen Mum in this state before, I talk soothingly but firmly to Indira, getting her to focus on her breathing, telling her everything's going to be OK. The shock must be devastating. I can't imagine what she's going through.

I try calling Max but keep getting voicemail. This is bad. He was my ride out of here. Indira's teeth chatter like castanets. Fearing she's going to have a panic attack if we don't get away from here fast, I resign myself to my last option.

Dad answers on the first ring.

'Dua, you OK?'

With a heart heavier than an anvil, I tell him I'm really not.

Twenty minutes later he pulls up and I do my level best not to cry. I think he does his best not to shout. It's obvious I've let him down. The coloured lights and music pouring out of the house leave little confusion about what sort of party it was.

'Please can we drop Indira home?' I ask. Dad looks at the tear-stained and scantily clad Indira and gives a curt nod. She manages to provide her address through shallow sobs. During the ride, I try speaking to her, but I think she's in shock as she doesn't reply.

Once we drop Indira off at her large house on the east side, Dad finally speaks.

'How could you?' he asks, shaking his head like he's about to cry. 'Did we raise you to behave like this? To go to drug- and alcohol-fuelled parties?'

Part of me wants to dig in and say, 'You didn't raise me.' But attacking him doesn't make me less guilty. I try a partial truth. 'I'm sorry, Dad. It was a party being held by those elitist Minerva kids – I wanted to know what goes on behind closed doors. You know? For my paper.'

'Are you crazy? That girl had clearly been through something awful. Look at you! You don't even look like yourself!'

'I was undercover,' I say feebly, touching the wig. The excuse sounds lame even to my ears. How could I compromise myself like this for a news story? My faith has always meant everything to me. Or did I remove my hijab cos I was trying to impress Hugo? The thought now makes me feel sick to my stomach as a sob rises in my throat. 'Please don't shout at me, Dad . . .'

'Your mum would've killed me if something bad happened to you. Don't you realize how precious you are to us? You are our only child. You are . . . Dua? Dua!'

An avalanche of sobs tumbles out of my throat. Finally, realizing I'm not in good shape, he gives the signal and pulls over. 'Have you taken something? Right, we're going straight to A&E!'

'I didn't take anything. I'm just so sorry I messed up!' How do I explain? Hugo showed me his world, but behind the glitter and the glamour was the ugliest place I've ever been. Taking deep breaths, I reign the sobs in. I can't afford to fall apart now I know the truth about Minerva. 'Please, Dad, just trust me.'

'That's the problem, Dua. I did trust you,' he says, rejoining traffic.

I stay silent.

'From now on you go to school, come home, do your homework, and study for your exams like your life depends on it. You think because we've got some black and brown faces on TV and in government that means the world is suddenly going to treat you fair? Those rich white kids can raise hell and no one's going to expel them. You might be naive enough to be flattered to be invited to a place like that and let these people change you, but mark my words, you will always be the first to be sacrificed to save their privileged arses. Don't let these people steer you off the path you've been carving for yourself since you were born. Remember who you are.'

Dad is kind of right. I have been trying to be like someone else. I realize, with real horror, that that person is *Keira*. Running a paper despotically? Check. Obsessing over Hugo? Check. Forgetting my true self in the pursuit of ambition? Check. Man, tonight I even have blonde hair, for crying out loud. This is not me.

But *TeaLeakz* is.

'But what about my paper? I have a team of people relying on me,' I plead.

'Do you have any idea how much stress you've caused because of that paper? Maybe Mr Aden had a point all along. It's time for you to stop this whole newspaper business – it's too dangerous and you can't handle it.' Before I can interject, he carries on. 'Be grateful I'm not confiscating your phone. Jubba went to raves when we were at school and got caught with ecstasy. You think the police cared that he was just a kid? Man, his mum bust him up so bad until Auntie Ismat intervened.' Dad rubs his eyes, recalling the traumatizing event. 'I saw her in Enley Market yesterday and you know what she said? Said she wished she'd done more to prevent Jubba from growing up into a thug.'

My heart sinks. Have I been wrong about everything? I think

of the twenty I gave him. 'But Jubba said Auntie Ismat died!'

'He's a pathological liar. I was seventeen before I understood I had to cut him out of my life, but not before he nearly dragged me down with him. *Wallahi*, I cannot and will not let that happen to you.'

I might have been wrong about Hugo, and Jubba, and running the paper the way I have been – but I wasn't wrong about the drugs. And I won't let Bodley down by not doing something about it. Dad's right – I have to stay true to who I am and what I want. And what I have always wanted is the truth. I *will* find it.

We drive the rest of the way home in silence and I head straight up to my room.

As I peel off the eyelashes and wash off the make-up Max painstakingly applied to my face, I think about my next move. Now I have video evidence of the Blue Bloods using, I must put any feelings for Hugo aside and reveal the truth to the world. I pluck out the SD card from the spycam and plug it into my laptop. I wonder why it's taking so long to load, until I get the shock of my life. *There is nothing to load*. The damn cheap-ass camera didn't work.

Swearing, I clutch the sides of my head, then remember I got some footage on my phone.

I hunt high and low until I reach a devastating conclusion: my phone is gone.

CHAPTER 22

On Monday, after battling through the crowds and, weirdly, the Bodley Football Team, who seem to be up in arms about something, I'm minding my own business, putting books away, when someone grabs me by my shoulders, spins me round and pins me down onto the lockers.

Renée stands before me, snarling '*Slut.*' Unbelievably Indira is beside her, though she has the decency to look at her feet when I glare.

A permafrost creeps over my shoulders. After the weekend I've had, I don't have the capacity to deal with this. I don't even want to think about Hugo. And I'm so sick of being attacked!

'Get your hands off me!' I shout, pushing her away and freeing myself. Grinning faces gather round us like they're getting front row seats at the Smackdown of the Century.

Keira emerges from the crowd and sidles up to me, her voice low. 'You do realize boys see your hijab and think you're an exotic parcel to unwrap, don't you? Once they've got what they want, it's over.' She strokes my hijab and I jerk my head back, seething. 'If you have one scintilla of shame, you will stop trying to steal my boyfriend and go back to printing your sensationalist lies in Tampon-LeakZ, or whatever your trashy tabloid is called.'

'*TeaLeakZ* is not trash,' I say loudly, folding my arms. 'No clickbait, no vendettas, just the painful, honest truth.'

'*TeaLeakZ* forever! *Chronicle* could never!' one of the onlookers shouts, setting off a wave of laughs.

'Look at you!' Keira spits. 'Acting like you own the place.'

'Bodley. Kids. Never. Asked. To. Come. Here.' I clap my hands, punctuating each syllable. 'It happened. Get over it.'

'You're dangerous smackheads and you're ruining everything!' Keira says, seething.

'This from the girl who pops $€x¥ like Tic Tacs?'

Keira's eyes widen. '*Hugo is mine!*' she raves, and with one aggressive, shocking motion, *she rips off my hijab*.

My hair tumbles over my shoulders, my eyes wide. A tremble works through my body as the horror of what just happened sinks in and I look up to the crowd with shock.

A hush descends as Hugo cuts through the oglers. They watch silently. Some in shock, some in curiosity, and too many in glee. I try to calm my racing heart. Keira turns to look at him.

I snatch my hijab from her and leave. As I'm battling my way through the ring that formed around us, I hear Hugo loudly declare, 'You vicious cow! You just pulled a Muslim girl's hijab off. That's a hate crime.'

A shocked gasp ripples through the crowd and I'm finally let through. Suddenly the Blue Bloods start shouting at Keira, turning on their own. Live by popularity, die by it too, I guess.

I run down the corridor and stumble into an empty classroom to pull myself together and process what just happened. Looking at my reflection in the windows, I put my hijab on and make sure my hair is fully covered.

Then the door opens.

'We need to talk,' Hugo says.

Can I not get one moment of peace? 'Not right now.'

He ignores me. 'You know how I feel about you, but I have no idea whether you're into me or not.'

I stare at Hugo in disbelief. Having my hijab pulled off is like . . . it's not like anything I've ever felt before. I feel violated. Exposed. Humiliated. And this guy is still banging on about something between us? Where was his attitude from thirty seconds ago when he faced Keira? His selfishness sends a wave of fury through me, but I swallow it. I don't have the energy to school him right now.

'You're a great guy and I enjoy your company,' I say, struggling.

'But you're just not into me.' He looks utterly baffled. 'Is it because I'm white?' My surprise makes him blush.

I shake my head. 'In my religion we're not supposed to have *boyfriends* of any colour.'

He looks at me, exasperated. 'Why are you letting your religion control you like that? You should be able to do whatever you want so long as you're not hurting anyone.'

This is why I don't usually talk about my faith. It seriously pisses me off when people think I don't have agency or worse: that I'm 'oppressed'. I swallow another wave of fury. 'I'm not a Muslim just because my parents are, OK? I'm under no one's control. I draw hope, power, and strength from Islam. And sure: some of the rules are tough, but I know they're there for a reason. I've decided I don't want a boyfriend.'

He studies me for three heartbeats before moving in for a kiss. I push him away, incredulous. 'Are you even listening? You're not going to change my mind with a kiss. You're looking for a physical relationship and I'm not.'

He starts laughing, running his hands through his hair. 'Wow! Is this because I didn't say anything when Tom was pawing that girl from your school? Everyone knows what Tom and Marlon are like.'

The bell clangs, announcing lessons.

'So what? Indira deserved to be stripped cos they have a reputation?' I spit, liking him less by the minute.

'Come on, I didn't mean it like that,' he says, annoyed.

'I've just explained my reasons. I've got a lesson to get to.'

He snags my wrist. 'You're lying. You *are* into me. I know you are.' There is something arrogant and even quite nasty about the way he says this.

I yank my arm free. 'I said what I said.'

I walk out, my heart racing, but also feeling oddly empowered. I haven't been myself in a very long time but Dua Iqbal has finally returned.

I sit alone at lunch like a pariah, casting surreptitious glances around the dinner hall, hoping someone will come and sit next to me. I haven't seen my news team since our last, admittedly disastrous meeting. In my mind I'm preparing an apology – something I've never been very good at. Will they even want to forgive me? Max seemed to think so.

Hugo is sitting at the best table by the portrait window along with Tom, Marlon and Oba, laughing and joking. Not once does he look my way. Logically I should be happy about this, but there's a part of me that is wounded. I prick holes in my jacket potato with a fork as I watch a Minerva student call a Bodley kid a 'crackhead' and push him away from his table.

As I'm coming out of the bathroom at the end of lunch, Indira walks in, sees me, then does a quick one-eighty.

'Wait!' I cry.

She pauses, her back to me.

'I bailed you out and you just stood by while Renée and Keira were attacking me?' I say, staring at her back in disbelief. After a while, her shoulders slump and she turns around.

'I don't owe you anything, Dua. I never asked for your help.'

Her words are like a slap. 'How can you go back to being friends with those girls after you've seen what they're really like?'

She folds her arms. 'Because I don't want to be like *you*. You might be OK having people laugh at you or hate you, or maybe thinking you're brave. I'm not like that. I'm sorry if you think it sucks but I want to be on the winning team. My dad told me making good contacts is the key to an easy life.'

Her response floors me.

'Oh, don't look at me like that! One day you'll learn that being idealistic is for babies. You have to go along to get along.' She pauses, dipping her hand inside her bag. 'Oh yeah. I picked this up by mistake.'

My phone. I grab it with an explosion of relief as she leaves. There are a whole bunch of missed calls from Max but the worst part is that my all my videos of the Rumbal have been deleted.

I rub my sore eyes. The Rumbal was the absolute worst night ever. But at least I found out that Minerva is popping pills like bubbles. If drugs equals an instant exclusion, Sir Reg would have no choice but to get rid of over half of his Year Elevens. That is IF I still had the footage.

Without evidence, I'm playing a dangerous game. And it's not a game I can play on my own.

I try to get Morowa's attention during maths, but she's hyper focused, so I grab her at home time. She glances at me then looks away.

'I don't want to talk to you, Dua,' she says as I approach.

Not the most promising start. She seems more downcast than angry, though.

'I know, I'm sorry. You were right and I was wrong. We need to publish your misogynoir article in full.'

'Whatever.' This is really unlike her.

'Are you OK?'

She glowers for a beat then rubs her eyes. 'You didn't hear? Josiah got excluded.'

For someone who's supposed to have her finger on the pulse, this news knocks me for six. Only then do I remember the Bodley football team this morning. Were they up in arms about losing their captain? 'Why?!'

'Why do you think? Drugs.'

I can't. That horrible word again. This *school*.

'Football means everything to him. He'd never . . .' I say, hoping she's mistaken.

'They found him carrying, Dua!' she tells me. I shake my head, still reeling. 'Did you know he sings in the church choir? Like, every Sunday?' Morowa says, her eyes wet. She folds her arms tightly, tapping her foot. 'Recently he's been slacking off. I thought the man might be having a crisis of faith or something, but turns out he was busy doing the Devil's work.'

I shake my head again in complete disbelief. 'We have to do something!'

'Don't you dare!' Morowa shouts, her braids flying. 'His family are embarrassed enough without this being turned into a juicy story for *TeaLeakZ*. Not everything is a way for you to get ahead.'

I stop in my tracks and take the hit. 'Another Bodley kid got busted for drugs last week too – not sure what kind. But Mor, I swear they were *everywhere* at the party on Saturday.'

Morowa raises a brow. '*You* managed to break into a Rumbal?'

'For espionage,' I confirm, which is half the truth. 'Minerva kids are using like nobody's business. They're just better at hiding it or privileged enough not to have to worry about being caught.'

My dad's words after the party come back to me: '*Those rich white kids can raise hell and no one's going to exclude them . . . you will always be the first to be sacrificed to save their privileged arses.*'

'Josiah knows it's exam year and he knows we're being targeted. There's no way he'd do something so dumb as to get involved with drugs right now. He must've been set up somehow?'

'I wish you were right,' Morowa says.

So Bodley excludes its greatest football captain ever and even Morowa is having doubts over Josiah's innocence. It's the Blue Bloods who are out of control, not us. I'm going to get to the bottom of this, even if it kills me.

I'm standing outside a small end-of-terrace house close to our old school with a 'For Sale' sign in the yard. There's a clipped hedge and a neat little garden brimming with snowdrops. Inside the porch, on a stand, are two porcelain figurines of Christ and Mary, their faces washed-out blurs. I ring the bell again and the door finally opens, revealing a Black woman with beautiful dark skin and a colourful headwrap.

'Yes?' she asks.

'Hi, I'm Josiah's friend from school, Dua. Can I see him, please?'

Her eyebrows furrow. 'My son has been excluded. I don't want him speaking to the people who led him astray. He'll begin a new life at a new school. Goodbye.' She starts to close the door.

'But he's a good kid!' I shout, grabbing the door. Her eyes widen like she's trying to work out if I'm crazy or high myself. 'Josiah would sooner die than let his parents down,' I persist. 'Please, please let me speak to him.'

She eyeballs me for the longest. 'Fine. You've got ten minutes then I don't want to see you around here ever again. And keep your voice down. My husband is very sick.'

I nod, take my muddy boots off, and hurry upstairs to the room she indicated. The door is partially open. Knocking on it, I call Josiah's name. His head is adorned with glowing headphones as he lounges in a giant beanbag watching anime on his phone. I tap him on the shoulder.

He rips off his headphones, looking like he's suffered a minor heart attack. 'Bruh, don't do that to me! What the hell are you doing here?'

'I heard what happened—'

'So? Everyone's talking about me. Good publicity, innit?'

I stare him out, frustrated by the weird front he's putting on. I've known him for years – this isn't him. 'I want to hear the truth from your lips.'

'I'm a drug pusher. End of.'

'I know you, Josiah. You're the kid who goes church, who won't pass someone's mum without asking if you can carry her shopping.'

'That was the old Josiah.' He turns *One-Punch Man* back on.

I study him then shake my head. 'Why'd you do it?'

'That's my business.' He pulls his headphones on.

I yank them off. 'Except it's not. We're not at Bodley any more, man. One of us gets caught, we're all suspects. Guilt by association. I know you: your body is a temple or whatever. You'd never risk your football career for a high and you wouldn't do it to anyone else either.'

Josiah blinks, scratching the soft curly hairs on his chin. 'I don't mean for anyone else to get in trouble. But you don't know me.'

'I know you're the best captain Bodley ever had and some day you'll probably be playing at Wembley. I know you won that prize for taking an amazing photo which Aden keeps displayed in his office to this day. And I know you stood up for weedy kids like Liam in PE when the Minerva boys were taking the piss. You're not the type.'

He looks at his *Naruto* socks, troubled. 'I used to think that if you did good, God made your life easier. It's bullshit! My dad's a pastor – a man of God – and he's lying next door dying of cancer.'

I cover my mouth, mumbling something feeble about being

sorry. Morowa never mentioned his dad was a pastor. No wonder she was so eager to keep it out of *TeaLeakZ*.

'Doctors gave up on him, innit? Can't be wasting chemo on that goner.' He finally puts his phone down, holding his head in his hands. 'Everything's been falling apart since we came to Minerva. That place is cursed! I'm failing and it's like even the teachers have given up on me. Like they're so stressed, they can only be bothered with the ones that get stuff right first time, you get me?'

I nod. 'Why didn't you say something?'

'To *who*?' he explodes. 'Aden don't give a shit. Minerva's his dumping ground. And the teachers here don't see me. All they see is a thug. I can't be dealing with all that you-have-to-work-ten-times-harder-than-white-people shit.'

'You saying you sold weed to help kids deal with the stress of moving?' I ask, trying to understand his fall from grace.

He sighs and shakes his head. 'It wasn't weed. It was this premium stuff called $€x¥.'

'Renée or Keira?' I demand hotly. He looks at me blankly. 'Who gave them to you?'

Josiah laughs. 'I'm not a grass!'

'So you'd rather get excluded than snake on the idiot who supplied the pills? You ever think maybe they gave you $€x¥ to get you excluded?' He doesn't seem to care, so I try again. 'Whoever you're protecting will strike again. It's divide and conquer. We're getting picked off one by one.'

'This is on me. I should never've sold that crap. I didn't think about the harm I was doing or what the consequences would be for my family.' I watch him cover his face. He's clearly broken up over this. Why couldn't Aden give him another chance instead of fast-tracking him to exclusion?

'Why is there a "For Sale" sign outside?' I ask.

'We're moving. Mum and Dad think Enley is basically Sodom and Gomorrah.'

'Josiah, *please*,' I beg. 'Tell me who's your supplier. You know me. I'm a nosy cow. Sooner or later I'm going to find out anyway. Just gimme a name and I swear they'll never know it was you. Think of all the other kids you could save.' I look at his socks. 'Don't you want to be a hero?'

Josiah stares at his sliders then slips the headphones back on. I deflate. His mum appears in the doorway. 'Your ten minutes are up.'

I nod, making my way down the stairs. Stopping at the bottom, I spin round with urgency. 'Your son isn't a bad kid, Auntie. Minerva is full of predators. Josiah just got played.'

Flames of suppressed emotion flicker in her eyes. She purses her lips and sees me out the door.

When I get home, I'm fighting tears. And not the usual angry tears – I'm truly, deeply sad. And I need my mum.

I get in bed and give her a call, wanting to confide in her about everything and hear her tell me everything is all right, but when she picks up, she's clearly been crying too.

I can't tell her anything. 'Dua, darling, is that you?' she says, sniffling.

I hang up.

The next day, in spite of my sinking feeling, I call a meeting.

Only Max turns up.

'Are you sure you want to do this alone?' Max asks, looking super-concerned.

'I know I screwed up. I just wish the team would give me a chance to apologize in person and explain why I made so many stupid decisions,' I cry. 'I'm just under a lot of pressure . . .'

'I feel you, but so is everyone else,' Max reminds me gently.

'Anxiety levels have been off the charts since we got here. Josiah was like the school mascot. With him kicked out, a lot of people have just lost faith.'

'Then I have no choice but to strike out alone . . .' I say, the gravity of my words weighing heavily on my soul.

'Rumbals in the Urban Jungle – An Exposé' by Nunya Byz

Change is happening in education. Privileged schools are merging with poorer academies, brains are being placed before money, and scholarships are boosting social mobility. This can only be a good thing, right? Well sadly, there's a darker side: drugs.

Our intrepid reporter managed to infiltrate a fabled 'Rumbal'. Known up and down the country by a variety of quirky names, these exclusive house parties have remained one of Enley East's best-kept secrets – until now. Grab a croissant, cos here comes the tea!

A variety of debauchery was witnessed at a recent Rumbal, fuelled by the reckless consumption of alcohol and hardcore drugs. The majority of attendees were from one of the best grammar schools in the area – none of them a day over seventeen.

Most alarming of all was the appearance of the newest psychoactive on the block: $€x¥, so-called because it gives the user an intense rush of pleasure accompanied by hallucinations of sexual encounters. But early research reveals some trippers have crashed and burned. While China and the US play the blame game on who exactly created these deathly beauties, young people are falling victim to its lethal charms. So far, five British people have died since the start of the year after suffering drug-induced cardiac arrest.

We've learned that headteachers at some academies have become trigger-happy with exclusions, even for a first offence with a class B drug like weed. Heads at grammar schools, on the other hand, have allowed parents to go on believing that the use of recreational drugs is something that only affects ethnic and working-class communities. In this journalist's opinion, heads should roll for failing to crack down on the Rumbals themselves.

Are the parent-governors of Minerva College too stoned to notice something's up? Or are they just busy working on another PR campaign to blame working-class kids for being a bad influence when it's almost always the other way around? And why hasn't Cllr Briggs made it a priority to stop the illegal drugs trade and save lives by coordinating with the police, hospitals and communities to fund drug outreach programmes and clinics?

Shifting blame onto society's marginalized communities just perpetuates harmful stereotypes. Exclusions put vulnerable kids on streets where they are even more likely to be exploited, and consistently stop kids from reaching their full potential.

All we can say is that someone somewhere is making a pretty packet by endangering young lives and there ain't nothing $€x¥ about it! We're making it our mission to find out who. Till then, stay safe and make sure your highs are all of the legal variety.

CHAPTER 23

Liam and I end up on the same bus into school for the first time in weeks. He maintains a four-metre distance as we get off and it isn't until the zebra crossing that he finally catches up to me and takes the plunge. 'Can we talk?'

I nod, trying to keep my shit together. I want to both hug him and tell him to jog on. But I owe him a conversation at least.

'I'm really sorry, Doo. I screwed up, but you still sent me that text at the Rumbal. Keira was joking, though. About drugging me, at least.'

'I couldn't take that chance,' I explain. 'You may have told Keira about my mum's mental health problems and joined her paper, but I'm not going to let anyone hurt you.'

'What? Is that why you were so hurt? Dua, I swear I never said a word,' he cries earnestly.

I frown. If not him, then who? Hugo? He's not the chill guy I thought but until the party we were great. Besides, he didn't know all the details.

'If it wasn't you, then why did you leave *TeaLeakZ*?' I ask, puzzled.

Liam's cheeks flush, his eyes watery. 'Mum lost her job at the shop.'

'I'm sorry.' I kick myself for not checking in with him and his family. I've been so wrapped up in my own crap, I didn't look beyond my own needs.

'She got fired for *stealing*.'

What?

Ten years ago, Liam's mum made him return a small ball of plasticine to our primary school teacher which he lifted from the art cabinet. Ms Akibo didn't even think it was that big of a deal but his mum still made red-faced Liam apologize and promise never to do it again. I remember cos that was the year I got him a plasticine set for his birthday and he made me an incredible model of Ariel bursting out of the ocean for mine, mermaid fin and all.

'She'd been asking Mr Tan for a raise for ages but he kept fobbing her off. Even with food banks and that, it don't help much. Sometimes we can't afford to put the heating on and Nan can't cope with the cold . . .' He looks at his battered school shoes, ears becoming red rosettes around his hearing aids. 'She was desperate and swiped money from the till. She can't get a new job with a criminal record, and Nan's dementia is getting worse so . . . so . . .'

I cover my mouth, suddenly realizing I made all the worst assumptions about my best friend. 'You got a job with the *Chronicle* so you could pay the bills.'

He nods.

My eyes fill with tears. 'And I screamed at you and called you a traitor instead of trying to understand. I'm such a shit friend. I'm so sorry, Liam!' I say, grabbing his arm and bringing our walk to a stop just outside the school gates.

'No you're not. I didn't tell you. I *couldn't* . . . you've been so caught up with the paper and Briggsy and the Blue Bloods . . . I know Keira's only got me on her paper to make you jealous and she only asked me to the Rumbal to make *Hugo* jealous. But we need the money so badly, I couldn't say no.'

I shake my head and take his hand. 'I'm so sorry you felt like you couldn't come to me because I was too busy or distracted. I always have time for you. Being with Keira on the *Chronicle* and dealing with our team's glares can't have been easy, but you're not the sell-out – I am. I let Hugo play build-a-bitch with me, pretending I was challenging myself instead of changing myself. I've got no conscience.'

'That's not true. I saw you stand up for Indira of all people in front of all those scary bougie kids, including Hugo. Can't've been easy.'

We're both wet-eyed, teary messes. He rubs his nose with his sleeve as we pass through the gates and walk to the lockers.

I swallow my pride. 'I did you dirty as the deputy editor. A gaming column is a great idea. I was so caught up in my war against the Blue Bloods, I didn't consider anyone else's feelings or ideas. Like Morowa's BHM article was fire. I think I edited it because I was afraid of losing the following we gained – and part of that was Hugo's admiration.'

'If Hugo likes you, Dua, it should be for who you are. I reckon you're too good for him anyway,' Liam says loyally. 'It ain't easy being editor. That's why you should share the load and trust your team will always have your back.'

I bite my lip, thinking it's too late, I pushed them all away.

'I saw your latest article,' Liam says, as if reading my mind. 'You exposed them but you didn't give any evidence.'

'I lost it!' I cry. 'I filmed stuff at the Rumbal but Indira deleted it.'

'You're brave,' he says. 'Wish I'd filmed stuff too as your back-up, but I spent the evening scared shitless. It's a good thing *TeaLeakZ* is anonymous otherwise they'd drag you for libel.'

'I don't care,' I say, fronting as I struggle with the dial on my locker. 'Josiah's the fifth Bodley kid to get excluded for drug use at this place. After witnessing what we both saw at the Rumbal, it's really messed-up that they're carrying the blame. Minerva is the problem, and they'll keep hurting Bodley kids unless they're stopped.' I try my combination again, but my locker remains stuck. I hit it, hoping to knock it loose, and try my combination again.

Liam groans, running a hand over his face, feeling Josiah's pain. 'The Blue Bloods will come for you with everything they've got. Maybe even Hugo.'

'Let them. I'm tired of their cover-ups. If nothing else, the article will have them looking over their shoulders.'

I finally get my locker open and scream, bringing the bustling hallway to a stop.

A naked Barbie swings from a string noose Blue-Tacked to the top of the metallic tomb. A marker has been used to give her 'brownface', a paper napkin glued to her head like a hijab. Taped to her plastic crotch is a typed note that reads:

Nunya,
SNITCHES GET STITCHES

Liam is nearly speechless as he glares at the doll wrathfully. 'Let's report it.'

I slam the door shut. 'What doesn't kill me . . . I published that article; I will weather the storm the way I choose.'

After lunch, Dr Sturgeon springs a surprise maths test on us. The Bodley kids moan but the Minerva kids don't seem that fazed. Maybe they were raised on surprise tests or maybe they're still stoned.

'Can't we delay it till next week, please?' Morowa asks bravely.

Sturgeon's jowls wobble like jelly. 'Certainly not! I want to know how much progress you've made *today*.'

'But supposing we're having a bad day?' I ask stupidly.

'If only that were the case! Your standards have been slipping for weeks and your homework has appalled me,' he tells me wrathfully, as if *TeaLeakZ* will write itself. It's not my fault I've recently had to do the job of five Duas.

'But, sir,' I persist, 'the actual GCSEs won't be a surprise that pops up out of nowhere. At least give us till next lesson to revise.'

'If you didn't waste so much time writing libellous articles about Minerva students, you wouldn't need the extra time to prepare for the test!' Renée sneers.

'Yes, your hit pieces suck,' Oba says coldly. I'm taken aback.

'Settle down!' Sturgeon says.

The test is super frustrating. He's even included a question on circle theorem which we only started learning last week. I skip it in favour of 3D trig.

There's a knock at the door and a Year Nine kid pokes his head round.

Sturgeon beckons the boy over, frowns at the note then scans the room, his eyes finally resting on me. 'Sir Reginald wishes to see you in his office.'

My heart drops into a bottomless pit. Renée cackles. 'Rest in Pieces, Dumya Bitchnez.'

'I beg your pardon?' Sturgeon glares at Renée, pale eyes bulging behind his thick glasses.

'This about *TeaLeakZ*?' Morowa whispers, tapping my arm.

'Probably,' I say sombrely, doubting it's about my homework record being on the slide.

'Need me for back-up?'

I smile at her. Her words of support bring on a wave of emotion. Even after I took an editorial axe to her passion piece, she still comes through for me. 'Appreciate it, sis, but I dug myself into this mess. Gotta get myself out.'

The corridor housing the offices of the highest-ranking teachers is seriously grim. Walnut parquet creaks underfoot as I pass ebony doors in tight white frames embedded into olive green walls. The cloying smell of wood polish scratches at the back of my throat. By the time I reach the last office, I'm half expecting to see Winston Churchill's name on the brass plate.

Sir Reginald Maurice Unwin KBE
BA (Cantab), MPhil (Oxon), PhD (Cantab)

He's not going to exclude you, I tell myself, staring at the engraved letters with foreboding. *He's not your headteacher, so he can't.*

Knocking, I enter Sir Reg's spooky lair of correction, bracing myself for the worst.

'Ah, Dua Iqbal!' says the man, who till now I have only ever seen from a distance. He's a silver fox with thick, dark eyebrows and Hugo's eyes. 'Do sit down, won't you?'

Using small talk, he tries to drop my guard: how are my studies going? What would I like to do when I leave school?

'Ah, journalism!' he replies, in a horribly loud voice. 'Of course. An ambitious pursuit, I must say, but one I have no doubt you are amply capable of.'

'Thanks.' Yep, mos defs about *TeaLeakZ* . . .

'In fact, one you have already forayed into. I must ask you, what on earth does "*TeaLeakZ*" mean?'

'*TeaLeakZ* is nothing to do with me,' I lie with practised confidence. 'I set up *Bodley Voices,* but as you know, it got shut down. Just as well really, so I can focus on my exams.'

'I see,' he says with an irony that makes my heart skip a beat. 'You'll have to forgive me for connecting the dots and thinking you might be behind this venture.'

'I'm sorry to disappoint,' I say flatly as my armpits start to weep.

He waves a hand dismissively. 'A school's good character and reputation are exceedingly important to its lasting legacy. Vulgar though it sounds, schools are businesses. I believe you *know* who wrote the salacious article about drugs, even if you didn't write it yourself, as you say. Would you be so kind as to ask them to remove it?'

I bristle. 'With all due respect, you've got the wrong girl.'

'The article smears Minerva College and by extension the Learning Trust and the right honourable councillor who helped set it up. *I don't like it.*' There's the steel I knew was lurking in those ice-blue eyes. 'It will be removed.'

I swallow thickly. 'The general public have been smearing Bodley students in the local press. The *Minerva Chronicle* ran an article with a thinly veiled attack on us lowering the tone. You want this article removed but not the other? That's hypocrisy. If drugs is a problem at Bodley, it's an even bigger one at Minerva.'

'I want you to do well in your mocks, Dua. I want the article to go away.' He pauses, his lips forming a smile which dies before reaching his eyes. 'Mr Aden tells me you wish to study A levels here? Certainly the Minerva name will place you in very good standing with any of the Russell Group here, or the Ivy League universities should you want to study abroad. No doubt your esteemed teachers have already told you that excellent mock grades are key for A-level study placements?'

My breath hitches in my throat; the kid gloves finally come off. If I don't make the exposé go away, Sir Reg will mess with my mock results.

'So I'm going to leave this with you to resolve – swiftly. You'd better get back to class.'

Check-fricking-mate.

CHAPTER 24

As I'm heading to English, Liam sends me a TikTok recorded outside Sir Reg's office. He bends over, rubbing his skinny arse on the doorhandle when it unexpectedly turns. Liam's eyes nearly pop out of his skull as Sir Reg's furious face appears behind him. A filter and some good editing make Sir Reg morph into a raging Godzilla. 'Shit!' Liam squeaks, running down the corridor as fast as his lanky legs will carry him. I burst out laughing.

Instead of freaking us out about the mocks like Sturgeon, Dr York chooses to start the lesson with a rousing speech. The perfect antidote to having to sit next to Keira. Man, how different life would be if I still had the video of her and Renée doing $€x¥. York dubs us his 'strongest cohort ever'. Maybe it's his usual pre-exam schtick but it means a lot to us Bodley kids. No one's really appreciated us like this since we moved here – not even our own teachers.

Suddenly Dr York clutches his hair, screwing up his face, and I'm afraid he's having a heart attack.

'Are you all right, sir?' I ask with concern.

'Oh, dear! After stating preparation is key, I'm afraid *I've* failed in that regard myself.' He blushes profusely. 'Gone and left the practice papers downstairs in the stockroom!'

Everyone laughs.

'Not a problem,' I say, rising to my feet. 'Dua Deliveries is good to go.'

'Teacher's pet,' Keira mutters.

'Islamaphobic thug,' I retort-whisper, not forgiving her for ripping off my hijab.

York looks at me doubtfully. 'There are four boxes. I don't want you putting your back out.'

'I'll go with her,' Liam says, giving me all the feels while Keira glares at him.

Grabbing a hastily scrawled permission slip and lift pass, I bounce out of the room with Liam in tow.

'So . . .' Liam says, 'guess who got fired from the *Chronicle*?'

'Keira fired you?! I'm so sorry, mate! Why?' I say, knowing his family is going to be out of pocket.

'Guess I failed to make either Hugo or you jealous.'

'I'm sorry.'

'Don't be. It's a relief. We need the money, yeah, but it's not worth me having to sleep with the enemy.'

I'm hoping he means it figuratively when we see Roshni stomping down the corridor, sobbing into a tissue. 'Roshni, you OK, hun?'

'You!' she marks me with a French manicured nail. 'You messed up my life! All I did was promote your stupid paper and jazz up your tweets and now Sir Reginald is treating *me* like a *criminal*. He interrogated me for an hour, trying to get me to confess to working on *TeaLeakZ*. Why did you have to go and publish that stupid article about their drug parties? Like who gives a shit if they want to snort drugs and kill themselves?!'

'Five Bodley students have been excluded for drugs since Sir Reg leaned on Aden. Our lot have never had a problem with substance abuse before – it's coming from somewhere within Minerva. It's not right, Roshni. I'm sorry but it's the hill I choose to die on,' I say, holding up my hands.

She runs a hand through her hair. 'I don't remember you asking the team if we were cool with dying on any hills.' Her large eyes well up. 'You have no respect for us. In your mind it's *your* paper and we're just the lackeys. Well, I didn't sign on for a war. If it wasn't clear earlier – I QUIT!'

'Roshni!' I cry, trying to grab her arm.

She thrusts a sanitizer spray in my face like a Glock 44. 'Don't make me use this.'

Backing down, I let her go.

I tell Liam once she's out of earshot. 'She's right. Though I did try calling a meeting, but after no one turned up I went ahead and published.'

He shrugs. 'Your methods are sus but I respect your integrity. In your own messed-up way you're looking out for Bodley kids even more than Aden or our parents. Just do me a favour and *learn* from this, yeah?'

'I promise.'

We approach the lift and I scan Dr York's ID, pressing the call button. There's a humming sound as the gears turn and I hear the disembodied sound of giggling in the lift shaft.

'Do you smell that?' I ask, turning my nose up at the smoky stench of rotting cabbage.

The lift doors hum open revealing three watery-eyed girls, one Bodley, two Minervan, enveloped in a thin cloud of acrid smoke. They're clearly blitzed. One shoots her hand for the DOOR CLOSE button, but my basketball-honed reflexes beat her and I snag her wrist.

'Where'd you get the weed?' I demand.

'It's finished. Go get your own!' chuckles her friend, swaying on her feet.

I think fast. 'OK, sure. Who's dealing?'

Liam flinches and I hope to God he doesn't give the ruse away.

'We don't know what you're talking about,' pipes up the girl at the back.

'Don't be annoying, fam,' I say, tutting. 'Exams are proper

stressful, you know? Help a sis take the edge off.'

'Jason Young,' the Bodley girl says. 'There are others, but his prices are the best. Last I saw he was heading for the loos on the second floor. You might catch him if you hurry.'

'And you never heard it from us!' The girls exit the lift. One face-plants and the other two prop her up between them as they stumble down the corridor, cackling.

Liam turns to me with concern. 'Dua, I know editing sucks, but drugs ain't the answer!'

'Thanks for the vote of confidence,' I say, rolling my eyes as the penny drops.

'Oh! So you're going to report Jason Young and those girls?' he says, following me into the lift, trying to scoop the pungent smoke out with his flappy hands.

I shake my head. 'It's called *investigative* journalism. Jason and the girls are pawns in a much bigger game. I want to uncover the source. That's the only way to stop this. If the dealers get taken out, a bunch of kids get messed-up futures and the supplier just finds new kids to funnel their product through.' Liam looks at me in surprise. 'I might have spent all night researching how this works in other schools,' I explain as I hit the ground-floor button.

'Are you serious?' he exclaims. 'You're playing with fire! What you're talking about isn't just a problem between two schools. It's a multimillion-pound business spread across virtually every school in the country. And you want to take them all down with an article?'

'Wish I could, but even I'm not that insane,' I say. 'I'm guessing there have to be smaller cells. I'm going after the Enley chapter.'

'Did you not hear me? It's *everywhere*. Bodley and Minerva are both guilty. People have to choose to do drugs, which is why people like us don't.'

'You seriously think it's a level playing field?' I say, getting annoyed. 'Minerva kids do drugs for kicks and zero consequences; Bodley kids do it to take a timeout from the reality of stressful homes and schoolwork that is way harder than it used to be and always get the full weight of the law.'

'You're generalizing. It's not all black and white.'

'No, it's not. But someone is profiting from the abuse of kids. They need to be stopped.'

'Then report them. The police have the means and contacts to uncover whoever's behind this. This isn't a game, fam. You've already got Roshni into trouble and been threatened with a creepy doll!' I make a mental note not to tell Liam about Sir Reg's threat, too.

'You trust the police to objectively investigate anything? I started this. I need to finish it.' The lift doors ding open. I throw Liam the keys to the stockroom and step out. 'You don't wanna be part of this, that's your call.' The doors close. I don't take it personally that he wants out: with his mum out of work and his nan sick, he can't play with fire. Thinking about my own mum and dad and what getting permanently excluded will do to them gives me pause. Then I remember Dad trying to convince Mum to sue her employers. I'm an Iqbal: we don't back down when the going gets tough.

I sprint down the corridor.

A Bodley kid emerges from the toilets with his hands in his pockets, a silly smile plastered across his spotty face.

'You Jason?' I ask.

'Nah, he's back there,' he says, pointing to the toilets. The sudden withdrawal of his hand causes something to tumble from his pocket and land between my feet. It looks like a tiny packet of green-brown moss. The air is suddenly electric and my heart starts to thump. I knew it was going on, but seeing weed with my own eyes at school really freaks me out. My conscience tugs at my heartstrings, telling me that getting excluded won't help Mum's recovery. But closing my eyes to the truth makes me as guilty as Sir Reg and I can't live with myself if I drop to his level. The kid snatches it up and scarpers.

Glancing left and right, I barge into the boys' toilets before I think too hard about what I'm doing.

'Yo! Jason!' The swagger is all fake, a cover for wracked nerves.

A cubicle door opens a crack and a slitted eye peers through. 'This is the boys' toilets. What you want?'

Wait – how do I even talk about weed? I've never done this before! I decide to take the roadman approach and hope for the best. 'Word is you've got ganja.'

The boy opens the cubicle and laughs. 'Who told you?' I notice he's wearing genuine Yeezys. Clearly the pill and potion industry pays well.

I tense up, my muscles vibrating like wound springs. 'Your mum.' Shock and outrage contort his face seconds before I give a double-handed push, forcing him to sit down on the toilet hard. I kick his unzipped duffel bag. It falls open, revealing a handful of small plastic bags of weed and a lot of those distinctive cherry-red pills stashed between an unwashed football kit and a pencil case. 'Who's your supplier?' I demand.

'Suck my dick!'

I grimace, snatching up his bag. 'I'mma flush this lot down the loo unless you start talking.'

He cackles. 'You and what army?'

I'm scrambling for my next move when out of my peripherals I see a tall figure step forward.

'I'm the army.'

Liam came through.

My heart does a little happy dance before switching back to roadman-hijabi mode and glaring.

Liam slaps Jason's forehead, showing we mean business. 'You gonna tell us your supplier's name, or are we gonna have to flush you and your drugs down the pan?'

'Ow! Why you asking me, though? Everyone's dealing here,' Jason says, getting up.

I roll my eyes, knowing Dad would kill me if he could see me right now, and get up in Jason's face. 'Don't waste my time. The name. Now.'

Liam reaches out and thankfully Jason finally cracks. 'I don't know him! He's outside the school gates every Friday at eleven.'

'How can you not know him?' I scoff. 'Was he wearing a Spider-Man mask or something?'

His scared eyes dart between us as Liam grabs his throat.

'Jubba!' he shrieks. 'They call him Jubba.'

The bottom drops out of my stomach hearing Dad's ex-mate's name.

Well, *him* we can do something about.

CHAPTER 25

Forcing myself to take another sip, I stick my tongue out, wanting to scrape it with a brush. My frappé tastes like an unhealthy cocktail of E-numbers, caffeine and over-processed sugar, which is exactly what it is.

We're just outside the coffee shop in Enley Market. My nerves are tingling. I can't believe Liam's following me into this, but I am so grateful I could cry. He kicks me under the table and nods to the right. 'That him?'

Spying him approaching from the direction of the antiques store, I nod, my palms suddenly clammy. Jubba's wearing a gold foil hoodie with a red cap like a teen from the Nineties. He scrapes back the chair opposite, manspreading without shame. ''Sup, princess? Did you manage to speak to your old man about pitching in for Auntie Ismat's funeral?'

'I did, actually. He said he spoke to her *last* week,' I say pointedly.

He blinks, his lips twitching then he sags. 'OK, ya got me. I need the money for chemo cos the NHS is pants. I didn't want to tell your dad cos it's embarrassing, you understand?'

Wow. This guy is every bit the wasteman Dad painted him as. 'Actually Uncle Jubba, I wanted to speak to you about something else.'

'I got a brain tumour,' he lies. 'I get blinding headaches. Here, gi's a bit of ya drink.' He snatches my frappé, rips off the lid and glugs it down in one. 'You don't mind, do you?'

I shrug.

'Not really . . . Actually, I need to talk to you about our school, Minerva College, and the Bodley kids that go there.' I take a deep, fortifying breath. 'Stop making my classmates into little drug pushers. You're exploiting them. You're from ends, you know how rough it is when your mum's struggling to put food on the table and you're too young to get a proper job. Have some compassion.'

'You accusing me of dealing?' he demands, sitting up straight, no longer pretending to be sick. 'You wanna watch your mouth. People get merc'd for less.' I feel a jolt of fear slither down my back and gulp. Have I miscalculated the danger I'm in?

'This is my town, Uncle Jubba,' I say, slowly enough to iron out the terror from my voice, 'and I care about these people, just like you should. Every time you get kids involved in drugs, you're robbing them of a childhood and setting them up for a life of crime or an early death.' I lean forwards, hoping I look threatening. 'So listen good and listen well: from now on, you are permanently closed for business.'

He laughs derisively. 'Dunno what you're talkin' about.' I look to Liam for support and he sends me a determined look that spurs me on.

'If I ever hear about you supplying drugs to any of the kids in Enley again, I will report you to the police.' I smile sweetly, hoping he can't tell I am literally shaking.

He grips my middle finger and begins to twist it back, sending shooting pain up my hand. It's all I can do not to cry out. 'You little bitch! You tryna threaten me?' I freeze in painful, paralytic terror. This wasn't part of the plan! I was so sure he wouldn't try anything in a public place.

Liam grabs Jubba's wrist and he lands a punch in Liam's guts, making him crumple up. I glance around, wondering why no one is helping us. 'My dad'll kill you!' I warn, tears of pain welling in my eyes.

'Not if I kill him first. You got no idea who I work for, girlie. They own the police, they own the town, and they own the government.'

'Javed!' an elderly Pakistani woman calls, waving a hand as she hurries over.

Jubba curses, releases my finger and shoots off. I massage my busted finger, asking Liam if he's OK. He's more in shock than pain.

'Where's my nephew run off to?' the lady asks in Urdu, catching her breath. 'Did he hurt you? That no-good rascal! Picking on a couple of kids.'

'We're OK,' I say, noticing a family resemblance. 'Are you Auntie Ismat?'

She places a hand on her hip. 'Why, yes I am. Who are you?'

I introduce myself, telling her about Dad, and she breaks out in a huge smile, swallowing me up in a generous hug, basting my face with a sloppy kiss and patting Liam on the head like a pet.

'I always hoped Rashid's good manners would rub off on Javed,' she laments, sitting down with us, 'but that one's bad to the bone! You know he cost the nice man that owned that tea shop his business?'

'Mr Steadman?' I say, making the connection.

'He gave him some "herbal remedies" for arthritis only they were illegal drugs! Winston and Fitzroy and Muneeb and Dilawar all lost their shops. Wouldn't be surprised if Javed didn't have a hand in that too!' She gives me a dark look. 'And that awful councillor doesn't care that there's a problem in the community. Javed is a dangerous man, beyti. Take my advice and keep away. Anyone who invites him into their lives has let the devil in.'

That afternoon her words come back to haunt me. All semblance of control I thought I was exacting over the situation, any ideas I had about being able to handle this on my own go out the window as I take in the words Dad's saying to me.

I hang up on him and sprint all the way to Mum's, ringing the doorbell with crazed urgency.

No answer.

I swear, scrabbling around in my bag for my old keys. If Jubba's hurt Mum, I will NEVER forgive myself. Just as I find them, Mum opens the door.

'Dua! What a lovely . . . surprise?' Her smile disappears, replaced by a snaggle of worry lines across her forehead. 'You're not all right, are you? Come in and tell me everything,' she says, pulling me in through the door and into the living room.

Sitting me down on the sofa, Mum comments on my cold hands. 'What happened?' she asks, helping me calm my breathing.

I am so relieved to see she's unhurt that I almost burst into tears. 'Dad's shop windows have been smashed in – and it's all my fault!' I blurt.

Mum shakes her head like that sentence made no sense. 'I— Is your dad OK?'

I take another calming breath. 'He's shocked and furious that someone would do that to him. Dad's got the police round right now, making a report. They checked both the shop and street CCTV, but the two men who did it had their hoods zipped up over their faces.'

'Your poor dad! This town's overrun with idiots and that stupid councillor hasn't done a thing to address it.' She wraps her arms round me to stop my shaking. 'Don't worry, this is what insurance is for. And I know it's not your fault.'

'But, Mum, it *is*.' I hesitate.

'Beyta, I told you you can come to me with anything. I meant it. I'm not made of glass.'

So I start at the beginning, telling her about the newspaper, meeting Jubba, the party, investigating the drug's presence at Minerva – all of it, right up until me and Liam meeting with Jubba this morning.

'You *threatened* him?!' Mum asks aghast. 'Dua, are you *mad*? You should've come to me or your dad!'

'I know but I didn't realize he was *that* dangerous. I thought he was just Dad's harmless loser mate who didn't know when to quit. I didn't know he was so connected!'

Mum looks like she's going to panic for a second, before she does some controlled breathing and steadies herself. Wow – therapy must really be working.

'OK, I'm going to make you a hot cup of tea before you catch cold, then I'm going to go over to the shop. We'll tell the police everything you've told me.'

'We can't!' I cry. 'This was a warning. Next time they'll do worse. Jubba as good as told me they've got the police in their pocket.'

Mum taps her lips worriedly. 'I don't know . . .'

'Mum, trust me – we can't go to the police,' I say firmly.

She steels. 'OK, no police *for now*. Not until we can find someone we trust. Our family's safety has to come first. We need to make sure we're all looking out for each other.'

'Mum, I'm so sorry!'

She squeezes my frosty hands. 'Oh, Dua. You know what your problem is? You need to stop trying to be a hero. This isn't TV. We only get one life and your father and I love you very much. You're still just a child – it's OK to not carry the world on your shoulders and try to fix everything all the time.' She turns on the fireplace, swaddling me in her shawl.

Mum is right: I'm no hero. It's time for me to stop trying to save Bodley kids. I'm just a scared sixteen-year-old playing at being an avenging journalist – I don't know how to help them, and rather than sharing resources, being a good friend or helping the news team tell their stories so they can have some kind of outlet, I used the belief they had in me to compete with Keira and push Sir Reg and Mr Aden's buttons.

Later, as we clear the glass and comfort my poor disheartened dad, I grow determined – it has to be over or someone I love is going to get hurt.

CHAPTER 26

'Congratulations,' Renée purrs, spotting me by the drinks machine. 'You finally made it onto the *Minerva Chronicle*.'

Oh no.

'Or at least your dad did!' Indira says, chuckling and shoving a printout of a page of their newspaper into my hands and flicking her bob triumphantly.

I hold it up, my eyes growing wide with terror.

'Mental mother, criminal father. Explains a lot,' Renée adds, bumping me as she walks past.

It's a report on the attack on !Komic Kingdom! – but it's essentially a smear piece on Dad's beloved business. Why, the reporter poses, should a modest comic book shop be targeted above all others? The insinuation is clear: Dad must have belonged to the shady underworld. I stare at them in utter disbelief as they strut off, too shocked and angry to bite back.

'Allow it,' Liam says, taking the article and scrunching it up.

'No!' I cry instinctively before I can help myself. 'If I keep it I can write a response—'

Liam grabs my shoulders. 'Dua, you need to stop! How is another article rehashing the same problem going to help?'

I hold my breath and nod slowly. In the last forty-eight hours, it's like a veil has been lifted and I can finally see the truth. I've been running around like a dog with a stick, making a nuisance of myself, refusing to let things go, and in the process I forgot to think about the people I love and how they could be hurt by my actions. Filled with remorse, I admit: 'I should have never turned *TeaLeakZ* into my own personal crusade. Things were so good when we were just using our platform to speak the truth, before I started thinking about our reach or who was reading and getting too big for my boots . . . Why can't I mind my own business? I've always imagined myself as some kind of warrior journalist, getting the truth out to the people, empowering them. But my actions endangered you and the team, damaged Dad's business, couldn't stop or reverse the exclusions, and brought the end of *TeaLeakZ*.'

'I know that wasn't the plan,' he says.

'Hi, Liam!' Tristan says, handing him a metal water bottle. 'Present from the planet to you. Reuse.' He doesn't so much as glance my way before he runs off.

'Everybody's airing me,' I say sadly.

Liam walks me out to a secluded spot on the corner of the field, where the twisted old oak tree grows. People generally avoid it cos it's infected with mould and looks like it escaped from Mirkwood.

'I've made a mess of everything, haven't I? Maybe it's not too late to knuckle down and get some revision done for the mocks.'

'Course it ain't too late,' Liam says kindly. 'Tristan's a pretty cool guy. He's been helping me revise for geography. He just doesn't appreciate someone clipping his wings the way you did at the last meeting.'

A large bumblebee drops out of the sky, clinging onto the tree bark, humming like a harmonica.

'Liam . . .' I say, my mind buzzing, 'I know you're gonna think this is crazy but can you call one last *TeaLeakZ* meeting?'

He studies me. 'Think they'll even listen to me after I worked for the *Chronicle*?'

'You're Liam. They'll listen.'

*

At 3.15, Liam and I settle down in 15C to see if anyone will show. Morowa's the first, just like on that fateful day back in September when we were filled with hopes and dreams about setting up our very own school paper. She sits down quietly, taking out some maths homework. Three minutes later Abdi arrives, eating a chocolate bar, grime leaking from his earbuds. He nods his head in greeting. Roshni and Max soon follow.

Just when I think this is it, Tristan arrives.

'Sorry I'm late,' he says. 'I . . . wasn't sure if I wanted to come.' He sits down gingerly.

I take a deep, steeling breath. 'Thanks, everyone, for being here. I know I'm not your favourite person right now.'

Abdi coughs. Liam kicks him under the table. Morowa just looks at me patiently.

'I wanted to apologize to you all properly,' I continue. 'For hijacking this paper and hacking up your work, for my tunnel vision with targeting the drugs problem at Minerva and not thinking about how it would reflect on you. I really thought I was doing the right thing, but I was being selfish and unhelpful. From the bottom of my heart, I am so sorry.'

Morowa turns to face me. 'It's not like you weren't trying to use our platform for a worthy cause. You just went about it the wrong way.' We exchange smiles.

I gauge the thoughtful expressions around the table, the flicker in their eyes. 'Nobody asked me to declare war on the school's drug trade. When ZayZay got us trending, I guess I lost my head, chasing after those clicks and likes; thinking I could actually do something to help those kids.'

'We've all been there,' Max says understandingly.

'It would've been a lot worse if you did what all the other papers do, which is pretend none of this shit is actually happening,' Abdi says, scratching his jaw.

'It's messy but reporting the truth is important,' Morowa says.
'One of my friends sent me a video of a teacher telling a Minerva
boy to go and study in the library when he was clearly blitzed –
the same teacher that reported Josiah. If that isn't a cover-up,
then I don't know what is.' Everyone nods.

'No one's hating on you for what you said,' Roshni adds
unexpectedly. 'It's the way you said it. Now we've all got eyes on
us, watching everything we do, trying to crack us – for something
we didn't consent to publishing.'

'That's fair,' I say, looking ashamed.

'I almost cracked,' Liam admits slowly. 'When Sir Reg kept on
at me about the paper and my future here, I almost told him
everything about *TeaLeakZ*. I couldn't handle that shit, fam. He's
like the frickin' Gestapo.'

'Ve haf vays of making you talk!' Abdi says in what he thinks
is a German accent. The tension in the room eases and we all laugh.

'I want to know how we're going to get Sir Reg to leave us
alone,' Roshni demands.

'I'll delete the article.' I announce. 'Truth be told it was
supposed to be a genuine exposé. I had video and everything to
back it up before sabotage from the *Chronicle* made me lose it.
Either way, it's not hitting the right note so it's pointless.'

'Sir Reg will think he's won,' Liam concludes. 'But then what
do we write about?'

'The stuff I should've let you write about in the first place,' I
reply. 'Your passion pieces. The stuff that gets you fired up.
Everyone's so fricking stressed about the mocks but people need
to remember that school isn't the be-all and end-all of life. We
need to combat those rising anxiety levels. Come on, hit me with
your best ideas.'

Sensing general scepticism, Liam elects to get the ball rolling.
He tells us he's going to write about the best video games to look

out for in the run-up to Christmas. Morowa smirks and says she's going to write a think piece on intersectional feminism in the church. Abdi says he'll forecast groundbreaking tech to look forward to in the new year. Roshni wants to share tips on how to make a career out of TikTok. Max is hoping to write an article about how annoyed he is by books and comics fetishizing gay male relationships for a female readership. Tristan is looking to court controversy by calling Christmas 'the planet's biggest environmental disaster'.

'I am so proud of you guys!' I say, getting a little teary. 'Your ideas are amazing and our readers will be here for it.'

'Will there be a word limit?' Morowa asks with irony hoicking up her right eyebrow.

I blush. 'No word limit, but if we could each include a little TL;DR section for the people in a hurry to get the gist, that'd make your work have wider appeal.'

'What are you going to write about?' Max asks.

I swallow. 'Mental well-being. The rumours are true. My mum's been going through a lot. I've picked up some self-help techniques and I'd like to share them with people stressing over the mocks.'

Liam touches my hand and the respect I see in every pair of eyes round the table nearly makes me cry.

'And then we're all going to work together on the drugs story. A real collaboration by Nunya, boosting the voices of the people most hurt by it, not doling out judgements. And it doesn't publish unless we're all happy with it.'

Buzzing with energy and passion, the *TeaLeakZ* crew leave and I feel I might have redeemed myself. Making tough calls is an editor's job, I realize, but working together as a team is just as important a part of that job. You'll have nothing to edit, otherwise.

Morowa hangs back. Sensing she wants to speak to me

privately, Liam says he'll wait for me at the bus stop.

'What's on your mind, Mor?'

'It's not everything, but here's another piece of the drug story puzzle.' She holds her phone up.

On the screen, Harrison follows Hugo down the corridor and into a stockroom. The camera person skitters forward, soundlessly pushing open the door a crack and zooming in on the two boys. At first it's not clear what they're saying, but Harrison is begging Hugo for something, waving a crumpled fifty-pound note. 'You're ripping me off,' Hugo says, pushing a hand inside his blazer. 'Don't go killing yourself.' He produces a small resealable plastic bag, tucks it inside Harrison's breast pocket, then walks towards the camera as the video abruptly ends.

Like an old-style projector, clicking and blinking with images, suddenly my mind casts back to the day Hugo grappled with the mugger at Rooke park. What was he even doing there? Word was Rooke park was a place to score drugs. Was Hugo dealing?

The projector fast-forwards to the day I caught Harrison and Hugo shaking hands – more evidence of dodgy dealings? And how could Hugo be immune when the vast majority of Blue Bloods at the Rumbal were high on more than just shits and giggles?

His father is the evil headmaster. Could Hugo be the reason so many Bodley students ended up excluded?

I swallow thickly. 'Send me everything.'

CHAPTER 27

'Drugs on Your Doorstep' – by Nunya Byz

Enley town has a serious drugs-related problem. Schools have recently been clamping down, handing out permanent exclusions – even for a first offence. Sends home a tough Stay-the-Hell-Away-From-Drugs message. Problem solved.

Or is it?

Well, before you start celebrating Enley as a drugs-free zone, read our exclusive interviews and make up your own mind.

Let's be clear: TeaLeakZ is completely against the proliferation of drugs in our communities. But to tackle a problem, you need to understand all the underlying issues. TeaLeakZ wanted to ask the difficult questions no one else is asking. Strap in then, cos here comes the tea, and this brew packs a punch.

Our first interview was with Marc Rembrandt (not his real name). Rembrandt was a popular Year Eleven student at a local academy. He played football for the school team, was the youngest-ever recipient of the prestigious Édith Amboise Photography Prize, and was really looking forward to sitting his GCSE photography exam. A couple of weeks ago things went decidedly pear-shaped when he was excluded for selling drugs at school. TeaLeakZ wanted to know what would cause a guy on the come up to trash his own future.

It's 4.30 p.m. when I meet Marc at a greasy spoon. He's

tall and athletic but his face is gaunt and his eyes look haunted, like a kid who saw way more than he ever bargained for. He is guarded and softly spoken. His eyes only light up when I ask him what got him into photography.

Marc: This is gonna sound super cheesy, but it was Peter Parker from Spider-Man! That character is relatable, man, cos he ain't some muscle-bound guy whose life is perfect. A long time ago they said 'the camera never lies'. Like way, way before filters, innit? I always wanted to be a photojournalist. A really good picture can tell you a whole story in the space of a few seconds. Words can't compete.

Nunya: Sounds like you're a man of ambition. So how does someone like you end up getting excluded for drugs?

Marc: (pauses for a while, eyes getting watery before he sniffs). Who knows? My parents always told me to stay away from drugs. But see, lately things ain't been going that well. We got moved to this elite school where the work is so much harder. My dad's been sick with cancer for a long time so money's tight. You feel me?

I used to walk this old lady's dogs every weekend, but since the local paper started chatting about kids from my school using, she don't trust me no more. Then someone told me about this man who pays a LOT if you shift merch.

Nunya: And by 'merch' you mean drugs?

Marc: Yeah. I know enough people getting stressed being made to go school with them rich kids. They got money and tutors and study rooms. What we got? I do homework on a busted mattress, trying not to get stabbed in the arse by a spring.

My guys aren't just looking for a buzz, they're desperate for a time out. Lots of kids at the elite school are stoners and nobody says nothing so I thought it'd be safe. Only it wasn't.

People are all like 'bro, bro!' and buy your stuff, then they get caught and grass you up to save their skins. Like the whole damn thing is your fault! People at my academy didn't even do drugs before. Yeah, maybe a bit of weed, but that was rare. The posh kids introduced us to the hardcore stuff.

Nunya: *Were you not aware that you could get excluded and even reported to the police for a drugs offence?*

Marc: *Not gonna lie: I knew. But you never think it's gonna happen to you? You get me? You believe you'll always stay one step ahead, and you swear you'll only do it till you make enough to help out at home then you're gonna quit.*

Nunya: *So what happened?*

Marc: *I made money, innit? Lied to Mum about getting more dog-walking work. So we don't have to worry about them turning off the gas or electrics. There's even enough left over to buy Mum some of those cakes she likes at Greggs. Fam! I'll never forget the day the principal of my school calls me into his office and says he's got written statements from kids saying I'm a dealer. Someone snapped a picture cos the camera never lies. Only sometimes it doesn't tell you the whole truth. Wish I'd never touched the stuff. I broke my mum's heart and Dad coulda died from the shock. I'll never forgive myself.*

Nunya: *Sounds devastating.*

Marc: *Those rich kids never get caught! I don't wanna make out like that's some kind of excuse, cos it's not. I shoulda never gotten involved. But I also think school rules need to be the same for everyone no matter whether you're black, white, rich, poor, Christian, Muslim or whatever.*

Nunya: *So what's happened to your dreams of becoming Peter Parker?*

Marc: *I got a court case coming up. I'm at a special*

school for bad kids. All I did was make one mistake. I got no future now. I don't wanna see any more kids from the west side getting their lives ruined. Rich people are like cats: they got nine lives. If you're from ends, you've barely got one, so live it the best you can.

TeaLeakZ pride ourselves on going that extra mile to serve truth. After days of negotiating, one brave member of Enley Police finally agreed to spill the tea, albeit anonymously.

Nunya: *So, Officer, can you give us the low-down on the rising drug situation?*

Officer: *There isn't a 'rising' drug situation. Enley has always had a problem, only it wasn't talked about because it only happened on the east side.*

Nunya: *Wait, are you sure? Cos we keep getting reports saying it's being imported from the west side of town?*

Officer: *The wealthy kids have held wild parties since time immemorial. We've been unofficially told to steer clear of their 'shenanigans'. There have been occasions where we've found it difficult to turn a blind eye and carried out a drugs bust. I can't mention any names, but a lot of the kids are well connected. A single call from a parent can downgrade an arrest to a simple caution which doesn't even get recorded on the Police National Computer. Without proper sanctions, why would anyone stop?*

Nunya: *That is truly disturbing. Do you have any idea who is behind the corruption?*

Officer: *It's more than my job's worth. I remember the pride I felt the first day I wore my uniform. Over the years I've become jaded. The rule of law seems to apply differently to different sections of society. This is not what I signed up for.*

Nunya: *What would you need to take down the local drugs empire?*

Officer: *(blows air at the enormity of the task.) There are just so many layers. At the bottom, you have kids using and dealing in schools. Adult pushers supplying them. The next level is a large population of adult users, and you would be surprised what high-ranking people this includes! You have gangs handling shipments and the people who have the power to protect them turning a blind eye in exchange for a percentage of profits. The whole thing is a disgusting menace!*

The only way things would change is if someone on the inside grew a conscience and presented evidence to the world in such a way it couldn't be hushed up.

Nunya: *Woah! This stuff is explosive!*

Officer: *It's been going on since before I joined the force! Early on, we're taught there's nothing that can be done, so don't even try. The officers who went against the grain lost their jobs. They became a cautionary tale for the rest of us to keep us in check. I'm Enley born and bred, but I'm thinking of moving out of town. I wonder if anywhere is actually better? I don't know what good speaking to you will do, but I'm tired of the whole thing. If my identity was known, I'm sure I'd be fired and would be banned from ever working on the force again.*

Well, there you have it folks: grim reading. Now you know this town is more crooked than a rusty hook and twice as fishy, protect yourselves and your friends. Drugs are hella messy and ruin lives. You gotta ask yourself: is a high that lasts hours worth an exclusion that lasts forever? Is selling a pill to pay a bill worth it when you're selling out? The world might not be fair, but if you're not going to watch out for your own safety, don't expect anyone else to either.

Scan this QR code for more advice about getting help for drug addiction, depression or just to have a friendly chat with a counsellor.

OMD! #TeaLeakZ killed it!!! 🤫 RESPECT to these kids for spotlighting social inequality and drugs. #understandingnotexclusions #mentalhealth 🔥🔥🔥
    @RealZayZay

Check this out! Tackling tough issues with fearless honesty. Wish #TeaLeakZ had been around when I was growing up. Nunya Byz for president of the world! 🙌
@MuznaSaleemAuthor

'Hey,'

I turn around and find myself cornered by Katie and Elspeth – the self-proclaimed 'goth' girls from my English class. Katie is wearing enough eyeliner to give a panda insecurities while Elspeth has given herself a pale glow-up worthy of an open casket.

'Everyone says you're the editor of *TeaLeakZ*,' purrs Katie without blinking. 'It's OK, you don't have to say anything. We just wanted to thank you for such a well-researched issue.'

'We think all the Bodley exclusions are evil!' Elspeth adds passionately.

'Also . . .' Katie pauses, glancing over her shoulder to check no one can overhear. 'I know you were pressured into deleting it, but the exposé on Rumbals was an eye-opener. We've been at Minerva our whole lives but nobody's ever invited us. We always knew something dodgy was going on.'

Elspeth covers her mouth with her blackcurrant nails and nods. 'This school might get great results but it's so backwards and pressurized and destructive. They call us "Satan-worshipping stoners" just because of the way we dress while they're the ones popping pills on a regular basis. Hypocrites!'

'So yeah: thanks for telling the truth,' Katie finishes.

'Well, if I ever see Nunya, I'll be sure to let her and her team know,' I promise.

'We're mangakas,' Elspeth says, haltingly. 'If you ever want a comic for *TeaLeakZ* about the adventures of a zombie warrior and her demon Pomeranian familiar, I hope you might consider us?'

'Webtoons!' I say, clapping my hands excitedly. 'Hell yeah!'

We exchange numbers. TeaLeakZ is finally fulfilling its mission in becoming a voice for the voiceless regardless of what school we hail from.

Liam is waiting for me a little distance away, grinning from ear to ear. We fist bump. After what feels like a lifetime of friendship, words are unnecessary. We walk down the stairs together.

'*TeaLeakZ* are trending again!' Roshni says, waving her phone as we join the queue at the refectory. She lowers her voice to a whisper. 'This might be our best issue ever and we pulled it together in a week!'

A good editor helps her team shine by telling the stories they want to tell. By dictating what they could and couldn't write, I almost lost them. Lesson learned.

'Omigosh, people!' Roshni announces, double-checking her phone. 'You'll never guess what. A couple of local businesses are reaching out, asking if we'll give them ad space. They're willing to pay!'

I know she's excited but I quickly hush her. It may be Bodley's worst-kept secret, but we've got to pretend *TeaLeakZ* is nothing to do with us unless we want to end up excluded.

'You know what this means, don't you?' Liam says quietly to me. 'We could potentially have a salary like they do at the *Chronicle*.'

'I dunno,' I say sceptically. 'When money gets involved, people think they can tell you what to write.'

'Not if we make it clear they're buying ad space and not influence,' he says pointedly.

Man, why do I keep looking at everything with tunnel vision? Liam needs the money more than any of us and this is work we deserve to be paid for. 'You and Morowa are the new finance team. Do the math, weigh up the pros and cons, make a decision then let me know.'

'Me?' he asks in surprise.

'You're the deputy cos you're amazing, Liam,' I say with a smile. 'Not because you're my best friend or you tick a box.'

Liam nods, his eyes glittering with pride. My phone beeps and I feel a burst of emotion when I realize it's from Josiah.

> Nice one G. X

I'm texting him back, thanking him for the brave interview, when Liam loses his shit.

'Aden! Run!' He tries to launch me with a shove.

'No need to run!' Aden calls, raising his hands as he cuts through the dinner hall. 'I just wanted to have a friendly word with you both. Follow me.'

With gulps as audible as unblocked drains, we're led into a languages classroom. Aden pinches the creases in his perfectly ironed trousers then perches on a desk. I notice he's wearing a tie with colourful birds on.

'I know the official line is you have nothing to do with *TeaLeakZ*. It *has* to be that way, and, of course, I thoroughly disapprove of sensationalism. But the most recent issue has raised some vital points.

'I've been under a lot of pressure to carry out certain duties.'

He pauses, eyeballing the Ghost of Christmas Past for all I know, sombre and regretful. 'I, uh, may have lost sight of what made the Bodley community special and perhaps wanted us to be more like Minerva. But what works for one does not necessarily work for the other.'

'Are you saying . . .' I begin, afraid to speak my thoughts aloud.

'Your article was very effective in humanizing the students who were permanently excluded. This is not how we do things at Bodley, so I have enlisted the help of an impartial third party to review the exclusions.'

'You mean all those kids that got kicked out will be let back in?' Liam asks, slack-jawed.

'I think Mr Aden is telling us that sometimes adults *might* make mistakes. Maybe even have their hands forced,' I suggest. 'But it's never too late to fix up.'

Aden smiles broadly. 'I always did think you were a very special student, Dua, even when you were cross with me.'

Scrambling to quash the defensive comment I know I'm about to make, I smile. The fact that Aden is having this conversation at all is pretty damn amazing.

'The Rumbals exposé was confrontational,' he says. 'But I think Nunya has hit the right tone with her latest article.'

'The entire news team want to do the right thing, sir,' Liam says.

Aden sighs. 'I'm counting on all of you to do well in your mocks. Never let your passions run away with you or jeopardize your futures. You can only fix the world when you've become a success yourself. Anyway, you'd better have your lunch.'

'I love your tie, sir,' I say, smiling with genuine warmth.

CHAPTER 28

'Dua, can we talk? It's urgent,' Hugo says, his hair as frazzled as the tinsel wrapped round the giant Christmas tree in the exam hall. It's the end of the day, our papers have been collected, and we're just waiting to be dismissed row by row.

Outside, kids throng the corridors, carrying out post-exam autopsies on questions they got wrong. The maths exam was killer and though Morowa's tutoring might push me up to an 8, I'm still pissed off at Sturgeon for sneaking in a question from a topic we haven't been taught yet. Guess only the Minerva kids with tutors are going to be getting 9s. Why am I not surprised?

'Dua?'

'Go away, Hugo,' I say tiredly. I haven't been able to get that video Morowa showed me out of my head for a second since I saw it. He should be glad I'm not handing it over to Sir Reg. Not that he'd do anything about it. 'We don't have anything to say to each other.'

'Please. It's important,' he says, his eyes glassy. 'It's about your *TeaLeakZ* article.'

Are those tears in his eyes?

'You've got five minutes.'

We hunt for a space, eventually ending up on the window seat in the English block. Hugo holds his head, breathing deeply. For a minute I wonder if he's lost the plot, then he suddenly starts babbling at me. 'I read your interviews and they made me feel so fucking sick of myself! I didn't realize what sort of a life "Marc" – or Josiah – was living or what he was going through. All he said was he needed to make money quick. He seemed desperate, so I hooked him up with a legit supplier. Minerva kids won't sell to Bodley and there are suppliers out there who deal in dangerous stuff cut with soap or lead. I thought I was doing him a favour. But *I* wrecked his life.'

The king of the Blue Bloods is breaking down right before my eyes. My emotions are a patchwork: fury, confusion and, yes, even compassion. 'Why?'

'It's complicated.' Miserable eyes plead for understanding. 'Do you have time?'

Journalism 101: you've always got to be prepared to listen even when you want to kick someone to the kerb so bad it hurts. Sighing in relief, Hugo steels himself. 'I know I'm privileged but even so I grew up in an incredibly pressurized environment. I'm the seventh son and largely unremarkable – Dad would always take the piss and call me the runt of the litter.'

I wrinkle my nose. 'Is he blind? You're more Thor than Chris Hemsworth!'

Guilt paints his cheeks pink. 'I wasn't, though. Not at first.

'Councillor Briggs – or Uncle Ethan as I grew up calling him— joined us every weekend for Sunday roast.' I try – and fail – to hide my shock. 'He saw how Dad constantly insulted me, so one day he asked me if I'd join him for a post-lunch stroll. Then he posed a question that would change my life. If there was a drug that could make me bigger, faster and stronger, would I take it?' He pauses, running a nervous hand through his hair. 'To be like my overachieving brothers? To finally have Dad be proud of me? I said, "Of course I would," and so he introduced me to steroids.'

My jaw drops. '*What!?*'

He looks ashamed but defiant. 'What would you have done if you were some weedy Year Nine kid whose own family bullied him?' I have no answer, so I listen just like I had after our first game of basketball.

'He sold it to me as muscles-in-a-bottle. The truth is, steroids only give you a boost, you still have to work out and eat right to bulk up, of course. But nonetheless, they mess you up.

'So suddenly I'm this sports star at school and my mum and dad are so fucking proud of me. That's when Uncle Ethan tells me I have to pay for the steroids, and it's just outside what I can afford, but it's too late because I'm hooked. I go to Uncle Ethan's son, Jack, and tell him my problem, and he says he'll smooth things over with his dad if I do him a favour: sell some drugs, get a year's supply of steroids for free.'

Oh.

My.

Days.

'So I sold supplies at Rumbals. It became so popular, I started buying extra stuff upfront and having it delivered.'

I recall the man who delivered the box to Renée at the party. Was the 'big man' he was after Hugo? Makes sense, but looking at the lost boy in front of me, I find it hard to believe.

'Why would you do that to yourself?' I ask, uncharacteristically lost for words.

A shadow falls over his face. 'Guess part of me was rebelling and hoping I'd get arrested, then everyone would know Dad had a dealer for a son. His fake reputation means everything to him, as you know.' He glowers. 'But the cops never came, so one night I tipped them off. Dad puts in a call to Uncle Ethan, and the cops let us go. There's even a blackout in the local press. That's why Dad and Uncle Ethan can't stand *TeaLeakZ*. They can't control you and that bothers them.

'Josiah and the kids that got excluded while I'm protected . . . I can't do this any more,' stammers Hugo. 'I need to come clean, and in doing so maybe I can finally break the cycle.'

'And if you end up doing time in juvie?' I whisper. I can't help but picture him thrown in with a bunch of bloodthirsty roadmen.

His eyes glisten as he swallows, then he slowly lifts his chin. 'Josiah didn't deserve to be sent to a PRU. I will take whatever's coming to me.'

I slip a finger inside my hijab, sliding it under my jawline. Big though this is, Hugo isn't the root of the drugs problem. 'Do you know a guy called Jubba?'

His eyes flicker. 'He's one of Jack's men. He does bits and bobs for Uncle Ethan too. How do you know Jubba?'

I frown, starting to formulate a plan. 'He's the arsehole that smashed up my dad's shop after I told him to stop dealing to my guys.' I shoot Abdi a text I realize I should've had the foresight to send ages ago, but there's no point beating myself up about it now. I turn my attention back to Hugo, who is visibly shocked. I tell him Dad is fine and insurance paid for the repairs.

Galvanized, he rises. 'Right! I'm turning myself in.'

I pull him back down. 'You think the police will do anything? As long as Councillor Briggs is in your corner, you're basically untouchable.' I rub my chin. 'Briggs is the problem. He groomed you. He keeps Enley a drugs-friendly zone. He's stopping the police from doing their job. And he's the one silencing the press.'

'Then we take Uncle Ethan down, Dua!' he says with fierce determination. 'I *have* to make amends. Whatever you need.'

My phone beeps – *Abdi*.

'Understand that there can be no coming back from this. It's all or nothing,' I warn.

His fists interlock like cogwheels, the wings of his jaw rippling. 'All or nothing,' he repeats.

CHAPTER 29

At three fifteen the next day, my heart is beating wildly as the *TeaLeakZ* crew gather round the table for the meeting I've called.

'What's he doing here?' Morowa asks, staring at Hugo with open hostility.

'Easy,' Hugo says, raising his large hands.

'Hugo's part of the story and he's willing to help,' I explain.

He nods. 'I was dealing. I'm ready to confess.'

There's a stunned silence round the table. I toss in a new bombshell. 'Abdi managed to hack into Sir Reg's email account.'

'Seriously?' Tristan asks, looking impressed. 'We could use a man with your skills to take down greedy gas-guzzling corporations.'

Abdi whips his hands like defensive swords. 'I ain't sayin' nuttin'!'

Clearing my throat, I hand them all a timeline of the damning email exchanges:

- 20th September – Briggsy advises Sir Reg to lean on Aden to exclude his own students for drugs.
- 28th September – Briggsy has a subordinate raise the alarm with Ofsted, suggesting that Aden is a crap principal who can't contain the drugs culture that has developed at Bodley High.
- 3rd October – an emergency school inspection is triggered. Briggsy arranges for Jubba to be there on that day handing out drugs like discount candy. Kids are caught carrying.
- 8th October – the Trust governors write to Aden telling him he

has till the end of the winter term to get the problem under control before they will have no choice but to sack him and appoint Sir Reg as 'supreme leader' of both Bodley and Minerva.

· Take away: Sir Reg is set to make a power grab, while Briggsy continues to manipulate the good people of Enley like puppets as he adds to his personal fortune with a cut of gross profits.

Everyone serves their best WTF faces.

'What a dick!' Hugo spits, summarizing the general mood.

'In spite of all our run-ins, my heart goes out to Aden,' I say, remembering our chat earlier. 'No wonder the man's been acting like a rampaging tiger, picking us off every time we failed to toe the line. He thought we were letting him down when all the time it was Sir Reg and Briggsy who were setting him up.'

'Even if we go public with this stuff, they'll deny it and use their army of lawyers to punish us. We can't leak the emails without risking Abdi getting properly in the shit,' Morowa says.

Liam and I exchange a glance.

Then I share The Plan.

'That sounds insanely dangerous, even by your mental standards!' Roshni concludes.

'If Hugo plays his part, it shouldn't be all that difficult to pull off,' I reply with false confidence. Technically, Hugo could throw me under the bus. However, the pay-off would be HUGE if things go right. It'll finally feel like we're making our own fate rather than letting rich arseholes push us around and take take take. It's worth the risk. 'Don't forget, this time we've got the law in our corner. Remember the officer who gave us the exclusive interview in our last issue? Baozhai Lu is Jenny's cop aunt. Jenny helped set up the interview, but still wanted to keep her distance from the whole thing, partly to stop people making the link between her, *TeaLeakZ* and her aunt.'

Fingers are snapped, mouths fall open and there are shouts of joy.

'I honestly thought you faked that interview for clicks,' Roshni says, getting a few laughs. I'm grateful my melanated skin hides my blushes.

'Dua may jump the gun sometimes,' Liam says, 'but she's solid when it comes to reporting the truth.'

'Here, here,' Morowa says, squeezing my hand under the table.

Smiling at her, I elaborate. 'Officer Lu swore an oath to uphold the law the day she put on the uniform, so she's said she'll help us if we deliver the goods. She's putting her entire career on the line and we only get one shot. We can't let her or the kids of this town down.'

'Wait,' Tristan says, furrowing his brow, 'if Hugo knows there's evidence, why doesn't he just steal it? Or why not get the police to do a search?'

'I'm not exactly sure where it is,' Hugo admits, scratching the back of his head. 'Tomorrow is a rare opportunity when Uncle Ethan – Briggsy – will be away so we can run a thorough search.'

'Secondly, have you not been listening?' I say tetchily. 'The police in this town are *corrupt*. Sending the evidence onto Officer Lu ensures they'll have no choice but to act to cover their arses.'

Everyone nods.

'Roshni, this whole thing is kind of riding on you. Because, without a shadow of a doubt, Briggsy and Sir Reg's legal teams will try to bury us, and you need to make sure that can't happen.'

Roshni flares her nostrils as if psyching herself up to be parachuted out of a plane. 'My town needs me. I get it. I'll call in some favours and pray *TeaLeakZ* lands one more round of celeb retweets.'

'Try posh celebs,' Liam says. 'That lot are tripping over their selves for woke points by pretending to care about grassroots communities.'

Morowa laughs. 'The insincerity is real.'

'Are you going to be OK?' Max asks me. 'If you and Hugo get caught—'

Dad's ominous words echo in my head: '. . . *mark my words, you will always be the first to be sacrificed to save their privileged arses.*'

I study Hugo. Under the layers of brainwashing, privilege, and arrogance is a good kid turned bad. I have to believe that. He needs this chance to fix up and I'm going to give it to him.

'Not gonna happen,' I say firmly. 'Hugo has intel we don't. Worry about yourselves and bring your A game.'

'Right!' Liam says, clapping his hands together. 'Let's recap everybody's roles. There's literally no space for anyone to mess up.'

This is it, I think, my insides turning to dust. *In twenty-four hours we'll either have the scoop of the century on our hands and Bodley kids' reputations will be restored, or else we'll be holding our next meeting in a young offenders institution.*

When I get home, I'm surprised and delighted to find Mum there.

'Your mum told me everything,' Dad says, forehead creasing, eyes alert.

'Everything?' I ask in a small voice. *OMG!*

Mum nods. 'Rashid needed to know what his awful friend put you through.'

'You should've told me straight away,' Dad says, looking sad instead of angry. 'When people like Jubba say they know people who own the government, they're talking crap. I told you, Jubba is a fantasist, and you can't trust a word that fool utters. Once your mum told me you thought Jubba was behind the attack on the shop, I made inquiries. We have a good community here, people looking out for one another. Those dumb yobs all went to the pizza joint after vandalizing my shop. The pizza guy's CCTV picked them up taking their hoods off. Then this really good police officer—'

'Officer Lu?' I interject.

'I forgot she was the one that interviewed you after the mugging!' he says, smacking his forehead. 'Anyway, once she'd worked them over, they admitted Jubba had put them up to it. Next thing: a warrant's been issued. Now guess where they found Jubba? *Outside your school, carrying class A drugs*. That idiot never learned a damn thing! Jubba's going to be put away for a long time. You don't have to be scared of him ever again.'

'Best news ever!' I cheer. With Jubba and his shady band of roadmen locked up, Briggsy's evil empire is already starting to crumble. Now all me and Hugo have to do is deliver the death blow.

'You don't need to hide things from us. No matter how angry you think we might get, we'll always be looking out for you because we love you,' Dad says earnestly.

'Family first,' Mum adds. 'It's time ours stopped letting the outside world spoil things for us.'

Do my eyes deceive me? Mum's looking over at Dad with a secret smile and Dad looks happier than I've seen in a very long time. 'What's going on?'

Mum chuckles. 'My little reporter; still as observant as ever! I'm feeling a lot more like myself after therapy. I've taken advice from a lawyer and discussed it with your dad. I'm going to quit Gwaine Academy and sue them for constructive dismissal.'

I can't help myself. Launching myself like an escaped bonobo, I hug the life out of my parents. 'I really love you guys!' And for a moment I want to tell them everything about Operation Briggsy's

Going Down. But they seem so happy together that I can't bring myself to spoil the moment. With Officer Lu backing us up, we'll be safe as houses.

IF everyone plays their part . . .

CHAPTER 30

The Uber drops Hugo and me off at the most exclusive precinct of East Enley — it literally feels like a different town. The houses are mansions, with patterned brick drives, hedgerows of privets, and Grecian statues of scantily clad women.

Hugo types a code at the gate and it pops open. 'You coming?' he asks, stepping over the threshold.

'There are cameras,' I say, indicating the discreet little black boxes with a jerk of my eyebrows.

'Not a problem. Sent Abdi a photo of the security system yesterday and he's given me instructions on how to delete our footprint.'

This is it then. The point of no return.

I say a prayer and step onto Councillor Ethan Briggs's private property. Standing before the impressive glass porch with trepidation, I watch Hugo twist a key in the lock.

W E E E E e e e e e E E E E E E E o o o o O O O O O O o o o WEEEEeeeeEEEEEEEooooOOOOOOooo . . .

I jump and cover my ears, desperately watching as Hugo unlocks the second door quick as a flash, swings round the doorframe, and taps the memorized code into the security system.

W E E E E e e e e e E E E E E E E o o o o O O O O O O o o o WEEEEeeeeEEEEEEEooooOOOOOOooo . . .

My heart drops as the siren gets louder, the ringing in my ears almost deafening.

'What did you do?! Has he changed the code?' I scream over the tidal wave of sound crashing around us just as I notice something move in the distance across the road.

'No, he can't have!' He nervously licks his lips. 'Lemme try again.' He re-enters the code, his face glazed with a nervous sheen. I'm seconds from grabbing his wrist and hauling ass out of there when suddenly – silence. He did it.

Hugo lets out a nervous chuckle. I push him inside and slam the door behind us. He looks at me questioningly.

'Curtain twitcher at six o'clock. Not sure if she saw us, but let's not take any chances,' I explain. Then I get a look at where we are. 'Oh, my days . . .'

The hallway is not only large and beautiful but there are luxury seasonal decorations everywhere, including a ten-foot Christmas tree and a light-up Santa on a reindeer-drawn sleigh on the stairs.

'He always did have the most gauche taste,' Hugo says, scowling.

'I can't believe we're inside his actual house.' My heart flutters inside my chest like a trapped moth, cheeks tingling from the shame of breaking and entering. Man, I hope I don't go to Hell.

'Clock's ticking. Remember, it's a gold phone we're after.'

'I'm doing a sweep upstairs, you're taking ground floor,' I say, reciting the plan. 'Any probs, send a text.'

'Good luck!' he says, bumping fists before we go our separate ways.

Resisting the urge to take my trainers off, I tiptoe up the stairs, patting Santa on his jolly face as I go. On the upper landing, I marvel at the length of the balustrade, almost like the balcony at a gallery. Gotta stay focused. Checking left and right, I try to recall which door Hugo said leads to Briggsy's son's bedroom. Apparently, the very official 'home office' on the ground floor was always kept immaculate in case he ever had the police commissioner over, so we're not wasting time there.

Walking to the end of the hallway, I push open the door. The room looks like a page straight out of *Architectural Digest*. A guest room, then. A car rumbles by and I freeze, petrified we'll be caught.

No, Hugo did his homework when he lifted the key. The councillor and his wife are at some outrageously lavish charity meal, while his son, Jack, is at an eCommerce expo at Olympia, London.

Calming my racing heart, I push open the next door – Bingo. Jack's bedroom.

Plastic boxes are scattered everywhere, with printouts and receipts strewn about on the floor like confetti. While I'm debating whether a messy room makes an easier search than a tidy one, I make eye contact with a model on a calendar. Miss December is lying in the snow with nothing but a twist of tinsel wrapped around her waist. Misogynistic wasteman.

Methodically turning over the room, I find nothing of interest, except a drawer of keys and memory sticks. Could he have taken the burner phone to the expo? Unlikely, since it would pose a risk of being discovered. On hands and knees, I check under his bed a second time, and just as I'm about to give up, I spot a cache duct-taped to the underside.

The box is locked. Remembering the assortment of keys I spotted earlier, I lunge for the drawer, selecting the smallest two. The second does the job.

Inside are bundles of used banknotes and a small bag with a few of those cherry-red pills. It's not enough for a dealer, but maybe Jack samples his own merch? I take a photo on my phone, replacing everything and moving on.

Outside in the corridor, I'm about to text Hugo for help, when I spot hazy light flooding from a partially open door. Following my instincts, I discover a large room, lit by a picture window looking out onto Enley East Park. One half of the room seems to function as an office, while the other has a leather gaming chair in front of a massive TV, a velvet chaise longue, and a small footstool to the side.

Centred on the desk is a PC. Another decoy from the looks of things. Hugo was definite about Jack using a phone for his shady deals. Hastily, I pick my way through his drawers and cupboards, growing increasingly frustrated as I fail to score the burner. A crash downstairs sends my heart leapfrogging into my throat. Must be Hugo.

'Where have you hidden it, you sick pervert?' I hiss, turning in circles. My eyes skim over every surface, diving into dark nooks and crannies, hovering over the well-stocked bookcase. Nothing. In desperation I imagine pulling a special book out will make the bookcase swivel round to reveal a secret room complete with incriminating phone and a cache of drugs to boot. Alternatively, he might just have shoved his phone down the back of some chunky books . . .

Excited to put my theory to the test and desperately aware of the small time frame we have to make this work, I rush forwards, tripping over the leather footstool.

The lid pops off and rolls behind the gaming chair.

'Crap!' I growl, about to chase after it when my attention is drawn to the footstool. Hiding inside is a golden phone, glittering provocatively like the lamp in Aladdin's Cave of Wonders.

'Jackpot!' I gasp, but there's no time for jokes.

Quick as a flash, I grab the old android phone and the cable Abdi gave me from inside my pocket and connect it to Jack's via its lightning port. I hold down the side button for ten excruciatingly long seconds. Nothing. Did I count wrong? Is the phone out of juice? Was it a decoy? Just as I'm on the verge of hyperventilating, the gold phone beeps as the two phones begin an illicit conversation.

Fountains of code cascade down both screens. I watch as level after level of security is breached in lightning-fast exchanges as Abdi's amazing phone works its magic. No sooner have usernames and passwords been asked for, than the boxes automatically fill up. Grabbing my phone, I call Liam. He answers on the first ring.

'We're getting it!' he confirms.

I hear Abdi's voice in the background. 'Oh, my days! This stuff is dynamite, fam!'

'What you got?' I ask, not able to keep up with the flickering screen.

'Contact lists of buyers, sellers,' Abdi cries. 'Messages from Jack to Briggsy telling him where major deals are going down and asking him to keep the police off his back. There's more but I'm sending it all over to Officer Lu.'

'That's brilliant! Hopefully we can—'

W E E E E e e e e e E E E E E E E o o o o O O O O O O O o o o WEEEEeeeeeEEEEEEEooooOOOOOOooo . . .

I nearly go into cardiac arrest. Someone has just entered the house.

CHAPTER 31

As pathetic as the naked statues on the front lawn, I am rooted to the spot in the middle of the room.

'Dua?' Liam says and it sounds too fricking loud. I hang up.

'Hello! Who's there?' calls a voice from downstairs. It's the Yorkshire accent from my worst nightmare.

Silence.

'Oh come on, don't be shy! Lovely lady across the street tipped me off. Two teens, she said. We operate a very good neighbourhood watch in Enley. Yes, I'm very proud of my town.' He pauses. When he next speaks his tone is all iron. 'Liam and Dua – if you two don't show yourselves on the count of five, you're going to be very, *very* sorry.'

My eyes swell like balloons as I try to break the wall of fear that has sprung up between brain and body. 47% – Jack's burner is still transmitting data via Abdi's phone. Glancing at my own phone, I get another shock when I see a series of messages from Hugo.

> You found anything? I've turned off the CCTV cameras but deleting the part where we arrived isn't working. Gonna call Abdi.

> Shit! I think someone's coming.

> DUA, GET OUT OF THERE! HE'S BACK!!!!!!

Wood creaks as someone heavy begins ascending the stairs. My cheeks burn while my vision goes blurry and the walls seem to close in around me. One message rises to the surface from the sea of dread crashing in my brain: *Abort the mission!* Gripping the burner tighter, I make a break for it. A door at the top of the corridor clicks open, causing me to throw on the brakes. *Oh God, he's upstairs!* Doubling back, I open an airing cupboard filled with files and boxes of copier paper and cram myself inside.

BAM!

I gasp, wondering what the hell that sound was as Briggsy swears.

Is he armed?

Frozen solid from fear, my brain goes into damage control mode. It tells me that when Briggsy finds me – *and he will find me* – he's not going to kill me. A murder is on a whole other level to letting your son run a drugs empire from your home while you embezzle council funds.

But then I remember the Briggs family have had the power of the local press at their disposal for years. Could a story be spun about a student, maybe high on $€x¥, breaking and entering the Briggs family home? Could my murder be dressed-up as self-defence? I glance at my phone, make a decision, and then with a couple of taps, I'm streaming. I pray to God I've got enough data to make it through this.

Whatever Briggsy does to me, the *TeaLeakZ* crew will know. It's cold comfort but it's better than nothing.

73%

Briggsy exits the first room. His laboured breathing acts like sonar, giving me a pretty good idea of his location. As he creeps up the corridor, my heart beats in my eardrums, deafening me with the sound of my own fear. I promise myself no matter how scared I am, the second he enters the room next door, I will run down the stairs and out of the house. It'll be my very last chance. As I psyche myself up, fully committing to the plan, the window of opportunity slams shut. Briggsy has just bypassed the second room in favour of his son's office.

I am so dead.

Through the ventilation slats in the cupboard, I see the large man himself poised with a baseball bat balanced over his shoulder. Never in my life have I been more afraid. One swing of that beauty and it's lights out forever.

'Oh! Pinched Jack's phone, have ya?' he says, looking down at the upended footstool. 'Let's make this easy, shall we? Hand it back now and I'll let you off with nothing more than a slapped wrist. We can even share a cuppa after.'

93%

Can Abdi's phone drain the last seven per cent of data from Jack's burner in the seven seconds it'll take Briggs to find me cowering in this cupboard? Can he dispatch Officer Lu and the cops in time to save my life?

NEED A DECOY! MAKE SOME NOISE!

I text, praying Hugo hasn't already left the building.

'Come on, Dua,' Briggsy calls with bristling irritation, checking under the chaise longue. 'This offer is about to expire. You and your white-trash boyfriend have committed a crime but we'll hush it up if you do the right thing and come out.'

SLAM. One of the books I failed to file properly suddenly hits the floor. I gasp, frightened into thinking Briggsy took a shot with his bat. Too late, I realize I've blown my cover. Briggsy's eyes lock on to the cupboard. A maniacal grin infects his face, moustache rising to reveal teeth like yellowing tusks. As he ambles over, grunting and wheezing, I get flashbacks of reading

Lewis Carroll's poem 'The Walrus and the Carpenter' at the age of seven. One of the problems of being an 'advanced reader' is you end up reading stuff you're just not emotionally ready for. The horrific fate of the gullible oyster children scarred me for life. That same, sickening childhood fear reawakens as Briggsy edges forward like a giant, murderous walrus.

Lights out – I close my eyes like a little kid who knows their game of hide and seek is over. In the darkness behind my eyelids, pictures dance and flicker. Your life is supposed to flash before your eyes when your time is up. That's not what I get. I see generations of hopeful people arriving and making Enley their home. Teenagers going to school, wanting to make their families proud, finding a way into the career of their dreams. A bolt of mental lightning reveals waves of drugs filtering through our town, spreading like an infection, entering our lives through parties, school-gate pushers, and hotspots like Rooke Park. Exclusions for Bodley; drug habits for Minerva. And in this moment, I finally realize *everyone* – rich or poor, black or white – loses out. Everyone, that is, except the Briggsys who have been growing rich on the back of human suffering, treating our town and its residents like chattel.

My eyes snap open, my anger transcendental.

100%

We've done it.

I pull out the cable and slip both phones into my pocket as Briggsy draws level with the cupboard. Liam must have alerted Officer Lu but I've run out of time. Briggsy's breath reverberates in the dank depths of his chest cavity. Timing is everything. With enough force to SLAM into his face, I throw open the door, darting out. He swings the bat too late and shatters something behind me.

'Come back, you little bitch!' he roars.

I hurl myself down the stairs, tripping and slipping, tucking and rolling.

Where's Hugo?!

Behind me I hear Briggsy thundering down like a tornado, knocking over decorations without a care. The electronic Santa and reindeer come alive with flashing LEDs as a boisterous rendition of 'I Saw Mommy Kissing Santa Claus' blares. In a blind panic, I run head first into the Christmas tree in the hallway. It sways left and right, before it comes crashing down between us, baubles and ornaments shattering on impact, swirls of tinsel zigzagging up into the air like sparks of electricity.

'You fucking vandal!' he spits, cheeks redder than rare steaks. 'Do you know what the law says about intruders? Homeowners may use reasonable force to protect themselves, including the use of a weapon.' He brings the bat down on Santa's head, blowing out the lights with a cranial crunch, the music track warping then dying. 'Hand over the phone and forget you ever saw it, or I make you forget.'

Briggsy points the bat at me, making my insides shrivel. With the data transfer complete, losing the phone is no great loss. I'm preparing to chuck it over when—

'Uncle Ethan, stop!' Hugo shouts, stepping between us.

Briggsy blinks like he's tripping on $€x¥. 'What on earth are you doing here, our lad?'

'It's over,' Hugo says. 'The police know everything and now Dua has the evidence to prove it.'

Briggsy's face twitches and darkens as I hold my phone up. 'Mad congrats, Councillor Briggs! You're a live-streaming sensation.' The comments are blowing up, everyone is live.

A notification pops up on my phone from Liam – they've done it. Morowa, Liam and Tristan have written everything up and published it, along with the evidence. And it's EVERYWHERE.

'You're done for,' I say, pride at my team radiating from me.

Shock and rage rolls over him. 'You sold me out?' he says, rounding on Hugo. 'After I treated you like me own flesh and blood?'

'You got me hooked on steroids!' Hugo roars with a grief that runs deep. 'Then you let your son groom me into becoming a drug pusher. You never saw me as family, just another person to exploit.'

'You ruined God knows how many lives with your filth in our schools!' I yell over Hugo's shoulder. 'We're going to make sure you go away for a long, long time.'

Briggsy's throat inflates like a toad, eyes blinking rapidly as he assesses the situation. Tossing the bat aside, he takes flight. Me and Hugo are stunned but a crusading burst of adrenalin gets me moving. Grabbing the bat off the floor I fling it, helicopter-like, at his feet. They tangle up, and Briggsy skips once . . . twice . . . three times. He recovers and my heart sinks. Then Hugo suddenly powers past, rugby tackling Briggsy to the ground.

'GERROFF!' he roars, foamy spit flying from his lips, dribbling down his double chin. 'You'll go down for dealing too, you little pest!'

In a stark callback to the day Hugo tackled the mugger in the park, he traps Briggsy in a choke hold. His eyes meet mine and though there is sadness, there's also a bold determination. 'No more running, Uncle. For either of us.'

The front door blasts open and cops surge in, led by Officer Lu, going full Valkyrie with her taser at the ready. 'POLICE! Everyone get up with your hands on your heads! NOW!'

CHAPTER 32

'Crooked Councillor Goes Pen!!!' – by Nunya Byz

For years we knew something was up with Enley. Like a tale of two cities, one rich, one poor, tensions have been reaching fever pitch in London's most unequal town. The utopian east always made it onto the brochure, while the west side story was one filled with muggings, poverty and high schools tarnished with a growing drugs problem.

No tea, no shade, no bitter tirade, but Councillor Ethan Briggs and his son, Jack Briggs, were both arrested on 16th December in a major drugs bust. After eight years of mismanagement of public funds and dodgy dealings, a criminal investigation into the running of Enley Council is finally underway. Things are not looking good for the Briggs duo.

This news will come as an unwelcome shock to locals who long held the belief that drugs were smuggled into town by ethnic communities. In a previous report, we revealed drugs have a thriving business at some of the town's top grammar schools and the uptake is spilling over into others.

The problem is not a new one. Successive governments have failed to deal with the illegal drugs trade in any meaningful way. The tea was some ministers were using on the down-low, so why bite the hand that feeds you?

The status quo might have remained but for the bravery of one whistleblowing teenager who cannot be named.

Enlisting the help of one of our undercover reporters, the pair were able to secure evidence and alert the authorities. The Briggs family home was raided by the police, who seized £1000 worth of the mega-dangerous new import $€x¥ which has recently been added to the Class A category. Jack Briggs's burner phone, containing records of illegal deals, was also seized and further arrests are expected within the coming days as the local drugs network is hopefully dismantled.

The problem won't disappear overnight, but the high-profile arrests demonstrate that nobody is above the law. Questions will be asked in parliament about how corruption on such an epic scale could have taken place. Serious safeguarding issues will need to be raised about exam pressure causing some students to resort to taking drugs. Now that it's out in the open, hopefully Enley can finally tackle its shameful drugs secret.

<u>Read our exclusive interview</u> with Jack Briggs's ex, who always suspected he was up to no good!

<u>Read an uplifting story</u> by a former addict who got help at Enley's No Judgements, New Start clinic and turned her life around.

Check the <u>LINKS</u> for more information about the very real dangers of taking drugs, how to get help, and reporting crime anonymously.

CHAPTER 33

After our final exam, we are done for the term, and a wave of relaxation and excitement rolls over us all. As I'm waiting for my mates at the bottom of the stairs, I see Keira trotting towards me. Too late to run, I pull my phone out and poke at random apps.

She stops beside me. 'Can we talk, please?'

Maybe it's the pinkness of her eyes or the knotting of her fingers that stops me from blowing her off. She leads me to a quiet corner, before turning to me, folding her hands over her heart. 'I apologize unreservedly for pulling your hijab off. I'm so ashamed of myself and no amount of sorries is going to change what I did or what I put you through.' She looks at her feet. 'I know you could have reported me and got me excluded.'

You don't even know your own privilege, I think. Super Reg would've moved to protect his Lois Lane. 'Are you expecting me to forgive you?' I reply with raised eyebrows. 'How would you feel if someone exposed a part of *your* body that you choose to cover up to everyone in the corridor?'

The tears she was holding back fall, her face suddenly blotchy, her lips quivering. 'I wasn't thinking straight. I felt like you were stealing my life. I wanted you gone!'

'You told your vicious friends about my mum's private mental health battles. You lynched a nude Barbie in my locker. You even sent me a death threat to boot.'

'No, no, no!' she says, waving her hands emphatically. 'I swear to God I didn't do any of those things. I couldn't. Renée heard the rumours about your mum from one of her friends at Gwaine

Academy. And the Barbie was her little sister's. When she told me what she'd done, I was mortified. She said it was the only way to make you understand your place.'

I shake my head in disgust.

'Look, I'll go and confess everything to Mr Aden right now.'

'Forget it,' I say, swallowing back bitterness. 'There've been enough exclusions and spoiled lives at this school. If I forgive you, you have to have a word with Renée. You and your friends have to back off *permanently*.'

She nods emphatically, 'I've been a real bitch to you and it serves me right I didn't snap you up when I had the chance.'

'I'm glad you didn't. The world needs both of our papers.'

Her eyes widen then she blushes. 'Do you think we could maybe be friends?'

'Maybe one day,' I say with a noncommittal shrug.

She nods. 'Merry Christmas, Dua. I'm glad I met you.'

'Happy holidays,' I respond, walking off.

Liam emerges from the gathered crowd, quickly dragging me away as I ponder why everything has to be such a competition: our GCSEs, our looks, our popularity, our newspapers . . . and probably most disappointingly, our romances. Maybe next term with Keira won't be so bad.

'Come on,' he says. 'You promised the team lunch and it's my sacred duty to hold you to it.'

Buying lunch is the least I could do for them after delivering our biggest and best issue ever in a *single night*. Everybody brought their A game – the video of Briggsy getting busted has over three million views and counting. Roshni hashtagged hard and this time it wasn't just ZayZay retweeting about *TeaLeakZ* but three celebs we collectively stan plus an anti-drugs charity to boot. The ad revenue means big cash bonuses all round. Liam said he's going to buy his nan the greatest Christmas present ever, so no amount of dementia can ever make her forget.

'Daaaarling,' Max says dramatically. 'Look at choo! They said stay in your lane and you sashayed across the whole damn motorway in your hijab lookin' snatched!'

The local places are fit to bursting with kids celebrating the dawn of the holidays, so Morowa takes us to a small Ghanaian takeaway tucked between a betting shop and a grocers. In spite of the halal accreditation, I go with the jollof rice and plantain option because Tristan has convinced me that less meat is kinder to the planet, though part of me still yearns for the goat stew.

We carry our aluminium foil containers and plastic cutlery over to the local park to sit together on the stone steps of the war memorial monument.

'You lot have no conscience,' Tristan says, clucking his tongue. 'Your plastic spoons are going to end up inside some poor whale's stomach.' We watch him shape his rice into a ball then flick it into his mouth. There's collective whooping and sounds of disgust but I actually think it's pretty lit and give him some applause.

'Tristan's a wild man,' Max says, grinning. 'And I'm down with saving the planet.'

'The only thing you're down with, is going down on him!' says Abdi, cackling, his mouth becoming a rice fountain.

'Why does everything always have to be about sex with you?' Morowa asks with a frown. 'Seriously, Abdi, your homophobic patriarchal brand of nonsense is not welcome.'

'I'd be offended if I knew what that meant,' Abdi says, laughing. Morowa cracks a smile then flicks a cherry tomato at him.

Trying to be extra dainty, Roshni nibbles her jollof rice one grain at a time while taking a selfie.

'Roshni, man, that is effort,' I say. 'Get your pretty face in there. It's the holidays. Forget updating your fans and live a little.'

'Some of us have some selfie-respect,' she says tartly. 'Serving flawlessness 24/7 is what I'm about.'

'I'll be more than happy to certify your flawlessness for you if you could send me some cheeky—' Abdi starts to suggest before Morowa slams her container down and he runs for his life.

'Such a shame!' Morowa says, sighing. 'The face of an eleven-year-old but the mind of pervert. I hope Abdi's voice breaks over the holidays.'

Liam sees me staring off. 'Dua, do you remember we used to have stone-skipping competitions in primary?'

I shrug, my mind on other things.

'Come on,' he says, grabbing my arm. 'Let's see if you've still got game.'

I get a vivid flashback of playing one-on-one basketball with Hugo and it feels like I got punched in the belly.

'What's up?' Liam asks gently as we move away from our friends.

'I don't know. I just feel really, really guilty.'

'Guilty? Come on, things turned out pretty decent. We made a difference.'

'Did we, though? I was never that popular but I feel like I'm killing it in the enemies department.'

Liam shrugs. 'Isn't that what every successful journalist's life is like? The truth isn't always the easiest thing to tell.'

'Hugo got arrested and has a hearing coming up. Sir Reg is on indefinite leave. Keira thinks I stole her life—'

'But none of that's your actual fault. Hugo was dealing, fam, even if he was exploited. The court will be fair to him cos he's under seventeen and rich, so stop worrying about that. Sir Reg tried to blackmail you into dropping the drugs story and harassed all of us. The Trust governors did him a solid allowing him to go on leave. They could've done a lot worse than making Aden acting head of both schools.'

'He's even started acting like his old self again,' I say, thinking of the triumphant return of Mr Aden's colourful ties.

'Exactly!' Liam says. 'And as for Keira, she needs to do some serious growing up over Christmas.'

'Out of all the boys I could've fallen for, I'm ashamed it was Hugo,' I say pensively.

'What, because he was so fit?' Liam says, teasingly.

I clear my throat. 'At least I now know I don't want to be dealing with those sorts of emotions for a *very* long time. Love or whatever is overrated . . . for now.'

'Think I'll join the club,' Liam says, chuckling.

I pick up a beige stone and fling it at the lake. It skips across the surface six times before drowning in a final sploosh. Liam whoops.

'I'm not coming back, Liam,' I say sadly. 'To Minerva, I mean. I passed the entrance test at Raymer's Grammar School.'

'Since when?'

'After the Rumbal. I didn't want to be around Hugo any more, so Mum made an appeal and Raymer's allowed me to sit their entrance exam.'

Emotions sizzle across Liam's face. 'But, Dua, you can't go! Who's going to keep *TeaLeakZ* running?'

'You are,' I say confidently.

'M-m-me? I'm rubbish!'

'No, you're not. You're a talented editor, Liam. I'm sorry for all the times I held you back and vetoed your ideas. Trust me: you are *so* ready for this.'

He stares from one sincere eye to the other looking like a spooked rabbit. 'I won't be able to keep everyone in line like you do. You pissed everyone off, but no one ever doubted you was the best person for the job.'

I suddenly feel an overwhelming rush of love, a feeling that is warmer than a log fire, sweeter than gingerbread, and more explosive than a cracker. I got lucky with Liam and the gang. Each one of them bringing the skills, commitment and loyalty of a pro. Turning my back on them now would be like Frodo abandoning the Fellowship so he could hide in his Hobbit hole. Maybe *TeaLeakZ* is just a paper for kids by kids, or maybe it's the dawn of a whole new resistance movement? Time will tell.

'Give me a couple of weeks to settle in at Raymer's and we could do meets after school?' I suggest with a shrug.

'Yes! Get in!' he says, pumping his fist. 'Acting Ed I can totally do.' He picks up a stone, weighing it in his hand, before flinging it out like a discus thrower. 'Mum and Nan are so proud of me for breaking the drugs story. The money's not bad either.'

I smile at him. 'Dad's invited Mum to come and live with us so we can look after her.' I pause, trying not to blush. 'This is gonna sound majorly childish but I'm kinda hoping they get back together. And if they don't, that's OK too. Happily Apart Parents defo beats Miserably Together Parents.'

'Amen,' Liam says, digging up a large stone with the tip of his shoe.

'Hey,' I say, watching him wipe the mud off his find. 'With Dad supporting Mum as she takes her school to court, he's gonna need someone to look after the shop. Think your mum might be interested?'

He grins, handing me the stone, as large and flat as a clam shell. 'You're too good, Dua. I'm gonna miss not seeing you every day. With you gone it's like Sir Reg got his Christmas wish.'

With my body stretched as tight as a bowstring, I whoosh round, catapulting the stone. 'Mark my words, mate, I'm not going anywhere.'

The stone cuts across the lake, skipping into the distance like it's never ever going to stop.

The End

ACKNOWLEDGEMENTS

I hope you enjoyed reading this book! The first draft was completed way back in December 2019 but events conspired to create delay after delay. In a way it worked out for the best as our world has been through some of the most dramatic changes in history and I am grateful for the opportunity to reflect this in my writing. It's strange to imagine that before the untimely death of George Floyd there were things we weren't allowed to say. Now I think the world is more open to discussions and that can only be a good thing.

Though my name goes on the cover, there are an awful lot of people I would like to thank for their amazing contributions without which this book wouldn't exist.

First and foremost thanks to my wonderful agent Penny Holroyde who has stood by me through thick and thin. I am so grateful to her for always fighting my corner and being one of my best friends.

I would like to say a HUGE thank you to my amazing editor Simran Kaur Sandhu! It's been an absolute pleasure working with you on this. Your kindness, humour, advice and masterful editing skills are all super appreciated. Your dedication to authenticity is beyond heart-warming. I'd also like to thank Pete Matthews and Lucy Pearse for their help.

Thanks to Amber Ivatt for running another brilliant PR campaign. Without you, no one would know about my books. You are one of the loveliest people I know.

Thanks to the students at my new school for boosting me every single day, for sharing your experiences and your slang, and making me excited to teach maths! Thanks also to all the students who inspired the characters in this book especially the confident hijabis who gave Dua her edge and love of her faith and the two boys who provided Max with his sass and laminated eyebrows.

Thank you to Jane Newman, Maryann Wright, Elena Koumi and Zeba Talkhani for your sage guidance with creating authentic representation. I have always been passionate about reflecting the wonderfully diverse society we are lucky enough to live in. It goes without saying, that any mistakes are my own for which I unreservedly apologize for.

Thank you to my brilliant author friends who never gave up on me as I struggled through one of the hardest times in my life. I'm talking of course about Patrice Lawrence, Andy Shepherd, Amy Wilson, Jasbinder Bilan, Francis Hardinge, E. R. Murray, Devon Cox, Russell Schechter, Angela Jariwala and Chris Mould.

Thank you to all the lovely teachers and librarians who continue to push my books on their students and the wonderful bloggers who are kind enough to write reviews.

Thanks to everyone at the Branford Boase awards for a lifetime of incredible support.

Thanks to Cassie Chadderton and everyone at World Book Day for being awesome and supporting my career.

Thank you to all the wonderful teachers, teaching assistants and overall good people who make schools work! Special mentions to Nick House, Lynda Wallace, Helen Dorfman, Carrie Goodgame, MC, Mary Mbema, Sam Warwick, Sarah Ernstzen, Dean Rollins, Sophia Daire, Francine, Sabah Mehmood, and Tanbir Hussain.

Thank you to the student I met in Warwick who wanted more representation for deaf teens. I sincerely hope Liam does your experience justice.

Thank you to the BBC for having me as a Young Writer's Award judge; to The International Agatha Christie festival for having me as writer-in-residence; and to Arts Council England for funding my work when Covid first struck.

Lastly, thank YOU dear reader. Your time is precious and I never take it for granted. I love to tell stories – sometimes with difficult themes – but always because I think there is something that must be said. My ideas are always born out of the real classroom environment. I hope my books will delight but also make ignored or bullied students feel just a little less lonely.

ABOUT THE AUTHOR

Muhammad Khan is an engineer, a secondary-school maths teacher, and now a YA author! He takes his inspiration from the children he teaches, as well as his own upbringing as a British-born Pakistani. He lives in South London and is studying for an MA in Creative Writing at St Mary's University. He is the author of the critically-acclaimed *I Am Thunder*, *Kick the Moon*, and the 2020 World Book Day title *Split*.